LOBSTER BLUES

Jacqueline King

First published in the UK in 2025 by ZunTold
www.zuntold.com

Text copyright © Jacqueline King 2025
Cover design by Isla Bousfield-Donohoe

The moral right of the author has been asserted.
All rights reserved.
Unauthorised duplication contravenes existing laws.

A catalogue record for this book is available
from the British Library

ISBN 978-1-915758-12-5
1 2 3 4 5 6 7 8 9 10

Printed and bound by Interak, Poland

Praise for *Lobster Blues:*

'An exciting and emotional story of courage, compassion and friendship. Beautifully told, with rich language and a delightful cast of characters, it is a perfect classroom read but great for all ages.'
Mel Darbon, multi-award-winning author

'A wonderful sequel to A Cake for the Gestapo. *Jacqueline King's immaculate attention to historical detail and use of oral testimony in Lobster Blues brings alive this often overlooked period in Jersey's history with music, laughter and humanity.'*
Dr. Sara Skillen, Cultural Historian

Praise for *Cake for the Gestapo:*

'Vivid and involving, woven together with a sensuous rhythmic prose.'
Anthony McGowan

'This might just be a classic in the making.'
Chloe Metzger

'A brilliant book; it's really engaging with a tremendously page-turning storyline, which kids will love. It would make a great film too.'
Lucy Coats, author of *Cleo* and *Chosen*

'A key part of recent local history.'
Sir Philip Bailhache, former Bailiff of Jersey

*'The writing is excellent
and the subject matter authentic.'*
Gilly Carr, Fellow and Director of Studies,
St. Catherine's College, Cambridge

*'A mesmerising account of the channel island occupation
told from the perspective of a plucky gang of kids who
waged their own secret war against the Germans,
utterly and completely unmissable.'*
ReaditDaddy

*'A Cake For The Gestapo is beautifully written, exciting
and dangerous, and quite heart-breaking. You find yourself
immersed in the children's world of mixed up innocence
and maturity, and you hold your breath when those worlds
collide, knowing that this is a real war, and bad things
really are going to happen.'*
The Brick Castle

*'A story that is often overlooked but incredibly important
to history with characters to fall in love with,
this might just be a classic in the making.
The group steal your heart and make you root for them,
I almost forgot what I was reading was based on reality.
Full of fun and mischief despite everything.'*
Chloe Metzger

*'If The Famous Five lived in Wartime Jersey and had a
penchant for revenge, Cake For the Gestapo would be the
ultimate adventure story. A fun, touching and fascinating
window into a mostly forgotten part of occupied Britain.'*
Sarah Churchill

*This book is dedicated to the Channel Islanders
who helped when they could,
during their very difficult and dangerous situation
from 1940 to 1945, and to all others
who take great personal risks for the sake of others.*

Jersey, Channel Islands
January 1942

Friday 9th January
7.30 pm

After supper, Clem put on a thick coat and went into the farmyard on his evening round, carrying a bucket in one hand and in the other, his heaviest torch.

He wouldn't switch it on unless he had to. The enemy had occupied the island for eighteen months. Everything was in short supply: food, clothes, soap, *everything*, even batteries. There was only a half-moon, but the stars were bright, so he'd find his way round the farm easily enough.

The torch had another use. In the right hands, it could easily knock out a grown man. Clem gripped it in his mighty fist. 'Try me,' he muttered.

But the yard was silent. There were no moving shadows.

Clem's grip relaxed as his eyes adjusted to the dark. Through the gate to his left, he made out Spinner's house next door. Behind it stood their garage with the flat above, where her cousins lived – the Martin family. Clem could hear Ginger strumming a lullaby on his guitar for his little sister. There was music in Spinner's house too - her father was playing the piano.

Clem listened for a while, then he headed up to the big barn, which they'd extended a couple of years ago, ready for the brand-new David Brown tractor they'd ordered just before the German occupation, to replace their old Fordson. But it had never been delivered, and now it wouldn't be until the war was over. Neither had the parts arrived to mend the Fordson.

Inside, he shone the torch around the huge space, checking the farm implements: piles of tools on the long bench, bill hooks and scythes hanging on the wall, the trailer and the pale bales of straw, heaped up against the wall. Ernest the horse was standing at his manger behind the partition that was his stable, his harness on wooden pegs. Clem stroked his soft, velvety nose and offered him a cold potato from his bucket, murmuring, 'I'm sorry you have to work so hard. We'll mend the tractor soon.'

Then he moved over to the pig in her temporary sty, a square made of sturdy railings slotted together, filled with straw and with a bucket wired to the rail. He took another potato from his bucket and put it beside the sleeping pig's snout.

'Good night, old girl.' He tickled behind her silky ears and Peggy opened one eye. Then she scooped up the potato in an easy gulp, turned her back on him and resumed her snoring. In the dim light, her huge belly gleamed white. 'Soon you'll be a mum,' said Clem. 'With lots and lots of babies.' He gave her a final tickle before padlocking the barn door and setting off up the hill, shivering at a sudden icy gust from the north.

The old store was empty save for potato barrels and

his punch bag hanging from a beam. As Clem opened the door, it twisted on its hook, dark and dirty as a hanged man.

There was a face on the bag, with a moustache. Clem began to box at the face with his bare fists, gathering pace until the bag swung in a slow, heavy rhythm. 'This is Hitler's face,' he grunted, punching harder and faster as the face swung away and then back, away and then back. *'This is Hitler's face.'*

After he was done, panting and sweating, he took the punchbag off its hook, and hid it behind the potato barrels. Then he stood on the doorstep.

He stared at the sea, picturing his older brothers, far away. He cupped his hands and shouted, 'Goodnight Bill. Goodnight George. We're keeping our chins up and hope you are too. God bless you.'

This was Clem's prayer. This was his fight.

His voice echoed back from the starry skies. But Bill was drowned, his ship torpedoed by the enemy in the Atlantic. George was in the marines. They hadn't heard from him for months.

8.30 pm

Next door, little Rosie Martin closed her eyes at last, in the flat over the garage. Her brother's lullabies had done the trick, although she'd asked, 'Will the giants come again?'

Every night, anti-aircraft guns shook the island, but tonight, they were slow to start, growling softly like caged dogs. Ginger sat on the end of her bed until he was sure she was asleep, then he went into the sitting room, where their mother was ironing by the fire. 'All's well,' he whispered.

'Thank you,' mouthed Mrs. Martin. 'Let's hope we have a quiet evening.' She folded a pillow case and hung it on the fireguard. 'We'll have to find a way of keeping Rosie busy, so she isn't frightened anymore.'

'Guess what she told me today?' Ginger said. 'She wants to play the harp.'

Mrs. Martin smiled. 'Next thing, I'll be cutting up my best sheets for an angel costume.'

'An angel? *Rosie?* Very funny,' said Ginger. 'But, I've had another idea. I thought she might like code breaking.'

'Really? She's not yet four.'

'I'd make it easy,' Ginger said. 'And it might stop her blurting out the wrong thing to the enemy.'

His mother picked up a small dress and shook it out. 'She'll certainly do that if we don't watch out.'

Ginger agreed. 'I'll see what I can do about codes.' He went back to the bedroom that he'd curtained off for himself on the landing. Then he sat at his desk and studied Rosie's favourite book, the animal alphabet. 'A for Apple, B for Bear, C for Cat, D for Dog,' he muttered. 'So in code, BAD can be Bear, Apple, Dog. PIG: Pig, Ibex, Goat. Rosie will get that, just about.'

He wondered whether or not to write the code on a page for his little sister, then he paused, listening. The growling of the guns had turned into snarls, then there was mighty explosion and the flat trembled. To the sound of breaking china, Ginger heard his mother muttering, 'Here we go again.'

'Good luck, boys.' Ginger pictured Spitfires and Lancasters far above the island amongst the stars, the Spitfires swooping and buzzing protectively round the bigger planes.

Rosie gave a muffled cry, but just as her brother

jumped up to comfort her, the guns stopped abruptly. Mrs. Martin looked round the curtain, her hands full of broken cup. 'I think it's a false alarm.' She held up shards of china. 'Too bad. Another cup gone. Never mind, I always hated this one.'

'So they've done you a favour,' Ginger laughed, keeping his voice low. He went on, 'They've done the pigs a favour too.'

'What? *Anti-aircraft guns*? How's that?' His mother looked puzzled. 'I thought the pigs hated the noise.'

Ginger explained, 'Clem gives potatoes to the animals every night about the time the guns start. Now they associate the guns with a reward, so they aren't frightened.'

'No one thinks about animals in wartime,' said his mother. 'Poor things. Mind you, Peggy's all right, but Hotspur's a nasty pig. He looks at me as though I'm a *menu*.'

'You're too thin for him.' said Ginger. 'He'd prefer someone fat.'

'No chance these days,' said his mother.

Ginger went on, 'Clem's probably feeding them right now.' He peered round the blackout curtains into the farmyard next door. The milking parlour door slammed shut and he saw that Clem was done with the animals and on his way past Hotspur's sty in the yard. As he went towards the orchard, Ginger saw his torch flash three times, as it always did. Then he heard the clank of a bucket and a long, low whistle. He murmured, 'Sometimes he puts out food for prisoners, if there's anything to spare. Turnips or apples, I think.'

'*Dangerous*,' said Mrs. Martin. She indicated Rosie and put her finger on her lips. 'For goodness sake don't tell Rosie.' Then she pointed upwards. 'The guns are starting again.'

9.30 pm

At the Brayes' house, Spinner Braye sat in bed wearing her yellow birthday scarf. To the east of the island, the big guns boomed. Her window was tightly closed but the candle flickered with the vibrations. She stared at it, thinking of her mother over the sea in England. Then she picked up her pencil and began to write her diary.

Clem says we'll have snow. The big animals are indoors and everyone's dreading it, except the children, of course, who want snowball fights. Lots of people in town are very hungry, but not as hungry as the prisoners. Those poor men are starving, so we help them when we can. In the paper, it said that prisoners ate weed from a stream which they thought was watercress. But it wasn't, so they were very sick and died. RIP.

The anti-aircraft guns have begun again, POM POM POM. Clem gets in a rage because the animals are terrified. Ginger's upset because Rosie's frightened and Joe is FURIOUS because the guns are turned on our boys in the RAF. Luckily, the enemy gunners here aren't clever enough to get them.

Ploughing starts soon. There are plenty of migrant birds on the marshes but there's a kind of prison camp there and Clem hopes the prisoners don't eat the birds.

The enemy is shutting off the beaches, painting red lines and planting mines. This makes Joe furious as he can't help his family. No more sand eels. It's also pretty difficult to find any lobsters, because they're usually beyond the red lines.

Joe says he's got the LOBSTER BLUES.

She drew a few crosses marked *RIP* for the prisoners who'd died of poisoned water plants, muttering, 'Rest in Peace' for them. Then she snuffed out the candle, pulled the blankets over her head and said a prayer for her mother in England.

As she settled to sleep, the cat jumped up beside her, nuzzled under the blankets and pressed flat against Spinner, trembling. 'They won't hurt us, I promise,' she murmured softly, stroking the cat's head until they were both asleep, despite the guns.

By the time they stopped, she was deep in dreams. So she didn't hear Ginger knocking on their back door at nearly midnight, well after curfew.

11 pm

Ginger whispered through the keyhole. 'Uncle Hedley, it's only me. I know it's late, but I need to ask you something and I can't open the door.'

'I'm so sorry,' said Mr. Braye from inside. He turned the key. 'All this locking up is such a nuisance.' He peered out at Ginger, his lamp held high.

Ginger said, 'Could you help me to move Hotspur into the garage?'

'That dreadful pig? *Into the garage? Tonight?*' His uncle pulled his nephew indoors. 'Why on earth? What are you thinking of? Moving a pig at this time of night?' He gave a low chuckle and locked the door as soon as they were both inside.

Ginger said, 'I'm sorry if I startled you.'

Mr. Braye managed a faint smile. 'These days, a knock at the door late at night can be nasty...' he paused, putting the lamp on the table. He put a chair by the fire for Ginger. 'You look frozen.'

'It's cold in the flat when there's a north wind,' said Ginger, warming his hands.

Mr. Braye passed him a cup of tea. 'Look, why don't you all move in with us for the winter? I've asked your mother, but she says no.'

Ginger pushed on his glasses properly. 'I think she doesn't want to be a nuisance.'

'Of course it wouldn't be any trouble, it would be wonderful for you all to be here. We have plenty of room.'

Ginger thanked him and went on, 'But Uncle Hedley, I meant it about moving Hotspur. You see,' he explained, 'Please don't tell Mother, but I heard a noise last night in the garage, right under my bedroom.'

'What sort of noise?'

'A person. Someone being creeping about. There were footsteps.' Ginger frowned.

'Oh dear. How worrying,' said Mr. Braye.

'The thing is, we haven't heard from Father for ages. So,' Ginger looked anxiously at his uncle, 'I feel responsible for Mother and Rosie. I have to protect them, but if Hotspur was downstairs, *he'd* protect us.'

'You're right. He certainly would,' said Mr. Braye. He ran his hand though his untidy hair. 'But he does smell terrible.' Then he looked serious. 'It's a very good idea for a night or two. We'd have to make a pen, or you won't be able to get out of the flat. He'll wait at the bottom of the stairs for you.'

'Mother doesn't like him at all, and as for Rosie…'

'She'd fight him off with a look.' Mr. Braye smiled, then said, 'But I really do think you should move in here. That would be the safest all round.'

Ginger nodded. 'I'd like that, at least till summer.'

'Also,' Mr. Braye went on. 'There's another reason for moving in with us. The German authorities are billeting soldiers in houses with spare rooms. So if you come here, you can save us from that. *Imagine* us having to face the enemy at breakfast and make polite conversation.'

'You'd feel like traitors.' Ginger drank up his tea and stood up. 'Right, we'll move over here as soon as we can, but until then, I'd still like Hotspur in the garage tonight.'

11.30 pm
Half a mile down Le Hocq lane, Joe couldn't sleep. His father was missing again, so he was in charge. He'd been listening to the guns and the planes roaring over the island, but they'd stopped at last. He tossed and turned under his blankets, but he was cold, even though he'd kept on his clothes and his dog, Beaufort, was pressed against him.

His small brother, Arthur, sniffled in his cot on the other side of the room and Diddie murmured in her dreams in her bed in the corridor.

Joe pushed back the blackouts and peered out, gazing below the cottage as the moon made a shining path over the sea towards France. Then, suddenly, he froze.

Someone was outside, crunching over the gravel.

He slipped out of bed, crept to the kitchen and put on his boots. Then he grabbed the rolling pin from its hook and opened the back door, his heart pounding. But as he stepped out, he gasped at the sight in front of him. In the darkness, the garden shimmered in a dazzling frost coat. A large white cat stared at him from on top of lobster pot. Then it tossed a mouse into the air, meowed and jumped down gracefully to the gravel.

Joe laughed softly. 'So it was *you*. What do you think you're doing, throwing your supper about when decent people need their beauty sleep?'

The cat gave him a scornful look and danced towards the sea wall with the mouse in its mouth. Then it raced down the wooden to the steps and padded down to the beach.

Joe wrapped his arms about himself. 'Blimey, it's like the North Pole out here.' He glanced up to the stars. For a moment, he was quiet, thinking of his mother and wondering if she was looking down from heaven at him. Then he hurried to the coal shed and felt for the coal bucket in the dark. 'I don't care that we aren't allowed to have a fire at night. I just don't flippin' care,' he muttered, shovelling coal. 'Blimming enemy rules.'

Just as he'd filled the bucket, he heard Arthur, crying again in his sleep.

Joe sighed and hurried indoors, dumping the bucket by the fire. It'd been like this ever since their mother had died. Arthur was always crying or wetting the bed. Wet both ends, Joe thought as he lifted the toddler into his own bed, next to Beaufort.

He waited until the little boy was quiet. Then he tiptoed back to the kitchen, laid a few coals on the embers and blew on them. Soon, they were glowing. By morning, there'd be some warmth in the house. Joe blinked back sleep, suddenly tired. He climbed into bed, top to toe with Arthur, the dog between them like a giant hot water bottle.

Saturday 10th January
8 am

When Spinner came downstairs, she found her father's shoes by the back door, covered in pig muck. He was humming to himself, making porridge.

'Daddy, there's straw in your trouser turn ups.' She reached down pulled some out, waving it front of his eyes.

'Thank you, darling.' Mr. Braye yawned. 'I'm not quite awake today. Ginger and I had a mission in the middle of the night.'

'You broke curfew?' Spinner's eyes widened. 'Someone might tell on you.'

Her father spooned porridge into bowls. 'We only went next door farm to fetch Hotspur from the farm.'

Spinner sprinkled a tiny pinch of sugar on to her porridge. 'I don't like Hotspur. He's such a mean pig. Where is he now?' She looked round the kitchen as if he might be under the table or in the cupboard.

'In the garage under the flat,' explained Mr. Braye. 'Out of the cold.'

'That was kind,' said Spinner. 'I bet he was pleased.'

'Mmm.' Her father put his own porridge bowl on the table and picked up his spoon. 'Not really. He didn't want to come with us at all, but Ginger waved a bread crust in front of his snout. Then he ran like mad for the garage

~ 11 ~

and Hotspur roared after him. Ginger had to jump right over him when he charged.'

'Crikey. That was brave,' said Spinner. 'Hotspur practically has flames coming out of his nostrils when he's cross. And he foams at the mouth. Ugh.'

'He was dead keen on the bread. Ginger really spoiled him. He even put on a scrape of jam,' said her father. He chuckled. 'We gave him a straw bed and he settled down as easy as pie.'

'But hang on a minute,' Spinner said. 'There are gaps between the floorboards. Poor Aunt Edie. The flat will stink like mad. She'll hate that.'

'Oh that doesn't matter at all. They'll only have to put up with the stink for a day or two, then the whole family's moving in with us over the weekend. He took Spinner's empty porridge plate. 'What do you think about that?'

8.30 am

In the flat, Rosie was holding her nose with both hands. 'Something smelly has happened,' she announced as her mother tried to dress her.

'Hotspur has moved in downstairs. He was cold,' explained Ginger. 'He's come to join the family.'

Rosie changed hands as her mother pulled on one sleeve of her jumper, then changed hands again. 'That's not very nice,' she said, her eyes welling up. 'He's mean and it's too smelly in here to eat my breakfast.'

'Then we'll eat it outside,' said Ginger. He helped put on her boots, then led her downstairs. 'Don't drop your toast.' As they passed the pig pen, Rosie began to wail, but Ginger said, 'I thought you were brave.'

'Carry me,' commanded Rosie.

'You're too big,' said Ginger. But he heaved her on to his back and took her outside to tell Clem why Hotspur had vanished in the night, in case he hadn't seen the note he'd slipped under the farmhouse door. While Rosie stroked the cows, he murmured to Clem about the sounds he'd heard underneath him.

'It was probably someone hiding.' Clem forked hay into the mangers for the cows, keeping his voice quiet. *'Don't tell anyone.* Not even Spinner.'

9 *am*

The woodshed was at the bottom of the Brayes' garden. Spinner's father opened the door and found the axe. 'Stand back, darling.'

He lifted the axe high above his head with an easy swing, then let it fall, splitting a log into perfect, halves. He chucked the split pieces to one side, then stood another log on the block, saying, 'There's something cheering about chopping wood. And it certainly warms you up.'

'Can I have a go?' Spinner held out her hand for the axe. 'Joe's been chopping wood all his life and I'm fourteen now.'

'Of course.' Mr. Braye stopped his work. 'But you have to lift it right above your head and let the weight of it do your work for you.' He placed a log on its end.

Spinner lifted the axe. 'It's heavy,' she said. *'Really* heavy.' But she forced herself to make it look easy and with a whack, the log was split in two.

'Brilliant,' said Mr Braye. He watched her split log after log, until she put down the axe, her face scarlet with effort.

'I'll do more next time,' She passed him back the axe and her father worked on.

Soon, they had a pile of split logs. A few snowflakes drifted through the hole in the shed roof, so after he'd finished, Spinner helped cover the wood with an old tarpaulin. Then she hurried after her father to the house, flapping her hands in the freezing air to warm them as the cat raced after them.

When they were indoors, Mr. Braye said, 'I'd better go and register the Martins into our house, so everything's legal.' In the kitchen, he scrabbled about in a drawer and held up a huge key. 'The woodshed key. Lovely isn't it?'

Spinner took the key and felt its weight in her cold hands, fingering the curved handle and wondering who'd used it over the years. 'Why do we have to lock the shed? Even Clem locks the farm now. It's so strange.'

'When the war is over, we'll go back to normal, when everyone trusts each other again,' said her father. As he knotted his tie, he said quietly, 'But for now, it's best not to give anyone temptation, I think. If someone needs wood, we'll share, of course. It's just that, apart from strangers wandering about, there's something else...'

'I know,' Spinner nodded. 'People steal things and sell them for lots of money. It's not very fair and it's not very nice. They might do that with our logs.'

'It's difficult for people. Sometimes they lose the good side of themselves when they're desperate.'

'We won't will we?'

'I hope not. And then, some people just make money out of bad situations.'

Spinner scooped the cat on to her lap. 'Be careful, Daddy. The enemy are watching us, ever since that business with Viktor…last summer, when we, erm… played tricks and he was taken away…'

'They're watching *everyone*, not just us,' said Mr. Braye, lightly. 'The whole island has to get used to it.'

Monday 12th January
7 am

Early on Monday morning, Joe heaved Arthur out of bed and sat him in their mother's chair in the kitchen. Arthur chewed on a piece of dry bread and spat soggy crumbs, but at least, thought Joe, he wasn't crying.

Their father still hadn't come home and the schools were closed because of the icy weather.

Diddie joined them, a green jumper over her pyjamas. She skipped from foot to foot to keep warm. 'I'm not going to wash today. Too flippin cold.'

'You don't have any choice. Auntie Vi's coming today. We'd better scrub up.'

Diddie groaned and smacked her head. '*Hell, hell, hell.*'

'Don't swear,' said Joe.

As Diddie slapped water on her face, she shrieked, 'Blimming heck, Joe. The water's nearly froze.' She held up a shard of ice, turning it the first rays of the rising sun so that it sparkled. 'Look, Arthur. Pretty.'

Arthur spat more crumbs, pointing at the glittering ice. 'Swords!'

Joe cocked his head as a plane roared over the cottage, so close that the walls shook. 'That's a Heinkel, landing at our airport.' He swore, then put his hand over his mouth. 'Sorry, Diddie. Quits, we both used bad words. No need to tell Dad.' Diddie nodded and he went on, 'I can't *stand* them enemy planes landing on our island. They've been fighting our own boys all night. *I can't stand them.*'

Diddie looked at the tin clock on the shelf and gasped. 'Look at the time! Auntie Vi will be here soon and Arthur's filthy.' She dragged Arthur out of his chair and tried to scrub his face with a rag.

'NO,' he yelled, pushing away the rag and trying to bite his sister.

'Stop it, you little devil,' said Diddie, jumping back and slapping the rag at him. 'You've got to be clean or you'll get nits and scabies.'

'Oi, Arthur, stop it, or I'll bite *you*.' Joe glared at him as he fetched the teapot and put it near the fire to warm. 'Cut it out, Diddie. It's not worth it. He'll start yelling.'

Arthur's cheeks were scarlet and his mouth had already opened wide in a square, a bad sign. He took a deep breath, but as he was about to bawl, the back door flew open and in stomped Auntie Vi. Arthur snapped his mouth shut and stared.

Her arms were full of packages, and she carried a laundry sack so big that they could hardly see her face over it. She wore her best winter hat, a brown felt with a stuffed bird on its brim. Its glass eyes glinted as icy air blasted into the kitchen. 'My word,' she declared. 'It's cold out there.'

At the sound of her voice, Beaufort charged into the kitchen and skidded to halt, his eyes fixed on the hat. He stuck up his nose and began to howl.

Arthur wrenched away from Diddie, grabbing the dog round his neck. 'Beaufort don't like that bird,' he said, sticking out his lower lip.

'It's not a real bird,' said Joe. 'Just pretend.'

Auntie Vi rolled her eyes. 'That dog,' she said, 'can put up with it or go outside. I'm not staying here without a hat, in this freezing cold.' Diddie sniggered, but Auntie Vi gave her a withering look as she took off her coat and put on her apron. Then, seeing tears gathering in Arthur's eyes, she knelt beside him, her voice suddenly gentle. 'It's a magic bird, Arthur. It frightens the soldiers.' She picked him up, adding, 'I had a little boy once and he liked this hat, long ago.' Then she let him touch the feathers until he cheered up.

Diddie threw her arms round her little brother. 'Brave Auntie Vi, scaring the soldiers.'

'I'd like to scare them *home*, back to their nice German mothers.' Auntie Vi scowled. 'This island's filthy since the enemy arrived. No soap, not enough hot water....' Then she stopped and reached into one of her bags. 'Never mind all that. We've a treat for breakfast.'

She held a cake tin high and Joe's eyes lit up. He knew at once what she'd brought.

'Sand eels!' yelled Arthur.

Joe put a dusting of tea leaves into the warm tea pot. 'Even better, Arthur.'

Diddie beamed. 'You made us Jersey Wonders, didn't you?'

'I might have.' The hat bird waggled again. 'But don't you tell no-one. I don't want talk that I've got more flour than anyone else.' She glared at the children as if they might tell the whole island. 'No breakfast until everyone's clean and tidy. I'm not having any nonsense and that means you too, Arthur.'

9 am

The flat above the garage was nearly empty apart from the furniture. Ginger took the last few things over to the Brayes' house on Monday morning, then went back to help his mother to clean it.

'It does smell dreadful,' said his mother, gazing round at the empty rooms above Hotspur. 'But I suppose that won't put off the billeting officer. They'll simply order us to move Hotspur out again and make us wash everything with disinfectant.'

'It might delay them for a few weeks,' said Ginger. He swept up some crumbs and put them carefully into a paper bag. 'I'll take these to Spinner's chickens later.'

Mrs. Martin sniffed one of the mattresses. 'I think the stink might have seeped into this.' She straightened the curtains and added, 'and these.' After a busy hour, the flat was cleaned, but as they went downstairs, she stopped. 'Who's that, in the yard?'

Ginger listened. 'Sounds German to me. I bet it's the billeting officer, sniffing for a spare room.'

'*Sniffing!*' Mrs. Martin laughed. 'That's so funny.' She glanced at Hotspur, who was eyeing her as usual. 'Oh gosh, what is it with that pig?'

Ginger listened again. 'I can hear Uncle Hedley talking in German. Let's go and find out what's happening.'

Over the yard at the Brayes' house, a soldier was standing on the back doorstep, his cap in his hand. He was gesticulating upwards, as if to say, 'You have a big house.'

Mr. Braye was listening politely. Then he said, 'Every room is occupied. But we have a charming apartment above the garage. Two of you could live in it. Although, I am afraid, there is rather a strong smell there right now.'

The German looked puzzled, but Mr Braye smiled graciously. 'I have informed the authorities that the present tenants, my sister and her children, have moved into our house because of the smell. But perhaps something can be done about that.' He indicated the flat again. 'Please. Come and look for yourself.'

10 am

Down at Joe's cottage, Arthur's face was shiny and his curls tamed, Diddie was dressed and her hair plaited and Joe had put out plates and mugs. Diddie rubbed her stomach. 'I'm starving,' she said, as Auntie Vi opened her tin. A wonderful sweet smell filled the air.

Beaufort crept towards the table as Auntie Vi lifted out a Jersey Wonder for each child, delicate twists of fried dough dusted in sugar and cinnamon. 'We'll say grace today, like civilized people who count their blessings.'

'For what we are about to receive,' said Diddie, 'may the Lord make us truly, very much indeed thankful.' Then, at a nod from Auntie Vi, they all began to eat, slowly at first, then gobbling and licking every trace of sugar from their hands.

Beaufort thumped his tail and Joe slipped him a scrap. He said, 'Mum used to make these.'

Diddie's face fell, but she turned to Auntie Vi. 'Yours are as good as hers.'

When every crumb was gone, Joe said, 'Thanks, Auntie Vi. That was a treat.'

But Auntie Vi had put her hand to her ear, then waved her hand at the window. 'Listen to those darn soldiers on the road. What a noise.'

Outside, the tramp of jackboots was close. Beaufort

growled as a soldier. shouted an order. 'Good job we finished the Wonders,' Joe said. 'None left for the enemy to steal.'

Diddie patted Beaufort. 'They might steal *him*,' she said, her eyes welling. 'My friend at school has an auntie who had a dog and one of the soldiers got his pistol out and …'

'They won't get Beau,' interrupted Joe, pushing Beaufort under his chair. 'Don't you worry. If they did, I'd kill them, just like that.'

'Bang, bang,' said Arthur, making a gun shape with his hand.

Auntie Vi told Joe not to put ideas into Arthur's head, then she ordered Diddie to take the sheets off their beds while Joe set up the wringer outside. She said, 'I'm going to boil the hankies and clean up before I do the sheets. You'll get in the way, so off you go outside.'

She held out Arthur's balaclava helmet and dressed him in layers, heaving boots over his thick socks and stuffing his starfish hands into mittens. Then she checked that Diddie was properly dressed too. 'Joe, keep them busy for a couple of hours, and no nonsense.'

'I'm ten,' said Diddie. 'I don't need Joe to look after me.'

'You look after *him* then,' said Auntie Vi. She looked sternly at Joe. 'I don't want any stupid business against the enemy. No silly talk.'

'Promise,' said Joe. He took Arthur's hand and pushed open the door into the morning sunlight. 'Look at the icicles, Arthur.' He broke off one the length of his arm and held it above his shoulder like a javelin. 'Watch it go,' He hurled the icicle into the road. As it smashed to bits, he turned to his sister. 'I reckon we could do a bit of damage with them. What do you think, Dids?'

He broke off a few more and whispered, 'The soldiers are on the beach, just below the wall.'

Diddle snapped off the biggest one she could find and whispered back, 'They deserve a treat.'

Joe grinned. Then he hurled his first icicle over the sea wall.

Tuesday 13th January
10 am

Spinner watched Clem from her attic bedroom. He was walking behind Ernest in the field beyond the orchard. His cap was pulled low over his face against snow flurries and Ernest, the old cart horse, was straining his shoulders ahead of him, heaving the plough through the hard earth.

She picked up her pencil and smoothed a piece of paper. First, she drew Hotspur with flames coming out of his nostrils like a dragon. Under her drawing, she began her letter.

Dearest Mummy,
Aunt Edie, Rosie and Ginger are staying with us. Hotspur has moved into the garage. So far he has eaten three trays of apples and one of seed potatoes. They were on a high shelf so he has been mountaineering. We had to barricade him with gates.

Everything is fine and you mustn't worry. Dad and I are making toothpaste with ground cuttlefish. Parsnip coffee still.

The soldiers made Mr. P walk in the road in town last week because they wanted the pavement. He was fuming. Town is very grubby with litter

*everywhere and half the shops closed. We are
not allowed to take any photos. All cameras are
confiscated.*

*Clem's mood is very dark. Sports are banned
in the island, and this includes BOXING. His
favourite. He and Mr. Percheron have spent
HOURS trying to mend the old tractor and Joe's
father has helped them too. NO RESULT. Poor
Ernest is being put to use and working so hard
because of it.*

*There are prisoners everywhere. Some of them
are so hungry. It's very sad.*

Loads and loads of love. Spinner xxxx

She wrote on the back of the paper: *If found, please deliver to Mrs. Braye, Exeter, Devon, England.* Then she stuffed it into a bottle, sealed it with her father's red sealing wax and slipped it into a canvas bag, which she tied round her waist by its handles.

She checked that the bag was hidden if her coat flapped open. Then she was off, racing down the lane through snow flurries, her plaits and new yellow scarf flying behind in the icy breeze. She waved at Clem and Ernest as the bottle thudded against her, but at last she was on the beach, blinking in the bright sunshine. Tiny shards of ice whipped from the sky into her face.

No-one stopped her. But who'd want to be out on the beach on such a wintry day? Even the soldiers seemed to be indoors for once.

Checking that she wasn't being watched, she hurried over the wet sand towards the rocks. From the highest one, she hurled the bottle as far as she could into the grey sea. It circled a few times, then bobbed off on the tide, moving away from the island.

'Good luck,' she whispered. She hopped back to the sand and began to search for winkles, glancing back now and then to check that the bottle had gone. Soon her bag was full, so she decided to head for home.

At that very moment, she heard the tramp of jackboots. Along the coastal road came a patrol, singing despite the icy wind. Spinner turned back one last time to see if the bottle had gone, then gasped. As the leading soldier marched into sight, the bottle turned and headed to the shore on the crest of a wave.

Her heart began to thump. 'Distract them,' she hissed to herself. So she raced towards the patrol with her catch as they halted at the top of the slipway. 'Would you like some winkles? They're lovely, a real treat.'

One soldier smiled at her, but their sergeant waved her firmly out of the way. 'We aren't peasants, living on sea snails like you islanders.'

The smiling soldier whispered *'Danke schon.'*

'They're really delicious,' insisted Spinner, her stomach heaving with terror in case they'd seen the bottle. Sending messages was against the rules. *They might think I'm an informer*, she thought. For a horrible moment, she pictured herself in prison, alone.

But the sergeant ordered his men to move on and soon they'd turned the corner, marching east, without a glance at the beach or the shining bottle as it bobbed and whirled at the water's edge.

Spinner trembled with relief as she raced back to it. 'Please, please, little bottle. I beg you. *Go.*' At last, as if it had heard her, it floated out of sight, twisting in another current and heading east. 'Phew,' she muttered. 'Safe at last.'

But at that very moment, there was a sudden, soft whistle behind her, three times. Someone chuckled, then whistled again. She grabbed a pebble and braced herself, but as she was about to turn and fight, someone sprang on to the rock behind her and grabbed her arms.

'Get off,' she yelled, pushing back with her elbow. She tried to wrench away, but whoever it was held tight and hissed in her ear so she could feel warm breath.

'What are *you* doing, Spinner Braye? Sending messages about the enemy? *Brave, Spinner Braye*. But stupid. Very stupid. I might have to tell.'

'PERCY,' she shouted, thinking of the school bully. 'SHOVE OFF.'

'I'm not Percy.' The person chuckled. 'Percy's a reformed boy these days, Spinner. He's cooking in the canteen; he has plenty to do and plenty to eat. Percy doesn't want to spend his time frightening girls.'

'Ow,' yelled Spinner. She stabbed her elbows backwards again, then whirled round. '*Joe*. You *beast*. And you stink. Don't do that again, or else.'

'Or else *what*?' Joe's scruffy jumper smelled of fish and engine oil. His voice sounded injured. 'What do you mean? *Stink*? We're clean as whistles. Auntie Vi made us have a bath yesterday.' He held his jersey cuff right up to her nose. 'But I wouldn't let her wash *this*. It's my best fishing outfit. A bit of dirt keeps it waterproof.'

'Rubbish.' Spinner shoved him away.

Joe whistled for Beaufort. His dog was splashing through the shallows, hooking up little crabs and tossing them in the air. He pointed out to sea. 'Your bottle won't make it you know. The tide isn't heading to England.'

'Course it is. I looked it up in the paper.' Spinner glared at him.

'Don't make any difference what the papers think,' said Joe. 'Mr. Hitler's given orders to King Neptune. He's in charge now.'

'Shut up,' said Spinner. 'What do *you* know?'

'I know everything. Ask me what you like about the sea,' said Joe. He grinned and said, 'Hey, I've got an idea. Why don't we escape? You can sail. I can sail. Easy.'

'Escape? Are you crazy?' Spinner waved her arm at the grey, unfriendly deep. 'Across that? I *couldn't* leave Daddy all alone.'

Joe shrugged. 'One day, they might take him away. We need to be ready.'

'What? Don't even *say* things like that.'

'In the middle of the night,' said Joe. 'That's what happens. Every time.'

Spinner's eyes were huge. 'Course they won't take him away. He's too useful, speaking German.'

'Righto,' said Joe, giving up. 'We can't escape anyhow. The Germans have nicked all the boats, except for big ones like Dad's.' Then he chuckled. 'Though my dad might be able to lay his hands on a nice little one. Just saying.' He tapped his head. 'I've got plans, Spinner, plans.'

4 pm

It was already dark when Clem's parents set off to evening chapel on the coast road. Clem handed them the big torch, with its blacked out, narrow beam. 'You take this. I'll use the hurricane lamp.' As they disappeared down the lane, he called out, 'Don't be late. It's going to snow later.'

Indoors, he filled the hurricane lamp with paraffin and lit it. First there was a blue flame, then a yellow, and soon the lamp was burning steadily. Clem sat at the table for a moment longer, enjoying the comforting smell of paraffin, the glowing lamp and the silence of the farmhouse.

Then he picked up the bucket a quarter full of potatoes that his mother had left for him. It was earlier than usual, but there had been snow flurries all day and the evening paper had warned them of blizzards in the night. The animals would need extra rations.

There was snow on the ground already, so the path up the hill was slippery. For once he wouldn't punch away his anger. Anyhow, boxing was banned, another rule that made him angry. Not that he took much notice of the enemy rules.

By the time he'd finished feeding and checking each animal in turn, snow was falling thick and fast. He turned down the lamp and felt his way to the orchard. As he put the potato bucket on the trailer, a great lump of snow fell close by. Then it happened again, further into the trees. Clem flattened himself against the wall. 'Who's there?' he called, glad that his voice had grown deep.

But no-one answered except the wind, blowing the snow into shallow drifts. 'Better check all round again,' he said to himself, keeping close to the farmhouse. As he made his way to the kitchen garden, he heard another soft thud, like a person landing from a height. He called out again, *'Who's there?'*

Again, there was no reply.

He peered into the darkness, but there was nothing except whirling snowflakes. He hurried indoors. Soon, his parents would be back, and if they weren't, he'd go and find them, so he kept on his coat as he went upstairs to pull the blackout curtains, first in Bill and George's empty bedrooms. He did the same his parents' room with its sea view and his own with its outlook on the farmyard. Then he headed downstairs to the sitting room, humming to himself.

However, as he pulled the last curtain shut, he paused. There *was* someone outside, he was sure of it, someone padding through the snow.

'You're imagining things,' he told himself. But as he closed the sitting room door, there was a sudden crash, the sound of breaking glass and a loud yelp. Light footsteps pattered past the hall window. Clem raced to the kitchen, thankful he'd left the hurricane lamp still burning on the table. Grabbing its handle, he tore into to the farmyard, yanking the door shut behind him.

By the lamp's dim light, he saw footprints leading towards the orchard. To one side of them were dark drops on the snow. Leaning down, Clem checked them. 'Blood,' he murmured. '*Blood.*'

He stood silently, his ears pricked. Then he heard a muffled cry. Someone muttered, 'Ow. Oh blinking, blinking heck.'

Clem held up his lamp, smiling with relief. Whoever was wandering about was a child. Prisoners and German soldiers never said, '*Blinking heck.*'

Through whirling snowflakes, a small figure shot between the apple trees, dragging a sack and panting, 'Come *on* you stupid thing.' The figure turned, pulling the sack with both hands and staggering backwards. 'Come *on.*'

'Oi,' yelled Clem. He sprinted towards the shadowy shape, the hurricane lamp swinging from his fist. But the figure had vanished, leaving the sack like a crumpled animal in the gathering snow.

Clem hurled himself though the hedge into the lane.

There he found a small boy, about eight years old, sniffing and wiping his nose on his cuff. Clem held up the lamp as the boy looked at him from under a filthy cap and stammered, 'I'm not the enemy...' He put his hands up as if Clem was a soldier. 'My dad sent me.'

Clem's voice was fierce. 'I hope you haven't been thieving.'

The boy stuck out his lower lip. 'I was borrowing some food. We're hungry.'

'Borrow?' Clem laughed. 'You can't give food back when you've eaten it.' Then he leaned down. 'It's Billy Cliquot, isn't it? Joe's cousin. What are you doing out here in this weather? You'll freeze to death.' Close up to the boy, he saw that Billy's face was smudged with tears and blood.

'Cut meself,' explained Billy. 'But I'm not blubbing.'

Clem took his arm. 'Come on home. We'll clean you up and you can tell us everything.'

'I ain't telling you nothing. 'Billy sniffed, pulling away from Clem. 'And you better not hit me.'

'I don't hit people.'

Billy looked up at Clem. 'You and Percy Du Brin had a fight at school. Everyone knows about it. You smashed him to bits, long time ago. When you had a gang and you tricked the soldiers and...'

'I was a stupid kid then,' said Clem. He led Billy through the hedge and round the pig wallow, with its thin ice covering. 'I won't hit you, but if you've got something of ours in that sack, I'll chuck you in that.' He pointed at the pig wallow and held the lamp above the sack.

'You'd never...' Billy stared at him through the gloom.

Clem looked closely at the sack, then roared, 'Hey. That's jam you've taken.'

Billy tugged away from Clem. 'It wasn't me that took the jam. Anyhow, it ain't jam.'

'Then what the heck is this?' Clem gripped Billy's arm and held a jar to his face. 'It's got Mum's writing on the label.'

'I didn't take no jam,' wailed Billy, struggling to free himself again. 'Someone else done it.'

Clem kept hold of Billy with one hand, picked up another two jars and put them back in the sack. Then he shouldered it and sighed. 'Look, it's too cold out here.'

When they opened the back door, Mrs. Percheron was home, making hot drinks. As soon as she saw them both, her face softened. 'Billy Cliquot,' she said. She crouched beside the younger boy, smiling at him gently. 'What's happened?'

'Nothing. I cut me head.' Billy looked round the kitchen. 'You got anything I can eat?'

Clem said, 'I caught him red handed, stealing our jam.'

'I *never*. My dad told me he needed some cause he's not well.'

Clem caught his mother's eye and sighed. 'Billy, your father's getting you to do his dirty work, isn't he? I saw him today, and he wasn't ill at all.'

Billy shrugged, then Mr. Percheron came into the kitchen, coughing. He gave Billy a stern look and sat down by the fire, his hand on chest as though it hurt.

'Sit down, dear,' said Mrs. Percheron. She handed him a cup of cocoa and turned to Billy. 'Let's sort out that cut, then we'll find you something to eat.'

Soon, Billy was sitting at the kitchen table with a bandage round his head. As Mrs Percheron gave him a slice of bread and dripping, he stuck out his tongue at

Clem. 'Cut that out,' said Clem. 'Look, Billy, if you're hungry, come and ask us. It's no good stealing because we deal with thieves and we don't want to hurt you.' He clenched his huge fists. 'See?'

'Clem...' Mrs. Percheron shook her head warningly. She changed the subject, reaching into her handbag and smiling. 'I would have told you straight away if Billy hadn't been in such a bad way. There's so much excitement in town – lots of Red Cross messages came today. There's one from George.'

'George?' Clem beamed. 'We haven't heard from him for months. I was beginning to think he was...'

'That's your big brother, ain't it?' said Billy, picking his teeth with his finger. 'So he ain't dead then, like your other one?'

'It's dated August last year. *Six months ago.*' Mr. Percheron wiped his forehead with a big white hanky. 'About ruddy time.'

Luckily, Mrs. Percheron hadn't heard Billy. She was busy putting together a parcel for his family. 'There's a loaf and some soup for you. Don't break the bottle, we haven't many left. Clem'll give you some milk and I've put in some apples and jam. There's a little cake, precious.'

Clem said, 'I'll take you home before curfew.' He tousled Billy's hair. 'And I'll stop anyone pinching it from you.'

'It's nice here.' Billy wiped his nose on his cuff. 'Our house is flipping cold now they cut off the gas. Thanks, Mrs. Percheron. Like I said, we're all dead hungry. We need the jam.'

Friday 16th January
9 pm

A couple of evenings later, Clem went to a secret boxing practice in town. He certainly wasn't going to take any notice of the ban on sports. Afterwards, he felt his way home along the coast road before curfew, glad he had grown into his brother's thick coat and boots.

He knew his way well and there was a full moon. In nearly every garden there was a snowman, some with soldier's caps on and one or two with sticks for guns. The children had been busy, but now they were asleep behind the blackout curtains.

To his right, grey mist rolled over the sea towards the island, the first wisps of it fingering the iron railings on the sea wall. Clem increased his pace, his boots crunching on frozen traces of the snow. The air was raw and the soldiers had kept to the barracks for days. However, as Clem strode along, one stepped out between two buildings, holding up his hand. 'Your identity card, please.'

Clem took his time, making a meal of finding it. He handed it to the soldier, who checked it with his torch then handed it back. He looked puzzled. 'Why are you out tonight? It is cold.'

'I visited a sick aunt,' Clem lied. 'She's hungry.' His voice was surly, but the soldier didn't seem to mind.

He nodded briefly, then indicated Clem's bag. 'Open that, please.'

Clem took a deep breath and showed him, thinking, *now I'm for it*. But when the soldier saw his boxing gloves, he smiled. 'I do this sport too, at my home.' He searched for words, then said, 'Sport makes people too hungry. So please, don't carry these with you. You are old enough to understand the rules. Sport is banned because there isn't enough food.'

And whose fault is that? Clem thought. But he said nothing.

The soldier searched for words again and said, 'These gloves are a provocation.'

'Your English is good, sir.' Clem put away his card and gloves.

'I was studying English at university,' said the soldier. 'Before this war.'

For a moment, Clem suddenly felt sad for him, stuck in a foreign island, far from home and all that he loved. So he nodded his thanks politely and set off into the dark again, after saying, '*Guten abend*. Good evening.'

'Good evening, Clem Percheron. My name is Helmut,' the soldier called back, 'One day, when all this is over, I'll challenge you in the ring.'

'And I'll win,' retorted Clem. 'You can bet on that.'

Soon he was at Joe's place, ready to turn left up the lane. Suddenly the mist was so thick that he could barely make out the shape of the cottage. As he was wondering if Joe and his family were warm and had enough to eat, the back door of the cottage squeaked open.

Joe loomed out of the mist, his face pale in the dark. Clem said softly, 'Wotcha, Joe. I hope you aren't wasting coal. Someone might tell on you. Like me or that soldier I just met.'

'Clem!' Joe dropped his coal bucket with a clatter. 'I thought you was a soldier, you're so flipping tall. What are you doing out this late? Aren't you a church boy, nice and sensible?'

Clem laughed quietly. 'Secret boxing practice.' Then he said, 'Best be off now, or they'll be sending out a search party.'

Picking up the bucket, Joe nodded, then asked, 'You doing anything tomorrow morning? I've got something to show you the other side of town.' He lowered his voice and explained. 'I saw some prisoners today.'

'Those poor blokes,' said Clem. 'And there are women too, working like slaves. Legs La Motte says…'

' Legs - your mate from out West?' Joe asked. 'The runner?'

'The best in the island.' Clem nodded. 'He says there are loads of them near where he lives, up St Peter's Valley.'

'Bring a few turnips or some spuds, if you can,' said Joe. 'They're flipping starving. Treated like dirt, all of them. It blinking annoys me.'

Clem nodded. 'You're not kidding. It winds me up no end.'

'It's no good lashing out.' Joe gave him a look. 'When my dad used to hurt me and I punched him back, it never ended well. I guess it might be the same thing with the enemy. Fight them and we'd end up in clink. That wouldn't help anyone.'

'It's hard not to have a go. Some of them are asking for it,' said Clem.

Saturday, 17th January
7.30 am

The next day, Clem worked quickly through his morning jobs, milking the cows and putting the full churns on the wall for collection. He swept the yard free of snow, then left a note on the table, explaining that he was going into town and would be back about ten. Then he tucked some boiled turnips into his pocket and set off through the mist.

Down the lane, Joe had made up the fire, swept the cottage and shaken the mats over the sea wall. His brother and sister were staying with Auntie Vi, so at least he didn't have to worry about their breakfast, something he'd done ever since their mother had died.

After that, he pulled on his balaclava so that only his nose and eyes showed. Then he put on his school coat with its special inside pockets, gave his dog a handful of dried crusts and a fresh bowl of water. 'Look after the happy home, Beau,' The dog thumped his tail, put his nose on his paws and closed his eyes and Joe went into the garden.

Outside, sea mist curled around the cottage, thick as a blanket. Joe felt his way to his father's shed through a clutter of ropes and lobster pots. Inside, everything was in its place as usual. The box he wanted was under the workbench.

Joe dragged it out and opened the heavy metal lid. Inside, there was a stack of flares, each one the length of his forearm, each in a green canvas bag. He chose two, sniffing their faint smell of gunpowder and wax. Then he pushed the box back in place 'Perfect for the job,' he muttered.

His father's fishing boat was in dry dock for the winter. No one would notice that the flares were missing.

After locking the shed, he nipped into the road, cursing under his breath as the gate hinges squeaked. Then he padded along through the slushy snow, the flares banging against his legs in the hidden pockets.

Clem was waiting at the end of his lane as they'd planned. He pulled up his collar to hide his face and walked beside his friend in silence, their breath clouding the freezing air. After a time, he murmured, 'Are you sure they'll still be there? It's Saturday.'

Joe laughed quietly. 'You don't really think prisoners have a day off do you?'

Clem shook his head and said, 'Legs said they usually work up on the North Coast, not in this part of the island.'

'Yeah. Where no one can see them,' said Joe. 'That's why we didn't realise what a flippin' horrible time they have. The ones I saw were in a bad way. Really vile.' He bit his lip, then went on, 'You got some food?'

'Turnips. Not much though,' Clem patted his pockets and added quietly. 'I don't understand. Most of the soldiers are OK, so why do they do that to the prisoners?'

'The guards aren't the usual soldiers. They're brutes, sent over specially by Adolf.' Joe slowed down. 'Look, we'd better not get caught helping the prisoners.'

'They won't suspect *us*. I'll just say that we're going to feed the cows.' Clem smirked. 'They know I'm a nice church boy who doesn't lie.'

'Not half.'

Clem fell in behind Joe as they felt their way along the road. More fog swirled in from the sea, salt and icy, making their throats tickle as they trudged on in silence into town, then out the other side. No one was about, except a few brave shoppers with empty baskets.

After a couple of miles, Joe slowed his pace. Then he suddenly stopped dead. Just ahead of them, there was a sharp command. Then there was a thump, followed by another command. Joe hissed. 'The guard's at it again. Same man, frightening the prisoners. He's flippin' scum.'

Joe had told Clem what to expect: a row of skinny prisoners in rags, digging out a ditch beside the road or mixing concrete. There'd be an ugly brute of a soldier standing over them with a length of hosepipe filled with sand. *I'd like to get my hands on him*, Clem thought, bunching his fists.

Joe whispered, 'Keep close.' He nipped into a field behind a thick evergreen hedge, through a tiny gap. Clem followed him and even though he crouched low, his shoulders caught on a twig. As he pulled it off, it snapped.

Instantly, a German voice called out, very close. 'Who's there? *Wer ist da?*'

'A hedgehog,' mouthed Joe, trying not to laugh.

'Idiot,' whispered Clem.

The man bellowed, '*WER IST DA?* WHO IS IT?'

Behind the hedge, Joe and Clem held their breaths, edging themselves further back into the field. The shout came again, together with a whack on the hedge. A few frozen leaves fluttered down on to Clem and a blackbird flew upwards into the fog.

The guard grunted and stopped hitting the hedge. He shouted, '*Es war ein vogel*. It was a bird.' His jackboots slammed on the road as he turned and marched away.

'He was frightened of a bird,' Jo sniggered.

Clem muttered, 'Let's get rid of the turnips.'

'Follow me,' said Joe. Further along, there was a small break in the hedge, at ankle level. Joe lay flat on the snowy grass, peering through while Clem crouched behind him. They could see the prisoners directly in front of them, their backs turned to the hedge as they dug.

'Look at their shirts. They've got numbers on them,' whispered Clem, under cover of the scraping shovels. 'That's horrible. Like they're part of a list.'

One was so close that they could see most of his number, until he staggered with the weight of his shovel. His ragged shirt barely covered him and his trousers were splattered with mud. His feet were bare and his hands purple with cold.

'*Poor bloke*,' Joe murmured, keeping his head down as the guard stamped back. The soldier's black, shiny jackboots stopped bang opposite them.

The prisoner lifted his shovel again. Just as he gave every ounce of strength, the hosepipe slammed down beside him, catching him on the shoulder and he stumbled into the bottom of the ditch, his face in filthy water.

The guard laughed and moved away.

Clem swore. He passed Joe the turnips and muttered, 'Give them to him, quick.'

'Psst,' Joe whispered, poking the turnips through the opening in the hedge.

The prisoner glanced behind him as if he expected another blow. His eyes widened and he reached out his filthy hands and grabbed the turnips. Quick as a flash, he took a bite from one and handed the rest along the line.

Joe put his finger on his lips as the prisoner held his

hand on his chest as if to say, 'Thank you.'

Clem backed away and growled, 'I'd best go home or I'll hit that guard.' As he stepped away, there was another thump of the hosepipe further away. He hissed, 'We must help them. Or we're *nothing*.' Then he stepped noiselessly away, heading up the hill to his home.

Joe waited until Clem was safely away. Then he hurried off and found a wall to hide behind. There, he fished out a flare and wedged it between two stones, muttering, 'Make them jump, you little beauty.' Lighting the touch paper, he leapt back as it caught. There was a woosh of blood red flame against the yellow fog and a bang. Joe laughed, staring up as the vapour trail melted into the mist.

There was a mighty bellow from the guard, followed by a whistle.

Joe laughed again, then raced along his secret footpath until he was safely up the hill. No one would find him there. Below him, he could hear jackboots thundering along the road as soldiers arrived from all directions, yelling.

He set off again, picking his way over the soggy fields towards the sea. The other flare banged against his leg. Before he was too far off, he set that one off as well. As it surged upwards, he heard the guard's whistle again, followed by a string of German commands and the sound of running jackboots.

Noon

Joe's brother and sister still weren't home. After he'd raced back, zig zagging over the fields in the fog like a hunted hare, he'd washed the gunpowder off his hands then settled down at the kitchen table to mend a lobster pot with string and wire. As he pulled the sides of the last hole together, there was a thunderous knock at the door.

Joe grabbed his dog's collar and shouted, 'Who's there?' Then he burst out laughing as the door opened. There stood his friend, Spinner.

Her eyes were huge as she said, 'The Germans are in a rage again. Something's happened.'

'Oh yeah? Something's always happening. So, what's new?' Joe grinned. 'Hey, what's in that bag?'

'I brought you some toffee from Clem's mother.'

'Toffee? I haven't had any for months.' Joe stared at her. 'You teasing me?'

Spinner laughed. 'Would I?' She held out a small square wrapped in brown paper. 'Mrs. Percheron made it out of beetroot syrup. Clever. But it's really sticky. I had a bit and I couldn't speak for hours after.'

'She's a genius,' said Joe, smelling the toffee. 'Mmm.'

'Actually, the toffee was an excuse in case a soldier stopped me. I really came to tell you there's an escaped prisoner on the loose.'

'Poor devil,' said Joe.

'The Germans are crawling all over the place trying to find him.' Joe pulled the paper off his toffee as Spinner lowered her voice. 'Someone threw flares at the soldiers and some prisoners took advantage of the panic and scarpered. The enemy's *furious*.'

'Oh dear, oh dear. What a shame.' Joe smirked. As he put the toffee in his mouth, there was another knock at the kitchen door. He tried to speak, but his teeth were glued together and he made a gurgling sound. He pointed at the door and waved his hand at Spinner to open it.

The knocking came again, so Spinner went to open

the door and when she saw two young soldiers on the doorstep, she leapt back and gasped.

The soldiers took off their caps. 'Sorry to frighten you, Miss. But we have to inform you that a dangerous prisoner has escaped. There may be others. You must lock your doors.'

Joe made another gurgling sound. Spinner tried not to giggle. 'I'm sorry about my friend. He can't speak.' Then she held out her paper bag. 'Would you like a toffee?'

8 pm

Clem kept to himself after the encounter with the prisoners.

The snow had started again, just a few flakes, but it was icy cold. He'd taken a pile of potato sacks to the shed where they kept the ploughs and harrow, together with a horse blanket. Then he put some of last autumn's apples on the window sill where they could be found easily. The shed was open to one side, away from the wind, with a small, unglazed window to let more light in.

There was thin soup and a slice of bread for lunch. Clem finished it quickly, saying he had homework to do. He spent the afternoon at his books before catching up on his farming diary, where he wrote about migrant birds on the marshes and the amount of milk the cows were giving. As he wrote, he kept to facts and didn't give away his feelings.

Before he went to bed, he spoke to his mother. 'I saw something today.' He swallowed, trying to control his anger.

Mrs. Percheron put aside her knitting and leaned towards him.

Clem went on, 'I don't want to upset you, Mother. But it was terrible. I feel so sad and angry.'

'Was it the prisoners?' His mother's face clouded. 'Poor men.'

'Joe showed me what's going on,' Clem said. 'I heard about it at school, but it's different when you see it.' Mrs. Percheron took his hand as he went on, 'I don't know what we can do to help.'

His mother glanced briefly at the window, then listened in case anyone was outside the back door. She spoke rapidly in Jersey French. 'Some of the farmers are hiding prisoners up in the north of the island, in the valleys.'

Clem spread his hands. 'I wish *we* could that. But you can see everything in our flat fields and even on the steep ones. There's no hiding place.'

'That's true.' Mrs. Percheron picked up her knitting. She looked up at the photo of Bill in its black frame. 'But you see, every prisoner is a son or a brother, or even a father. So...'

Clem finished her sentence. He said slowly, 'So, we'd want someone to help George, if he was alone and hungry somewhere.'

His mother kept to Jersey French. 'Perhaps we might be a safe house – someone could hide in our barns for a night or two, then move on. They could arrive in the dark and leave in the dark, while it's winter.'

At last, Clem managed a smile. 'What does Father think?'

Mrs. Percheron began to knit. 'He wants to help. But it's dangerous to chatter about these things. A passing soldier might see something, a tiny thing that gives everything away. A lost shoe, a torn piece of shirt. Then there'd be a search.'

'Like last year,' said Clem. Then he whispered, 'There are two men on the loose this evening. They could be anywhere, terrified.' He explained what he and Joe had seen and that he'd put potato sacks in the implement shed. 'They can escape through the window.' He spread his hands. 'I had to.'

'If *we* don't, all of us, then we will *all* be worthless,' said his mother. She got up and said she'd try to find a little extra food to put out, in case someone needed it, adding again, 'But remember, son. This is very dangerous. Fear makes brutes dangerous and the guards are brutes. I have heard about what is going on and so has your father, God help us all.'

Clem stood up. 'I said to Joe we'd be nothing if we don't help. That's the same thing as worthless.'

In Jersey French, or Jerriais, Mrs. Percheron said, '*Le Bouon Dieu a lit dans nos schoeurs*. God hath shined in our hearts. And we must keep that light shining.' Then she smiled. 'There's an old well in that little shed, with a trap door over it. It's very difficult to see. No one would notice it unless they knew. It could be an extra hiding place.'

Sunday 18th January
11 am

The next day, Ginger had the Brayes' house almost to himself, so he could read to his heart's content. There hadn't been any guns in the night, and Sunday was always the same, with a little extra food and usually church, where there was the comfort of friends all sharing news.

Mr. Braye had lit the Sunday fire in the sitting room, so it was warm. The sun was pouring in through the large windows, and that made the room even warmer. Everyone else had gone to church to hear Clem sing a solo, but Rosie had a cold and someone had to stay at home with her.

Although Clem hadn't mentioned the escaped prisoners, the news had got round the island. So it was best that someone stayed in the house with the doors firmly locked.

Rosie was still in her dressing gown, sucking her thumb and snuffling as she trailed her doll along the floor. 'Vera's ill,' she explained to Ginger. 'She has a bad cold.' Then she settled on the sofa, pulled a rug over herself and the doll. 'DOG. ORYX. LEMUR LEMUR,' she muttered.

'Clever Rosie,' said Ginger. 'When Father comes back, you can tell him your alphabet.'

Rosie said, 'Vera's tired.'

She closed her eyes, so Ginger concentrated on his book, *The Riddle of the Sands*. The book was a spy thriller and he was in the middle of a description of a dramatic race at sea. However, just as he was at the most exciting part, a shadow fell on his page, as though the sun had suddenly gone behind a cloud.

Ginger glanced up briefly, but then he gasped.

A stick of a man stood at the window, dressed in grimy rags. He was trembling and there was a dusting of snow on his black, matted hair. As Ginger looked at him, the man edged closer, his nose almost pressed to the glass.

Ginger jumped to his feet, his book tumbling to the ground with a thud. Then he caught his breath. The man wasn't just looking into the room. He was staring at Rosie, almost as though he recognised her.

'I have a gun,' shouted Ginger. 'Go away.'

At that, Rosie woke up with a cry. She caught sight of the stranger and pointed at him. 'Daddy,' she shouted. 'Daddy's out there.'

Ginger kept his voice calm. 'It's not Daddy,' he said. 'Daddy's in his battleship.'

Rosie pushed the blankets back, jumped off the sofa and ran towards the window to show him her doll. 'Look, this is Vera.'

Ginger grabbed her other hand and tried to tug her away. The stranger's eyes were blinking, as though he was trying not to cry. Ginger noticed his filthy bare feet and his shabby blue and white clothes and the number on his pocket. *Prisoner*, he thought.

The man moved his glance to Ginger, then put his finger on his cracked lips, glancing behind him as if he was being watched. As he did so, Ginger saw terror flickering over his hollowed-out face. His own stomach turned to water. The man was so thin, his filthy clothes flapping around his skinny arms and legs in the icy breeze.

Rosie tugged at her brother again as the man pointed again at his mouth. He pressed his hands together in prayer, his eyes boring into Ginger's.

Ginger held himself still. He couldn't leave Rosie alone. The man might break through the window. He pointed to the left, showing him to go to the back door, then rushed to the kitchen with Rosie firmly in his grasp. 'Bread, cheese, apples, water,' he said, opening and shutting cupboards. 'That man needs some food.'

As he searched, Rosie clung to his leg. 'I want Daddy,' she yelled, suddenly.

'Shh, Rosie. Daddy will come back when the war is over.' Ginger found his tiny ration of chocolate and shoved it into a precious paper bag together with the food.

With Rosie still attached to his leg, he opened the kitchen door and put the bag of food and mug of milk on the shelf outside. Rosie suddenly let go and shoved past him. 'Come and fetch your picnic,' she yelled, racing towards the prisoner as he came round the corner.

Ginger charged after her, wrenching her back as the stranger sidled towards the food. 'Take it,' he said softly. 'Quick.'

The stranger gave him a nod of thanks. Then he vanished through the farmyard and into Clem's orchard, leaving a strange smell and patches of blood on the snow.

'That man stank,' said Rosie, holding her nose. She looked up at Ginger and her tears welled up. 'He has bare feet.'

'Let's try to be kind.' Ginger picked her up. 'Maybe he fell in the mud and now he can go home to a lovely bath and eat his picnic.' As he carried her indoors, he found that he was trembling. He locked the door again and bolted it as well, trying not to weep himself.

Not long after, Spinner returned from church, banging on the door so Ginger would unbolt it.

'Clem was brilliant,' she said, taking off her church hat. 'He sang so well. You should have heard him...' She stopped, mid-sentence, staring at her cousin. 'What's up?'

'Nothing at all,' said Ginger, blinking, as Rosie came into the kitchen. 'We had a lovely time, didn't we Rosie?'

'Ginger told the man he had a gun,' said Rosie. Then she went off to find her mother, the doll trailing on the floor as usual.

Spinner stared at him. 'But we buried the guns, ages ago. Rosie doesn't know anything about them, surely?'

Ginger shook his head, 'She definitely doesn't. But a prisoner came here today, in a terrible state. He scared the stuffing out of me at first. So, I told him I had a gun.'

'Where?' Spinner stared at him. 'Did he break in?'

'No. He was very weak.' Ginger said, as Mr. Braye arrived back form church. He repeated his story. 'Uncle Hedley, a prisoner came here today.' He pointed at the window. 'He stood there, close to the glass and he looked terrible, so cold and hungry and his clothes were in rags.' He swallowed, then went on, 'I'm so sorry, but I gave him all the cheese. I had to.'

'Did anyone see him? Apart from Rosie?'

Ginger shook his head. 'I don't think so.' He bit his lip. 'I'm sure he wasn't a spy or anyone dangerous. He was desperate. It was awful to see someone like that.' He looked at his uncle and added, 'He hadn't eaten for weeks. I could see that.'

Mr. Braye sat down and indicated that Ginger and

Spinner did the same. 'I'm so sorry, Ginger. That must have been a horrible shock.' He put his head in his hands for a moment, then glanced at them both. 'My guess is that he's a slave worker on the run.'

'*Slave?*' Spinner gasped. 'What do you mean? We don't have slaves in Jersey.'

Upstairs, Rosie was silent, as though she might be listening, so Ginger lowered his voice. 'I heard about them. They're prisoners from the Eastern Front. Soviets and they've been marched here through Germany and France.'

Mr. Braye opened an atlas and showed them where the Eastern Front was. 'It's Russia, Ukraine, Lativa, all those nearby countries,' he said quietly. 'The fighting's been savage, hand to hand stuff. Awful things have happened there, so Hitler wants revenge. They're being made to build gun sites and bunkers here and in Guernsey, and they're being brutally treated.'

'*In Jersey?*' Spinner bit her lip. 'That's terrible.'

'Where do they live?' Ginger looked puzzled. 'The camps near here are a bit basic, but I never saw anything bad going on. Anyhow, the workers in those camps are Spanish, mostly. They get paid.' He pictured them, and added, 'Not much, but a little. Though they're hungry.'

'The Soviet slave labourers are a different matter altogether. They live in the west of the island,' said Mr. Braye. Suddenly, his voice grew fierce. 'Don't go near them. It wouldn't help.'

Spinner stared at him. 'That's miles away. So why was this one hiding near us?'

Mr. Braye shrugged. 'I don't know.' Then he gripped Spinner's wrist. 'Look, you *must all understand* that sheltering and feeding the Soviet prisoners is against the rules. The punishments are severe.' He let go of Spinner's wrist and added, 'If we're caught feeding even one of them, we'd all be in dreadful trouble. It would be the very worst punishment of all.' Then he smiled gently. 'But if we're very careful, there might be a way.'

8 pm

Later, Clem came over to the Brayes' house after locking up. He said, 'Mum and Dad told me about the man you saw.'

Ginger explained what had happened and then went on to talk about Mr. Braye's warning, but Clem frowned. 'It's not that simple. I reckon we don't have a choice.'

'What do you mean?' Spinner spread her hands. 'Not that simple?'

Clem took a deep breath. 'Joe and I saw some prisoners yesterday, like that man. They were being treated very badly, like your father said, Spinner.' He flinched and carried on, 'I mean REALLY badly. And they were starving.' He explained about the turnips. 'I've never seen anyone so desperate. And now two of them have escaped, and it might have been our fault. So it's up to us to shelter them.'

'Why is it *your* fault?' Spinner looked puzzled. 'You didn't help them to escape, did you?'

'We planned a diversion and that gave them a chance to run for it,' said Clem. 'Joe did it after I'd left but we both planned it, with the flares.'

Spinner beamed. 'So it was him that lit the flares? He never said.'

'It wasn't you,' Ginger offered. 'It was the fog that gave them a chance. Without, zero gamble.'

'Maybe,' said Clem, looking more cheerful. 'But either way, we've got to help them, or else we're just...' he searched for the word...'cowards. They'll be out on their own in this weather, with nothing.'

'Nothing but their freedom,' said Ginger. 'Actually.'

Spinner frowned. 'But the Germans said the prisoners are dangerous. They warned me and Joe when I was down at his place.'

'And you believed them?' Clem laughed. 'Who does *that?*'

'The one I saw didn't look dangerous in the least, except at first glance. If there was a strong wind, he'd blow over,' said Ginger. He fitted his trumpet together and blew a few notes, pulled on a pair of grey fingerless mittens and said, 'I'm going outside now.'

'In the dark? What for? It's freezing out there.' Spinner looked anxious. 'And there are *two* prisoners. The other one might be desperate...'

Ginger set his mouth. 'I'm going to play the Russian national anthem for them this evening in the garden. I hope they hear and it gives them hope.' Then he headed for the door.

'For goodness sake,' said Clem. 'Now you're the one that's playing with fire. It's illegal to play *any* national anthems, except the German one.'

Spinner hung back. 'We don't want the very worst punishment. Do we?'

'Do or die,' said Ginger over his shoulder as he headed into the dark. 'But I'm not flipping stupid.' He moved away, heading for the gate into the Percheron's garden.

Clem flung himself after him, grabbed his sleeve and hissed, 'If the Germans hear, they'll take it out on the prisoners as well as us.'

'You say you want to help the prisoners,' said Ginger. He looked at Clem scornfully, then shook off hand, striding towards the end of the garden. '*So do I*. This is what *I* help with. Music. And I'm not giving in.' He took a deep breath.

Clem tried to wrench the trumpet away, but Ginger elbowed him in the ribs and said, 'Cut it out Clem. Don't be a coward.' Then he began to play. The notes soared to the stars, but he varied them, so that no one would recognize the tune, unless of course they were from the Eastern Front.

Clem turned on his heel and stomped away, but after a while, the music was so wonderful that he forgave his friend and quietly stepped nearer to listen. When Ginger had finished, he asked, 'What was that tune you ended with?'

'Russian ballet music,' said Ginger. 'The men dancers can leap to shoulder height. They love ballet in Russia.' He pushed his glasses back in place and said,

I just hope it helps the man I saw today.'

'The horrible thing is,' muttered Clem, 'they've taken away his name. He's been turned into a number. We saw that yesterday. And you saw it today.'

Ginger said, 'They're going to make everyone over fourteen have identity cards. That's us, Clem. We're all numbers now.'

Clem glared at him. 'No we aren't.'

'No need to be angry,' Ginger said quietly. Then he added, 'Everything used to be so blinking hilarious. What's happened to us all?' He held up his wristwatch with its luminous dial. 'Let's not go back inside. I'm going to play my trumpet to your cows. It might cheer them up.'

Clem laughed at last. 'What are you going to play?'

~ 52 ~

'Obvious, isn't it?' Ginger said, *'Away in a Manger.'* He burst out laughing too and soon they were rolling on the ground clutching their stomachs as if they'd never stop. When they picked themselves up, Ginger went on, 'You've got flipping cow muck in your hair.'

Saturday 24th January
9 am

A week later, Joe and Diddie arrived at the farm not long after breakfast. They turned into the yard just as Clem finished milking. 'There's not much, this time of year,' said Clem, showing him the half empty churn. 'And we have to give most of it to the Germans. Blooming cheek.' He filled a tin mug. 'Half each,' he said, offering it to Diddie.

'Thanks, Clem.' Diddie downed her share and handed the mug to Joe. As he drank his, she stroked the old horse. 'Arthur loves Ernest. He wants to ride him.'

'Maybe another day,' Clem replied, taking Joe's empty mug. 'Anyhow, where *is* Arthur today? And Beaufort?'

'It's Arthur's day with Auntie Vi,' Joe explained. 'Beau's staying with them. He's very useful. He licks Arthur's face clean.' He took one handle of the milk churn and helped Clem with it to its stand, ready for collection. 'Auntie Vi said your dad's not well. I thought you might like a hand today.'

'*I'm* not helping,' said Diddie. She crossed her arms. 'It's too cold.'

'Yeah, well, don't go mucking about on your own, or getting in with Billy Cliquot.' Joe rolled his eyes. 'Auntie Vi said I have to keep you out of trouble after you chucked icicles at those soldiers last week.'

Diddie giggled. 'It was funny. The icicles went down their shirts and they were furious.'

Clem interrupted the discussion. 'Auntie Vi's right, Dad's not well. He's still coughing and that's not like him at all. Mum doesn't want him going outside, so I'd appreciate the help. Thanks, Joe.'

Diddie headed off to find Spinner and Rosie at the Brayes' house. 'We're going to speak in code,' she said. 'It's Elephant, Apple, Snake, Yak.'

When she was safely out of hearing, Clem told Joe about the prisoner that Ginger had fed the week before. 'I think he was the one we saw digging the ditch when it was foggy. Probably Russian.' He handed Joe a bucket of pig swill for Hotspur. 'We've been putting out extra food and it always goes.'

'No one would suspect your mother. She's like a saint.' Joe stuck his finger in the bucket, then sniffed it. 'Crikey, this looks like sick, smells like sick and...' He licked his finger. 'But it don't taste like sick, not really.' He shook the bucket so that vegetable peelings rose to the top. 'Still, I might fancy some if I was hungry enough.'

'Watch out,' said Clem. 'Hotspur's in a bad mood. I am too. I can't get the blooming tractor started. Tried all week.'

Next door, Hotspur was ramming the garage door, desperate for breakfast. As Joe crossed the yard from the farm, he called out to the pig. 'Calm down. Your old pal Joe's here.' The door shuddered as Hotspur butted his enormous head against it. Joe shouted through the keyhole, 'Oi, you nasty old pig, I thought you had a brain. This is your personal waiter service, you idiot.'

He heard Hotspur's trotters reversing across the

concrete floor, then there was a gentle grunt. Very carefully, Joe edged round the door, wrinkling his nose. 'Blimey. What a pong.'

The pig looked at him expectantly from the other side of the garage. 'Sit,' said Joe, expecting nothing. However, Hotspur sat on his haunches with his mouth open, his mean little eyes focused on the bucket. 'Lovely teeth, mate,' Joe said.

The barricades lay flat across the floor, one in a deep pile of pig muck. Hotspur licked his lip, stood up and stepped delicately towards Joe, his muscles rippling and his trotters gleaming.

'Brekky wekky,' said Joe, nipping behind a straw bale. 'Blimey, Hots, you're looking a bit flipping dangerous today.' He dumped the bucket in front of the straw bale as the pig thundered towards it. Joe whipped his fingers away, then grabbed the two barricades, lifting them up and slamming them together and tying them with string from his pocket.

'No chance of escaping again, big fella,' he said from behind them, testing his knots and adding a few more.

The pig finished, then licked out the bucket, rolling it round and grunting as he scooped out every last scrap. After that, he worried at the handle so that the bucket clanked on the concrete. Joe said, 'Don't do that after curfew or someone might hear you, nip in and take you home for a nice pork dinner.'

Hotspur gave him a shifty look and settled in a pile of straw. 'Flipping heck,' Joe muttered, as the food took its effect on Hotspur's digestive system. 'I reckon we could use your smell against the enemy.'

The pig began to snore, so Joe decided to check the flat above the garage. 'Not that anyone would come and sleep here,' he said to Hotspur, 'with your stink.'

Upstairs, the smell was seeping through gaps in the floorboards. Joe laughed. 'Hot air rises. No German soldier would put up with this.'

Ginger's place on the landing was the smelliest of all because the cracks between the floorboards were the widest. Joe knelt down to peer through to see if Hotspur was still asleep. Then he leapt up, ran back down the stairs, yelling, 'Hey! You wretched pig. What are you doing?'

In the garage, Hotspur was chewing through his knots on the barricades, working his way down them. He looked sideways at Joe and kept at it.

'Strewth.' Joe grabbed a coil of thin wire that hung beside the work bench. He chopped it into lengths, eying Hotspur all the time and muttering to him. 'Blimming pig. You and Peggy are just the same, always wanting to escape.' As fast as the pig undid a knot, Joe twisted wire in its place, and as he worked, Hotspur blew at him with his special morning breath.

At last everything was pig proof. Joe hung the rest of the wire back on its hook, but as he turned to go, his eye was caught by something glinting on the work bench. Tucked between two hammers, there was a coin.

Holding it up to the light from the dirty garage window, he turned it over and spat on his hanky to rub it clean. When the coin shone, he examined it. 'Blimey,' he whispered. It's gold.' He tucked it into his trouser pocket and left Hotspur to sleep off his breakfast.

11 am
Joe didn't say anything about his find when he went to

the field to help Clem with the ploughing. He wanted to think about the coin before he showed anyone. Anyway, Clem was grappling with Ernest. The old horse didn't want to work.

Clem glanced at Joe when he arrived. He stopped Ernest and handed over the reins. 'Here, Joe. The poor old boy's feeling the cold in his bones.' He patted the horse's neck. 'Can you take over now? I want to check on Peggy. I reckon she's about to have her piglets.'

'I'll ask Dad to help with the tractor next time he's home,' Joe said. 'Except he never is. Just as well.'

He stepped into place behind the plough and as Clem walked away, he urged Ernest to walk on. Sensing Joe's calm, the old horse moved forward and the plough sliced easily through the soil. Joe began to whistle, enjoying the work and thinking about the coin. At each end, Ernest turned without needing directions, and Joe followed on, whistling every tune he knew until the sun began to sink and the field was finished. Then he unhooked the plough and led Ernest to the farmyard in the dusk murmuring to him, 'An apple for you, old boy, after all your hard work.'

As he undid the harness, he noticed Clem walking back into the yard smiling, then going into the farmhouse. 'Something's made him happy,' said Joe, under his breath, 'about blimming time.'

He brushed Ernest, sweeping over the horse's glossy coat as the animal pulled hay from the rack. When he was done, he held out an apple. 'There you are boy,' he said, as Clem came out of the farmhouse and walked into the barn, quickly followed by Ginger and Spinner.

'Follow me,' said Clem, still grinning. 'Come and look at Peggy's babies. I've just been to tell Mum and Dad.'

He led them through the open barn door and glanced in. Then he whirled round to the others. 'There are even more than I thought. She's popping them out like a machine gun. Three more already.'

'Oh!' Spinner clutched her hands together and beamed as she looked into the sty. 'Piglets! Loads and loads and loads. Oh well done, Peggy.'

Joe counted, 'Thirteen. An unlucky number. Excellent. It's a sign that the enemy are going to lose.'

Peggy lay on her side, as some of the tiny piglets suckled and others scrambled over each other to find the teats. Clem scratched behind her ears and round her neck. 'You clever girl, Peggy.' He picked up a piglet and handed it to Joe. 'They're really small. Probably because there are so many.'

Joe's piglet had its eyes closed, but its tiny tail was a perfect squiggle. As he held it in mid-air, it let out a stream of liquid, which spattered far and wide. 'Blimey,' said Joe. He wiped a yellow trail off his jumper and offered the piglet to Spinner.

Spinner pushed his hands away. 'It's got a sweet face, but...'

Ginger was counting again. 'I say. There are fourteen. I just spotted another.'

After counting again, Clem beamed, then he said, 'I might sleep here for a few days in case she squashes them by mistake.'

'Or eats them,' added Joe, helpfully.

Spinner shoved him, but Clem said, 'They do that. Anyhow, I want to find homes for them as soon as possible. The enemy makes us give them half after we've fed them for a few weeks. They take half of everything. Much better to let Jersey people have them. If they check up, we'll just say they died or something.'

'Auntie Vi might like one,' suggested Joe. 'She could keep it in her best front room.' He cocked his ears. 'Guess what? I can hear her now, collecting Diddie. Shall we ask her?'

6.30 pm
After trying to sweet talk Auntie Vi into taking a piglet home in the pram, without success, Joe stayed on for supper at the farmhouse.

After grace, Mr. Percheron tried to eat his soup, but in the end, he put his spoon down and said to Clem's mother, 'It's very good soup, my dear. But I'm not hungry. Give it to the boys.' He pushed the soup bowl to Joe, who shared it with Clem.

'It's flipping delicious,' Joe said, scraping the bowl.

After supper, Mr. Percheron handed Clem the family bible. 'You read tonight, son. I'm not up to it.'

Clem glanced at his father and noticed that his hands were trembling. So, he opened the right page and read the part about fishermen putting their nets on the other side of the boat when they didn't get a good catch.

'That's a bit blinking obvious,' said Joe. 'If the fish aren't one side, of course you try the other, stands to reason.' Mr. Percheron gave him one of his looks, so Joe changed tack. 'My Dad fished a dead man out of the sea the other day. He was swollen like a balloon. Nasty. We kept his boots. Had to wash them though, in case there was any toes left inside.'

Clem kicked him. 'Shut up, Joe.'

Mr. Percheron patted his wife's hand, then said he'd go to bed without listening to the news.

Mrs Percheron exchanged glances with Clem, and mouthed, 'He's not well. Bad chest.'

So Clem said, 'Joe and I'll wash up. You look after Dad.' He hung the kettle on its hook over the fire for a hot water bottle for his father.

As she left the kitchen, Mrs. Percheron said to Joe, 'Don't forget your fish cakes, my love.' She pointed at a fat parcel on the dresser, wrapped up with newspaper. Then she hurried after her husband.

Joe stacked the soup bowls by the sink. 'Sorry, I shouldn't have said that, about the drowned man. And the boots.' He grated a little soap into the washing up bowl and took the last of the hot water to melt it. Then he added cold water and started his work.

Clem filled the hot water bottle and took it upstairs. When he returned with a pile of blankets and a pillow, he said, 'I'm going to stay in the barn to keep an eye on Peggy and her family.'

'Good idea.' Joe hung the cloth to dry on the rack above the fire. He said, 'I know Bill died at sea. I'm such a stupid idiot, saying that. Sorry, Clem.'

'It doesn't matter. Mother didn't even notice, she's so worried about Dad.' Clem gave Joe a wintry smile. 'War makes us all idiots and anyhow, you lost your mother. I lost my brother. One each. We're quits.' Then he ladled the last of the soup into a small metal can, screwed the lid on it and said, 'We're still putting out what we can. Those prisoners haven't been caught yet.'

'They're lucky chaps,' said Joe, 'if they're eating your mum's cooking every day. She can make anything out of turnips.' He picked up his parcel of fishcakes and added, 'If you need some help, if your dad gets really ill, I'm up for it. There's no fishing at the moment, and I don't go to school much. Can't stand having to learn German.' Then he hurried into the dark.

'Thanks Joe,' Clem called out. He put the soup can outside on the shelf beside the back door before going off to do his evening round, the blankets rolled up under his arm. As he walked up to Peggy's barn, a shadowy figure nipped across the yard. Clem pressed himself against the barn door, watching. The figure picked up the soup can, retreated to the orchard and disappeared into the night.

Tuesday 3rd February
7.00 am

Clem stayed in the barn for the first few nights after the piglets' arrival into the world. The straw was warm and he slept fully dressed, heaped up in blankets, at peace because he put extra bolts on the door. There was plenty of company: the rustle of mice in the straw and Peggy shuffling about in her pen, the piglets squealing softly in their sleep. Ernest whinnied gently in his sleep.

Once night, Clem heard light footsteps outside. Someone tried the handle, gently turning it. Shadows crisscrossed the strip of moonlight that shone under the door, then vanished. Another time, he heard a soft conversation and peered through a little window to the side of the entrance. Two men, their faces obscured by caps, stood together, watching the farmhouse. Then they moved off, still chattering in a foreign language.

'Checking us out,' Clem thought, clutching his heavy torch. 'Wondering what they can steal.'

Before he slept each night, he added to the false wall that he was making behind the pig sty, using straw bales, securing each bale with wooden pegs to keep it stable. Each evening, he took a few more things over from the farmhouse: a jug and bowl for washing, a precious piece of soap and a towel. He climbed over the false wall with them, making ready for anyone who might need them. There was one of his brother's shirts, too and a pair of socks, tucked out of sight.

And each evening, he put out soup and apples in the shed for anyone who might need. The food had always gone by daybreak.

At school, he kept yawning, trying to focus on Latin and Algebra, but when he looked round, he saw that half the boys in his class were yawning too, either from hunger or exhaustion.

When the piglets had learned to keep away from their mother's dangerous bulk, he went back to the farmhouse to sleep. He left the barn door shut, unlocked. If anyone tried to steal a piglet, Peggy would defend them, he was sure, but at least someone could find real shelter.

The morning after his first night back at home, he found a scrap of paper on the back door mat, and on it were two words in capital letters, *THANK YOU.*'

Clem's heart raced. He shoved the paper in his pocket and looked outside, but it was not yet light. He listened, but all he could hear was the owl on her last flight back to her nest. So he walked cautiously to the barn. After he'd fed Peggy and Ernest, he climbed into the hiding place and smiled with relief. Someone had used the washing bowl in the hiding place. The mattress had dents in it.

He tore the paper into pieces and fed it to Peggy, checked that all her piglets were with her and went back to the house for breakfast. Over their porridge, he spoke to his parents in Jersey French.

Mr. Percheron kept his voice very quiet. 'Tell no-one.' He tilted his head in the direction of the Brayes' house. 'Not even our closest friends. Not yet.'

Clem nodded then said to his mother, 'Be careful

with the soup can this evening, mother. Anyone could see you.'

Mrs. Percheron gave him her sweet smile. 'I can be a little forgetful. Leaving soup outside, or a few apples or turnips isn't a crime you know.' She laughed gently. 'Especially if you make it look like a mistake.'

'Sometimes, *informers* pretend to be prisoners,' said Clem. 'Someone told me at school. Or even soldiers, dressed up in rags, just to catch us out.'

'How wicked,' said his mother. 'But perhaps they need food too.'

A sudden gust of wind sucked the black out curtains in and out, as though someone had shaken them. Clem went to pull them back. The sunrise was bright painting the frosty garden as red as blood.

Clem shivered, for no reason at all. He put his arm round his mother. 'It must be horrible to be out there, alone and frightened even when the sun rises.'

Wednesday 4th February
7.30 pm

It was time to start band practice again. For a time, the weather had been so cold it was almost too painful to play their instruments. There was still a hard frost this evening. They gathered in the kitchen, the only warm place in the house.

'Keep an ear out for Rosie, will you?' Aunt Edie said, on her way out to visit Mrs. Percheron. 'She's in bed, but she's found that wretched potato gun again.'

Ginger groaned. 'I put it on top of the tall bookshelf. Giving it to her was a big mistake, but I thought it would explain why I shouted about having a gun. You know, when that man looked through the window.'

'Oh dear,' said Spinner, putting together her saxophone. 'She'll go too far one day and get us all into trouble.'

'*So what?*' Joe shrugged. 'We haven't done anything much. I've flicked a few stones at them, you've spread a bit of manure on the roads. Ginger has played a bit of music. There's nothing to see here and no one to find. Not even escaped prisoners.'

Spinner changed the subject. 'Daddy's been into College today. He's fetching some music.' She looked at the clock. 'He'll be back any minute.'

Clem flushed red, then blew into his sousa, warming it up. Soon, they were playing through their music, tapping their feet to keep the rhythm.

Mr. Braye arrived, pushing open the door with a blast of cold air that made everyone jump. He said, 'Hello everyone. That sounded great outside. Sorry to be so late, but I've found some new music for you. It's called 'Ain't Misbehavin.'

'Perfect,' said Joe. 'Because we never misbehave, do we, chaps?'

After they'd run through it a few times. They stopped for a break. Mr. Braye made everyone a cup of dandelion tea. As they drank it, Joe said. 'I've made up a new song. It's called The Lobster Blues. It's about not being able to catch lobsters because of the mines.'

'The mines?' Spinner said. 'I know they've put lots out but is it really impossible to find a lobster.'

'Hopeless,' said Joe. 'Unless they get bored under sea and decide to explore the land.' He put down his cup, took out a pair of spoons from his pocket and began to thump them up and down on his thigh, making a rhythm, then he sang *'I woke up this morning, feeling blue, thought I'd catch a lobster, but then I knew, I knew, it's true about the mines, man, about the mines.'*

Ginger said, 'Are there mines on every beach? Poor old Lobsters. One false move and they learn to fly.'

'Poor old *us*,' said Joe. He rubbed his stomach. 'I love a nice lobster claw.'

'That's an excellent idea,' said Mr. Braye. 'Maybe Ginger could compose the tune? And Clem, you could play the explosions on your sousa.'

Everyone laughed and finished off their drinks. Mr. Braye said he had work to do in his study and went upstairs. When the four of them were alone, Joe fished in his pocket and held up the coin. 'I found this the day the piglets were born. Meant to tell you, but I forgot in the excitement.'

'Gosh,' said Spinner, touching it. 'It's *beautiful*. Where was it?'

'On the garage workbench, gleaming away.'

'Crikey. It's gold,' said Ginger, holding it to the light. 'I'm sure it is.' Then he frowned. 'But I don't understand. I was in the garage the night before Hotspur moved in, working on my model plane. I'd have noticed a coin.' He took it from Joe. 'Russian,' he said. Peering it at more closely, he added, 'It's old Russian. There's a Tzar's head on it. Pre-revolution. These coins are rare.'

'Maybe the man at the window was a Russian aristocrat,' said Spinner. 'And he's been hiding in the garage for ages.'

'No one would hide in the same place as Hotspur. Being in prison would be miles better than that,' said Joe.

'Actually, it's probably a perfect place,' said Spinner. 'Because the soldiers would be far too frightened of Hotspur to search there.'

Ginger said, 'But how could a prisoner keep a coin? They take everything from them, even their names. Also, they usually shave their heads and the man I saw had longish hair, so he must have been on the run for a quite a time.'

Spinner picked up the coin. 'Daddy used to collect things, toys, shells, coins, all sorts. Maybe it fell through a crack in the floorboards. I'll ask him.'

Clem checked the clock and turned to Joe, 'You'd better go home. Curfew starts soon.'

Joe gave the coin to Spinner so she could ask her

father. 'I want it back, mind. It might come in handy. I could buy a boat with that.'

'Hurry up,' said Clem. 'It's really late. You'll be in trouble if you're caught.'

'Me? In trouble?' Joe laughed. He held up his pen knife. 'I always have an emergency plan. See you soon, chaps.'

10 pm

Joe crept down Spinner's garden, crunching on the frozen grass. The moon was behind the clouds, so he edged towards the gate into the lane, noticing that the woodshed door was open. Spinner had told him they always locked it these days.

At that moment, the clouds parted and the moon sailed into view, throwing silver. 'Blimey,' muttered Joe, looking up. 'Don't overdo it, mate.'

Holding his breath, he sidled along the shed wall until he was below its dusty window, wondering if it was safe to carry on into the lane. He flicked open his penknife, ready, cursing the sound of his own breathing. *Someone's in there*, he thought, tensing his muscles. He listened, but there was nothing, only the rustle of dead leaves on the old conker tree.

But somehow, he knew he was not alone.

Stilling his breathing and his heart, he waited. Then there was a faint crunch inside the shed. Joe pressed himself against the wall. The crunch came again, then suddenly the dark shape of a tall skinny man shot out of the door, followed instantly by another, much shorter.

'Ruddy hell,' Joe whispered, shrinking even further back. 'It's like Piccadilly Circus out here.'

The men leapt over the gate and ran down the lane,

scattering gravel. In the moonlight, their faces were white as skulls. The first man's hair was long and wild, but the second man's head was shaved. The moon lit his naked skull like a beacon. Joe watched them for a minute, then set off behind them.

'*Prisoners,*' he muttered. 'I must have scared them.' He raced down the lane, following the second man's moonlit head bobbing up and down until they reached the corner where the lane met the main road. Suddenly, they vanished through a gap in the hedge.

Joe stood at the crossing, listening to their feet pounding through the fields, then he shrugged. 'What's the point of following?' he muttered, turning east and heading for home along the coast road. 'It's too blimmin' cold to hang about any longer.'

Sticking to the edge of the road, he ran silently along in his old gym shoes, humming to himself, but with his penknife still open and ready. But just as his cottage came into distant view, a soldier stepped out of a gateway ahead of him, the tip of his gun glinting. 'Who's there?' he called.

'Not me,' gasped Joe, looking round frantically. Each side of him, tall granite walls edged the road, easy enough to climb, but in full, moonlit view. 'Oh ruddy hell,' he muttered, 'this is the last thing I need.' Then he picked up a handful of gravel and hurled it high so that it flew in an arc to the other side of the soldier.

The man jumped, tearing his bayonet out of its scabbard. As he waved the blade, he bellowed, 'Who goes there?' Then he began to march along the road in Joe's direction, the bayonet flashing in the moonlight. After staring wildly into the dark, he turned and stamped away again, peering into gateways and shouting, 'Show yourself, or you will wish you had.'

'Nothing for it,' Joe muttered. Then he stabbed himself sharply in the palm of his hand. Trying not to shout with pain, he tucked the gory penknife into a crack in the wall and ran out into the road form his hiding place. Blood dripped on to the road. 'Oh heck,' he muttered, wincing. Then he shouted, 'Help, help.'

The soldier spun round to face him, yelling much louder than Joe. '*Hande Hoch*. Hands up.'

Joe gave a shriek. As he put up both hands, blood oozed down his wrist and into his cuff. 'Help, sir. I need a lift to hospital.' Then he managed to wobble dangerously without falling over.

'Keep both hands up,' shouted the soldier, running with the bayonet blade pointing directly at him. 'Show you have no gun.'

Joe managed a sob. 'Sir, I was running to get home before curfew and I slipped and fell on a piece of glass.' He jiggled his arm and blood dripped again. As the man came to a halt, he spoke to him in the few German words he'd been forced to learn at school. '*Bitte, der herr.* Please, sir.'

'Where is this glass? Show me.' The soldier glared at him, then slowly put his bayonet back into its scabbard.

'Flipping heck,' Joe said, stumbling towards him. 'I'm bleeding to death. My mind is going. I can't remember where the flipping glass is.' He grabbed the German's woolly sleeve. 'Sorry, if the blood stains,' he whispered, closing his eyes as though he was about the faint, 'but I'm going to die. It will look very bad for you if you don't help a young man in need.'

The soldier sighed then said, '*Kommt*. Come, I will help you.' Then Joe passed out without having to pretend.

Midnight

When he came to, he found himself being carried by two soldiers on a makeshift stretcher. He could hear the sea to his right, so he knew that they were carrying him east. The moon shone brightly above him, swaying from side to side with the soldiers as they marched. Joe shut his eyes again, cursing so much that one soldier said, '*Sei ruhig*. Be calm.'

'OK, mate,' Joe murmured. 'We've learned that at school.' Then he blacked out again.

Sometime later, he found himself indoors on a table. Instead of the moon, above him were the wooden beams of a hut. Someone had covered him with a blanket and he could feel that his hand was bandaged. On one side, there was warmth and he could hear the low rumble of men talking. He opened his eyes properly, tried to sit up and patted his empty pockets, muttering, 'I hope you blokes ain't stole my money.'

A cup was pressed to his mouth. 'Here. Tea,' said a man, supporting him with a strong arm. 'We are not thieves.'

'*Real* tea? Flipping heck. You lot live like kings.' Joe held up his good hand. 'Thanks for this.'

Soldiers sat on all sides of the hut resting on benches, some playing cards, others smoking and reading. All wore German uniform. Joe drank the tea and afterwards, he said to the nearest soldier, 'Give us a smoke. There's a shortage in the island, in case you didn't know.'

The soldier smiled. 'My name is Helmut, the man with the bayonet. Help is coming for that cut.' He lit a cigarette and handed it to Joe. 'Don't tell your father I gave you this.'

'He wouldn't care,' said Joe, puffing. 'Anyhow, how do you know my dad?'

Helmut laughed. 'Everyone knows of your father. And *we* know your, how do you say it, gang? The little girl who tells everyone her brother has a gun.'

Joe raised his eyebrows. 'Rosie? She'll say anything for a sweet.' He concentrated on his bandage so Franz couldn't see his face. There was blood seeping through and his arm throbbed. His head swayed, but at that moment a soldier arrived carrying a box. He wore a white armband with a red cross to match the one on his box. 'I can help you but you must be brave.'

'I'm a Jersey boy,' said Joe. 'Not a flipping coward. Anyhow, what's with the crosses? A prayer meeting?'

The medical orderly laughed. 'I am going to bathe your cut with iodine to stop infection. It will hurt badly then I will stitch it together. I have no anaesthetic, but if we wait any longer and try to go to the hospital, it might take too long. You will lose a lot more blood.'

'Righto,' said Joe. He took another drag on the cigarette. 'You speak good English, so I suppose I can trust you. Carry on.'

The man gently removed the bandage. As blood welled up, Joe said, 'Blimey, I think I'm going to faint.'

'Don't look,' said the orderly, pouring iodine.

Joe bellowed and tried to snatch his hand away. He said, 'Flipping heck that stung.' He took another puff of the cigarette.

'This is the bad bit, the stitching, but there will be only a few and so after it is done, you will be safe.'

'I wish my dog was here to hold my other hand,' said Joe, biting his lip as the needle went in and out of his palm.

The orderly knotted the last stitch and patted Joe on the shoulder. As a bandage was applied, one of the soldiers gave Joe a toffee and another pressed a square of chocolate into his good hand. The orderly helped Joe off the table and sat him in front of the brazier. 'Wait there. I will fetch you some food.'

Joe's hand throbbed, but when he dared to look, there was no sign of blood on the new bandage. He closed his eyes, and by the time the men returned with a plate piled high, he was almost asleep.

'Hey, wake up,' said the man who called himself Helmut. 'We have something special for you. Marmalade sandwiches. Very British.'

Joe perked up immediately. 'Can I take them home? My sister's hungry and so's my brother.' He looked at the clock. 'I need to go. They're alone.'

After he'd eaten two sandwiches, Helmut put the rest in a bag and said he'd walk Joe home. 'I have a brother like you,' he said. 'A funny boy.'

'No need to walk me home. I'm a big boy now,' said Joe.

Helmut insisted. 'You have lost much blood and there are bad people about who might steal the sandwiches.'

'In that case...' Joe agreed. Half an hour later, they were at the cottage gate. 'I'll be all right now, thanks,' he said.

'I'll stay to make sure you aren't locked out. Then I promise I will leave.'

Just as he reached the cottage, the door burst open. His father stood in the doorway, lit from behind by a paraffin lamp. 'What the hell are you doing out so late?' He grabbed Joe by the collar, dragged him inside and slammed the door when he spotted Helmut watching him.

Saturday 7th February
8.30 am

Dearest Mummy,

It's all drama here. Joe's cut his hand (it's healing well) and Mr. P has suspected pneumonia. Mr. Le Carin gave him a tin of PINEAPPLE. Can you imagine it? We haven't seen any of that for months.

But Mr. P threw it out of the window and it broke the greenhouse. Pineapple's black market, of course. ILLEGAL.

We've begun band practice again. Joe's made up a lobster one and Ginger's working on a pig one.

Clem was right ages ago about not giving names to the rabbits as we ate Nigel for Sunday lunch in a pie. There is no meat to be had and we're not allowed much fish either. Joe continues to be angry about lobster fishing.

There are piglets everywhere, squealing and escaping.

Otherwise, everyone's bored because we can't go anywhere. No buses, nothing in the shops, loads and loads of rules. ANNOYING. Clem isn't bored. He is doing all the farm work as well as his usual rounds because his father is so ill.. That's a lot. His mood is even darker than usual, except when he is

> *with the piglets. No one can feel dark with them.*
>
> *We have been expecting soldiers to stay in the flat for ages, but so far, no show.*
>
> *This might be my LAST letter. There is a bottle shortage.*
>
> *Dearest Mummy, we miss you and send loads of love. xxxxxx*

Spinner decorated her letter with pineapples, piglets and rabbits, then went downstairs to find a bottle to put the letter in, although she didn't want to send it yet. The tides were all wrong and it might end up in France.

Her father was in the kitchen studying a Red Cross message. He patted the chair next to him. 'Lovely news from Mummy,' he said, holding out a thin piece of paper. 'Clem's brother George safe. He's got married.'

'That's good news for the Percherons,' said Spinner.

Mr. Braye said, 'It's dated September 10th. Months ago.' He handed her a cup of tea. 'What are you up to this morning?'

Spinner was putting on her coat. 'I'm going to find some winkles for Lizzie's cat. Or maybe some limpets. She seems to have eaten all the mice.' Then she said, 'I meant to show you this. Better not take it to the beach.' She fished the gold coin from her pocket and laid it on the table. 'Joe found it.'

'How extraordinary,' said her father. He peered at it more closely. 'A Russian coin from the old days.'

'Did it belong to you? From your collection when you were a boy?'

Mr. Braye shook his head. 'I never had such a wonderful coin. This is a beauty. Mine were mostly French, or Jersey pennies. Nothing valuable.'

'Joe will be pleased if it's worth something.'

'I'll look it up in my book of coins,' said Mr Braye. 'And I'll keep it safe until he wants it back.' Then he wished her good luck with her expedition to the beach, so Spinner took a bag and a screwdriver and hurried down the lane. Soon she was on the beach, levering limpets and winkles off the rocks. After a while, Joe turned up with his dog, looking cheerful. 'Wotcha Spinner. Guess what? I've just seen a lobster.'

'A LOBSTER?' Spinner stared it him. 'Don't believe you. They don't come in this close.'

'Yep. Un flipping believable. One great big blue lobster. Supper in a shell.' He pointed up at the sky and said earnestly, 'I had my doubts but now I know there is definitely a God and He has arranged this, with the help of Mum.'

'Spinner laughed. 'Where did you see him?'

'He must have missed the tide and got stuck in a pool. Silly clot. Want to help me catch him?'

Spinner shivered. 'I don't really like touching lobsters. You know, the claws…they're…'

'Get a grip, Spinner. This is war. We haven't time to be frightened of food. Even if it moves.'

With Beaufort bouncing beside her, Spinner followed Joe to where the tide had left knee deep pools. 'I saw it here an hour ago,' said Joe. He splashed through the shallows, poking the stick under likely looking rocks. 'And now there's *nothing*. Not a blimming thing. They've scarpered.' He picked up a couple of cockles and handed them to Spinner. 'We can't go out much further. Maybe we could look there.' He pointed at a shallow gully slightly further out.

'I hate those gullies. They're so seaweedy.'

'This one isn't. Cross my heart.'

So Spinner put the cockles in the sack, took off her boots and socks and tucked her skirt into her knickers. She shrieked as she waded into the water. 'If my feet drop off, it's your fault. It's so *cold.*'

'Shut up,' said Joe. 'You'll scare the lobster away.' Suddenly, he whistled so loudly that she jumped, glancing up at the slipway.

'What is it? Soldiers?'

'Much more important – *I told you there was one.*' Joe grinned at her, then he eased his hook under a rock. Wiggling it to and fro, he muttered, 'Come on Mr. Lobster. Come and meet Uncle Joe.' Then he gave a yell of triumph. '*Got it!*' Pulling hard, he yanked out a huge blue lobster, its claws snapping.

Spinner jumped back. 'Oh, the poor thing.'

'Not at all,' said Joe. 'It's going to have a treat soon, a nice hot bath.' He thrust the lobster at Spinner, who screamed, so he said, 'Don't be so wet, Spin.' He tied up the claws with string, wincing with pain from his injured hand. 'Put it in the basket. And don't let Beaufort have it. He loves lobsters.'

Spinner splashed back to dry sand with the lobster flailing in her hands. 'Ugh, ugh, I hate doing this,' she shrieked, trying to put the lobster into the bucket. 'It's rattling about. I bet it'll get out and chase me.'

Joe laughed. 'You're a quick runner, Spin. But I tell you something, lobsters can move at twelve miles an hour. Best get your boots on.'

'Let's go home,' Spinner clapped the lid on the bucket and tried not to look at the lobster as it stuck out a claw. She dried her feet on her scarf and pulled on her boots. 'My feet are like ice blocks.'

But Joe didn't hear her. He was poking his hook under the rock again. 'There's something else.' He leaned closer, grunting. 'It's not a lobster. It's soft.'

'They find dead sailors and pilots in the sea all the time.' Spinner looked away, tying her laces.

The water bubbled near Joe's legs, and he said brightly, 'It's OK. I can't see no hand or nothing.' Then he suddenly shot backwards, yelping. 'It's a conger eel, a flipping *conger*. It must have got stuck at low tide.' He grasped the hook handle with both hands and heaved, but then yelped. 'My hand still hurts. Come on girl, help me pull. I can't do it with only one hand.'

'Give you a hand? With *a conger?*' Spinner turned white. 'If they get hold of you, they pull you under the water and eat you.'

'I said get a grip. It's a *giant*. We'll have enough to eat for days. Come on Spinner, chuck me a rope.'

Beaufort barked, his tail whipping from side to side. Spinner edged forward and tossed Joe a rope from a distance. 'It's probably an old tyre.'

Joe gave her a look, then lashed the rope round the lobster hook and splashed back. 'Pull, girl,' he urged. 'Put your back into it.'

Spinner grabbed the rope and braced herself, digging her boots into the sand. Joe pulled with his good hand.

'HEAVE, girl.' He gave one last pull, then sprang back onto the sand, as a long grey shape shot out of the water and landed beside him, frothing and writhing on the end of the hook. Joe punched the air with his good hand and roared, 'It's *massive*. Must have been after the lobster.'

The eel's tail suddenly convulsed, smacking Spinner on her legs. 'EEEEUGH,' she shrieked, hopping out of reach. 'Look at its *teeth*.' Then she gasped, 'It's looking at me.'

'No it ain't. It's looking at the lobster.' Joe whacked the conger on the head and looped a slip knot round its neck. It was still twitching and coiling. 'Got a newspaper, Spinner?'

'Course I haven't. We keep them for the lav.'

'If you roll a conger in newspaper, it goes quiet. Probably reads the news.' Joe yanked the rope as the head lunged from side to side. 'Stop it, you little beggar.' He slid the tail into a sack. 'Very clever, congers,' Joe went on, pulling the slip knot tight with difficulty. 'They can swim backwards.'

'That's horrible.' Spinner wrinkled her nose. 'Imagine one chasing you, tail first. Spooky.'

Joe lugged the rest of the conger into the sack. 'Nice and easy, mate,' he murmured. He dumped the sack in his home-made fishing cart, then he picked the lobster out of the bucket and thrust it at Spinner. 'Hide this under your coat.' He pointed at a couple of soldiers, who were sitting on the wall with their backs to them.

'No way,' Spinner gasped. 'Under my coat? You're crazy.'

'*Needs must*,' said Joe. 'Hide your scarf in case they nick it to send home to their little sisters.'

'Course they won't. It's against the rules.'

Joe looked at her. 'They've taken our island. They wouldn't give a toss about taking a scarf.' Then he looked at his injured hand. Blood was seeping through his bandage again.

Noon

Back at Clem's place, a man sat at the Percheron's kitchen table, his whole body trembling. His eyes darted to the window, then towards the sitting room, where there was the rumble of men's voices.

'That's the doctor, seeing my husband.' Mrs. Percheron explained. 'You can trust Dr. Harris. He's one of us.' She put a bowl of vegetable stew in front of him. 'Eat that, my love.'

The man stared at the bowl, his eyes huge in his starved face, then back at her, as if he couldn't believe what he had been given.

'Eat, please, my boy,' Mrs. Percheron urged, leaving the kitchen.

Suddenly, he grabbed the bowl and gobbled down the stew almost in one gulp, clutching as though someone might knock it out of his hands. He glanced at Clem, who was keeping watch in the porch, then back at the bowl.

Clem looked away so that the man could lick the last scraps with dignity. When he heard the bowl being put back on the table, he looked back. The man touched his chest in thanks, then said, 'I am Russian prisoner. But I speak English.'

Clem glanced at his scarred hands and arms, trying not to stare, even though he was sure that he recognized him. He said quietly, 'You are safe with us. I have seen how they treat you.' He edged past him again back to the porch, where he leaned down, then held up his brother's boots. They'd been kept in their place ever since he'd gone to war, even though he wouldn't come back. 'For you?'

The man touched his chest again thanks, shaking his head. 'I cannot. They would know, they would find you.'

Clem said that he understood. 'I will leave them for you in the barn, behind the pigs, if you need them.'

The man nodded slowly. Then he searched for the

right words. 'I have a sister like the one I saw. There.' He pointed at the Brayes' house. 'I'm sorry I frightened her.' Suddenly, tears welled up and he gulped. 'War is hard for everyone. I wonder if my sister will know who I am, when I...'

At that moment, there were footsteps in the hall. The prisoner shot under the table, shaking even more violently.

Mrs. Percheron stood quietly at the door, repeating Clem's words. 'You are safe.'

The doctor followed her into the kitchen. He waited until the shaking had slowed, then opened his medical case. He said, 'I will not hurt you,' and held out this hand. The man looked up, his eyes full of terror.

The doctor kept his voice calm, saying, 'May I help you?'

The man took a deep breath, then showed his hands and his feet, criss-crossed with bleeding scars and chilblains.

'Take this.' The doctor tipped a bottle on to a piece of clean cloth. He held it out and the man dabbed it on his wounds, gasping as the disinfectant stung.

Suddenly, in the distance, there was a shout in German. The prisoner froze for a second, then shoved the doctor away, jumped up off the floor and out into the hall. When they followed, he'd vanished, leaving the window open and the cold wind blowing away any sign of his presence.

'Leave him,' said Dr. Harris. 'He'll know how to hide. Give him a minute.'

After a time, Clem went outside, but there was no sign of the man, so he covered up his footprints in the flower bed. When he was back in the kitchen, his mother said, 'I wish I'd given him more. A good fish soup, or some meat. Vegetables aren't enough.'

'They're probably more than he's had for months,' said Clem. 'From what I hear.'

Dr. Harris put on his hat and turned to go. 'It's good that he trusted you. But don't let them into the house. You will be complicit. If they are found outside, you can deny all knowledge.'

Mrs. Percheron said, 'This isn't the right part of the island for them. They usually go north and west. So no one will notice if they come in now and then.'

The doctor shook his head. 'There are eyes everywhere, searching.'

Later, Mrs. Percheron went to her women's bible class, leaving instructions that Mr. Percheron was to keep warm. However, as soon as she was safely out of sight. Mr. Percheron put on his thick coat and said, 'I'd like to find a really good place for young men like that one to hide. Come on, son.'

In the implement shed, Clem levered up the hatch over the dry well. 'It hasn't been moved for years,' he said, heaving on it.

'There's a ladder down the side of the well. It always used to dry up,' said his father. 'And there are grips under the hatch.'

'I'll see what it's like,' said Clem. He lowered himself into the well and felt his way down the ladder. 'The rungs are strong,' he called up, 'and there's a little escape shelf down here.' He climbed up again, and checked that he could pull the hatch over his head. 'Don't leave me under here,' he said, his voice muffled. 'If I get stuck.'

Mr. Percheron laughed painfully and through his coughs said, 'Now, there's a thought.'

But Clem pushed up the hatch easily, and when it was shut again, they swung the harrow over it. 'It's easy enough to get into,' said Mr. Percheron, swinging the harrow back and forward. 'Takes a couple of seconds.' He put his hand to his chest. 'I'd best go indoors, son. Your mother will kill me if she comes back from her bible class and finds me out here.'

'But we can sleep easily,' said Clem. 'Now there's another safe place for the prisoners.'

1 pm

After Spinner had bandaged Joe's hand with her hanky, she helped him to drag the cart up the slipway, the lobster struggling in the bag against her stomach. As they reached the road, the two soldiers stood up and turned round, stubbing out their cigarettes. Beaufort dropped to his belly and Spinner folded her arms across her coat.

'Those two are easy. I know 'em. Nothing to worry about.' Joe grabbed Beaufort's collar. 'Tuck the lobster feelers under your coat.' He stamped towards the soldiers and touched the sack. 'See this?'

The pair turned smiled feebly. Spinner could see they weren't much older than Clem. One was spotty and the other had big lips. The spotty one kicked at Beaufort.

Joe pulled his dog close, his eyes narrowing, then undid the knot on the conger bag. Reaching in, he half pulled out the conger.

'*Gott in Himmel*,' yelled the big lipped one, jumping back. '*Was ist das?*'

Joe waggled the conger's face at them, working the jaw so the teeth stood out. 'My friend here,' he pointed at Spinner, 'thinks conger eels have lips like yours.'

'I never...' began Spinner. 'Shut up, Joe.'

'They don't understand. These two are stupid ones. They can only say about three things in English.' Joe smiled pleasantly. 'I could give you the head.' He made cutting signs with his finger across his throat, showing them his bloodied hand in its bandage and bloodied hanky.

Big Lips puffed smoke at him, then said abruptly. 'Identity card, *bitte.*'

'Identity cards?' said Joe. 'Blimey, you're eager. Listen mate, I might look like a man of the world, but I'm only thirteen. I don't need one yet.'

'Don't muck it up,' said Spinner, showing hers. 'It's brand new.' She took it back. 'Come on,' she said to Joe. 'Let's go.'

'Au revoir, boys.' Joe pushed the conger back into the sack. 'Hurry up Spinner. They're looking at your birthday scarf.'

Spinner tucked her scarf further into her coat and glanced back as they gathered pace. The soldiers were talking rapidly, watching them. She held one side of the cart handle and pulled. As they reached her house, she said, 'You shouldn't provoke them.'

'They're scared of a conger eel,' said Joe, scornfully. 'And they call themselves fighting men.'

Saturday 14th February
9 am

Each evening that week, Mrs. Percheron put out hot conger soup in her special soup can. Even though it was emptied every time, the prisoner hadn't been seen again. Clem looked for signs that he'd slept in the barn. Once or twice, he thought he, or someone else, had slept there. Once, he thought he spotted a stranger near the potato store, but when he looked again, he'd gone.

'I think he was the one Joe and I saw. And maybe that Ginger helped that Sunday. But they all look like each other, so thin and desperate,' he said to his mother. 'I can't be sure.'

Mrs. Percheron answered in Jersey French. 'Whoever he was, he's gone, son. He knows that he mustn't hang about too long in one place. That's what a safe house is. It's not for ever. Just a day or two.'

Mr. Percheron wouldn't agree to another visit from the doctor, but even though it was time to plant the potatoes, he didn't go outside to help. It was almost spring and the sun was shining, but it was icy in the wind. Anyhow, he couldn't walk more than a few steps without stopping for breath.

He gave a few instructions to Clem and settled by the fire.

Soon, they were all spread along the big field, planting potatoes. Even Diddie was putting in an effort.

When the field was half planted, Mrs. Percheron and Auntie Vi brought bread and tea. Arthur sat on the grass while Rosie played her home-made harp, five strings attached to a triangle of sticks.

'For goodness sake,' said Auntie Vi. 'What's wrong with the girl?' Then she frowned, staring towards the road. 'There's a soldier watching us.'

Clem bunched his fists. 'He's on our land. He has no right. He'd better...'

'Cut it out,' Joe interrupted. 'They trample everywhere, so it's no good getting wound up.'

The soldier looked at them for a while, as though he was counting. He took out a note book and wrote for a minute. Then he moved off.

'Nosy beggar,' said Joe, making a rude sign at his back.

By dusk, the whole field was planted. Ernest pulled the trailer load of empty potato trays back to the farmyard.

'Time for bed,' Auntie Vi said, 'Off we go. Come on Diddie.' She pointed at the farmhouse. 'Let's go and tell Mr. Percheron that we've finished the field. It'll cheer him a lot.'

Mr. Percheron was sitting in front of the fire with a rug over his knees.

'We planted the whole field,' said Rosie.

Diddie added, 'Thousands of seed potatoes.'

Mr. Percheron thanked them and said he was proud of them. Then he pulled three shiny Jersey pennies from behind his ear and gave one each to Rosie, Arthur and Diddie. 'Thanks for your help, kids.'

Saturday 21st February
9 am

Mr. Percheron still wasn't well enough to climb the steep little fields they called *the cotils*. Dr. Harris had visited and issued strict instructions for him to rest. He'd said to Mrs. Percheron, 'His chest is very infected. Pneumonia's dangerous. He needs to get back his strength.'

Mrs. Percheron suddenly became very fierce, even banning her husband from seeing his cows. She fed him all the best things she could find from her carefully managed store, such as calves' foot jelly. 'Thank goodness for Joe,' she said, 'finding that big conger. Such good food.'

Meanwhile the piglets were growing. 'I've given the biggest ones away,' Clem said to Spinner. 'But soon they'll be too heavy to move in secret. We need to send them to new homes soon or the Germans will come to take what they think is their share.' He rolled his eyes. 'As if.'

'It's a good job they were tiny in the first place,' she said, picking one up and stroking it. 'This one will still fit in a handbag. And it's so sweet. Everyone will want one.'

'With roast potatoes,' said Clem.

A week after planting the flat field, everyone set off up the hill to deal with the last of the potatoes, leaning into the sharp easterly wind as it swept over the island. Even Clem's friend Legs came to help, all the way from

St Peter's valley.

'You look like that man we saw in the snow,' said Rosie, staring at him. 'He has dirty feet and he smells.'

'Nice,' said Legs. 'I like a compliment.'

After a couple of hours, they sat down for a break in the spring sunshine. Joe pointed down the hill. 'There's a motor bike coming...German.'

'That's a Zundkapp,' said Ginger, listening. 'The latest design.'

Clem leapt up. 'Mother doesn't like it when they turn up and Dad's not well enough to cope with them. I'll nip down.'

Spinner watched him running towards the farm, the soft earth rising in clouds about him. She mouthed at Joe, 'Do you think they're still looking for the prisoner?'

Joe shook his head. 'They won't bother about him anymore. He's been gone too long.' He glanced down the hill and turned to Ginger. 'You said it was a Zundkapp and it flippin' is. Good one, brainy.'

At the bottom of the hill, Clem reached the farm buildings as the motor bike came to a halt. A soldier climbed off.

Spinner said, 'Clem's much bigger than the soldier.'

Ginger pushed his glasses back on his nose. 'He always stands his ground. You watch.'

They saw Clem shake his head, then take a letter from the soldier, who climbed back on to his motor bike and roared off.

'See,' said Mr. Braye. 'Nothing to worry about.'

But when Clem joined them ten minutes later, his face was grim. 'They say we've got empty rooms.' He kicked a tuft of grass, his face red. Then he shouted, 'They want Bill's room and George's room to put soldiers in. How *dare* they? How ruddy dare they?'

Nobody said a thing for a moment.

Then Joe laughed. 'It's a good job you put in a bathroom last autumn. Germans think people with outside lavs are sub human. We don't want that.' Clem glared at him, but Joe went on. 'Imagine it. You might have to share bath water with them.'

'Don't worry, Clem,' Mr. Braye said quietly. 'I offered them the flat a few weeks ago. It's got quite a fancy bathroom and a nice smell from Hotspur. They'd prefer that, I'm sure.'

Clem managed a tight smile but his fists were clenched. 'Thanks, sir.'

Spinner thought, *I bet the soldier was frightened of Clem. He looks like Samson from the Bible.'*

Saturday 28th February
2 pm

Clem checked the hiding place behind the straw every day. But there was still no sign that anyone stayed there. What's more, the soup was no longer taken, so Mrs. Percheron kept it for themselves. The only good thing was that their friends in the north had told them, when they had visited, that they had a couple of prisoners hiding in their farm buildings.

'They say they're clever ones, they speak good English,' Mrs. Percheron said, speaking Jersey French again.

'Maybe that's our prisoner,' said Clem. He took his piece of bread off the plate. 'We're going to the beach this afternoon, just for a breath of fresh air. As if we don't have enough of it.'

'Take some more bread.' She handed him another slice. 'Your father's still not eating enough and you need it, with all this extra work.'

'There's so much to do that I can't get up to mischief,' said Clem. 'So that's one good thing.' He smiled wryly, then went into the yard to meet Ginger and Spinner. 'Let's go. I've got plenty of bread.'

They set off through the orchard to the potato field, then on to a narrow road lined by low walls with trees behind them, heading east towards the castle. Suddenly,

Clem skidded to a halt. Dead ahead, there was a group of soldiers standing round an army truck. The bonnet was open.

Ginger said, 'I spy with my little eye a nice little opportunity. He stepped towards the soldiers. 'Can I help, sir? I know everything about engines.'

The soldiers turned. A reedy young sergeant in a forage cap sneered at Ginger, looking him up and down and taking in his red hair and long legs and arms. 'You don't look strong enough or clever enough. *Schwachling.*'

Ginger said, 'A weakling, eh? *Schwachling.*' He gave an easy smile. 'Have it your own way. I was just offering, that's all.'

The sergeant talked to the others, his face impassive and unfriendly. Then he beckoned Ginger and said in a commanding voice, '*Kommen Sie.* Come.'

Ginger took his time. He motioned the soldiers out of the way and leaned in on the engine, staring into its innards. 'Mmm,' he muttered. '*Du hast ein problem.*'

'Gosh,' Spinner whispered, 'He's being really rude. You can't say *Du* to grownups in German. We learned that at school. You have to say *Sie.*'

Clem gave his best lazy, contemptuous grin. 'Ginger's brilliant at being rude with a smile.'

Ginger chatted on, half in English, half in German as he checked the oil and fiddled with the battery. Then he said, 'Try now.' He made a twisting gesture as if he was turning on the key.

Immediately, the van started. The other soldiers cheered and the sergeant nodded curtly. Ginger wiped his hands on some grass and sauntered back to Spinner and Clem, humming *'Ain't Misbehavin'.'*

'*Gut, zehr gut,*' shouted the driver. The men climbed

into the back of the truck and soon they'd roared off into the distance.

'Oh dear,' said Ginger, a few minutes later. 'I don't think they'll go very far. I undid a few other little things while I was under the bonnet.' He grinned. 'Actually, just about everything. How about we move on?'

Clem slapped him on the shoulder. 'Nice one. I knew you were up to no good.'

Spinner burst out laughing. 'Serves them right.'

They turned into a track through the fields until they were out of sight of the road. Then Ginger said, 'Oh dear again. My shoe laces have come undone.' He bent down and with one hand fiddled with the shoe lace and with the other, poked some of his bread crusts into a crack in a wall.

Taking a couple of stones, he clicked them together.

Clem and Spinner stared at each other. 'What the heck?'

'We need a code for the prisoners. Signs, sounds, maybe even morse code,' explained Ginger. 'It's vital that no one notices what we're doing.'

The others agreed and further along the track they found plenty of places to hide the crusts, twisting grass in knots above them as signals or clicking stones. 'It's a start,' said Ginger. 'If we can get away with putting out food this way, while we have some to share, then we can move on to more difficult ways. Poking bread through the fence of one of the nastier camps, maybe.'

'That might be too dangerous.' Spinner shivered and changed the subject. 'Let's go to the beach, like we said we would.'

'Race you,' said Clem, sprinting away.

Spinner charged after him, but soon Ginger was loping

past them both, running as fast as Clem's friend, Legs, the island runner. As they reached the slipway, skidding to a halt, Spinner gasped. 'Gosh, they've barricaded off our beach.' She stared at the scene ahead of her. Prisoners toiled on the sand, carrying enormous loads of stones in hods.

Ginger said, 'I bet they're building another anti-tank barricade.'

Spinner pointed at a German in black uniform. 'That soldier has a whip. He's *threatening* them as if they're donkeys.'

'I wouldn't treat a donkey like that.' Clem began to move forward. 'I'm not going to stand here and do *nothing*.'

Ginger and Spinner held him back and Ginger said, 'If you do *anything*, you'll spoil *everything*. They'll watch us forever. And that would be a bore.'

Saturday 7th March
9.30 am

A week later, Clem made a sandwich from one thin slice of bread after breakfast. He put it with an apple into a canvas bag and a spare sweater. It was still cold, even though the first daffodils were almost showing, and the sun was shining.

He said to his mother, 'Thanks for giving me a day off, Mum.' He picked up his woolly hat and turned to his father, who was warming himself by the fire. 'Will you be all right, Dad? I've done the heavy feeding.'

'I'm much better now, son. Nothing to worry about at all.' Mr. Percheron gave him a bright smile. 'Off you go, son. You deserve time off. You've worked so hard keeping the farm going while I've been under the weather. And you worked like a Trojan on all your school work too.'

'Like I said to Mum the other day, it's keeping me out of mischief,' said Clem. 'Sorry I've been grumpy. Everything got me down last week. It's not the war, just what's happening here. I keep thinking about Bill and what he'd make of our island, covered in hungry prisoners and bunkers. I'll be better for a day away.'

'We all feel like that now and then. Chin up, son,' his mother said, adding, 'Auntie Vi's coming up soon to keep us company.'

Clem hovered on the doorstep, 'Are you quite sure you can manage?'

Mr. Percheron father coughed, a deep, painful sound. But when he'd stopped, he gave a thumbs up.

'Your father will be perfectly all right,' said his mother. 'I wouldn't tell you to go if he wasn't. And there's another thing, Clem Percheron. We were farmers long before any of you boys were born.' Mrs. Percheron smiled, then added, 'Have a wonderful day. You've earned every minute of it.' She sliced a tiny piece of bread pudding for him and wrapped it in a square of newspaper. 'Where will you go?'

'I'll head towards St. Catherine's.'

His mother said that was a lovely walk. 'Best if you avoid the coast road. It's full of soldiers and prisoners, turning the island into a fortress.'

'Best if I don't go there, in case I lose my rag.' Clem packed away the bread pudding and thanked his mother, then he slung the canvas bag over his shoulder, said goodbye and set off up the hill behind the farm. For once, the skies were empty of planes, but the sound of busy building and shouts floated up to him on the breeze from the coast road below.

He trudged happily on up and down the little hills of his part of the island, until he was at Grouville church. Half an hour later, he was up beside the castle, his shoulders back and his face to the sun. On the horizon, a fishing reef could be seen so clearly in the early spring light that he could see fishermen's huts on it, and beyond it, the French shore that circled the huge bay of St Malo all round them.

Puffs of smoke hung over France, like little mushrooms. 'Poor blighters,' he muttered, marching on and wondering what was going on over there.

An hour later, he was nearly at the big breakwater that stretched half a mile out to sea, St. Catherine's, but even at this lovely place, there was the echo and clang of building and clumps of ragged men working and being shouted at.

'Ruddy hell,' he muttered. 'Mum was right. They really *are* turning Jersey into a fortress.' He narrowed his eyes, trying to work out what lay ahead of him, wondering if he could pass it and reach the breakwater.

But just as he'd decided to walk on, a soldier jumped out of nowhere and glared at him. He marched towards Clem like a clockwork soldier, left right, left right, his jackboots ringing on the road. At once, Clem recognized him as the brute of a guard he'd seen on that foggy day in January. He thrust his hands in his pockets, kept his face blank and walked on.

When he was so close to the guard that he could see the hairs in his nostrils, the man raised his hand, palm out, almost touching Clem's face. '*Halt,*' he spat out. Then he pointed. 'Your bag,' he ordered, not smiling.

Clem scowled. '*Why should I?* Do you think I'm carrying a gun?'

The soldier's eyes widened. Then his hand shot out and grabbed Clem's bag. Using his bayonet, he ripped it open and shook it out onto the road. The sweater fell into a puddle and the apple bounced into the gutter like a cricket ball, then tumbled towards the beach.

The sandwich lay between them, with the little slice of precious bread pudding in its carefully wrapped paper. The soldier sneered, then ground the picnic with his boot. 'You *will* obey orders. Understand?'

Clem took in the man's soft mouth and narrow chest

as rage boiled up in him, pumping his heart so powerfully that his ear drums hurt. The soldier twirled the ripped bag on his bayonet. Clem clenched his fists, trying not to react. Then he muttered, 'I bet your mother's proud of you.'

At that, the man shouted at him, threatening him with his gun.

Clem stood his ground, bracing himself. He held his enemy's gaze.

The soldier stamped again on the picnic until it was just a smear on the tarmac.

At that, Clem lost it. He barged forward. 'We have *so little* food, and *you* have plenty.' He shoved the soldier, hard, so that the man staggered backwards. His words echoed against the rock face behind them. There was a horrible silence, then the soldier dashed forward and smashed his rifle butt across his face. As Clem gasped with pain, he did it again, across his nose.

'You do what *I* say.'

'Jesus,' yelled Clem. He reeled back and fell on the mashed up food. Hot blood poured from his nose.

The soldier shouted. 'This is a warning. You are old enough to be interrogated.'

Clem tried to stumble to his feet, but the man pressed him back with his rifle. Then he stamped on Clem's hands before strutting off like a pigeon, his toes pointing inwards.

Clem wiped blood out of his eyes and yelled, 'Who let *you* into the army? You can't even march like a soldier.' He wiped his bleeding nose on his cuff, then picked himself up and climbed slowly and painfully down to the beach that lay below the road. He sloshed sea water over his throbbing nose and swollen lips until the breaking waves swirled pink with his blood.

The cold water helped to calm him down and he set off for home over the hills again, holding his bruised fingers up against his chest and swearing at every step. He thought of the prisoners and what they endured. That gave him strength. 'I won't be beaten,' he muttered. 'I won't.'

Blood crusted his shirt and jacket and his whole body throbbed with pain. He found that his legs were shaking. 'Steady on,' he told himself. Twice, he stopped at roadside wells to drink and to wipe off oozing blood, but at last he reached the orchard. He longed to lean his head against Ernest, the horse, for comfort.

As he turned the corner, he caught his breath. Billy and Rosie were standing under a tree. They were talking to a soldier. Rosie's voice was high and clear. 'We saw a dirty man one day at my house. He had no shoes.'

'Oh,' said the soldier. He lit a cigarette. 'I see.'

At that, Clem sauntered through the trees towards them, trying to look nonchalant, but blood was oozing from his nose to his chin. The soldier raised his hands in horror. *'Ach. Zo*, what happened to *you?'* He offered a clean handkerchief.

Clem brushed it away. His voice was terse. 'I slipped.' Rosie burst into tears and rushed up to him, pressing her scabby face into his leg and sobbing.

'This is a German,' Billy said Clem. 'He's called Helmut and he is very nice.' He turned to the soldier. 'Clem's the best fighter in the island. He's a boxer so he's probably had another fight.' He glanced at Clem with hero worship. 'So watch out, Helmut.'

The soldier grinned. 'I know. And I will.'

4 pm

The doctor came as soon as he could. When he and Clem were alone, he said, 'What happened?'

'A wall hit me,' Clem shrugged. 'It whacked me when I wasn't looking.'

'And broke your nose? And your hands?' Dr. Harris applied ointment gently. 'Your hands are your family's livelihood whilst your father's ill.' He felt each finger. 'I'll strap those two together, but they're only bruised. You'll live.'

He handed Clem a splint and asked him to hold it while he bandaged it tightly. 'Good job it's not your writing hand, with school exams coming up.'

'Sometimes,' said Clem, 'I feel that school exams aren't in the least important any more' His face reddened. 'Soon the enemy will tell us how to *think* and *what* to think. And the way they treat the prisoners. It's disgusting.' He began to raise his voice. 'I've seen…'

'Shh, Clem. Don't get over excited.' The doctor kept his voice low so that Clem's parents didn't hear. 'Most of the soldiers are ordinary men. They don't hurt women and children in the island. It could be worse.'

'One of them hurt Rosie once. On the beach,' Clem countered. 'And they've hurt Spinner by being here, so that her mother can't come back, and they've hurt Joe because his mother died because she couldn't get her medicine and they've hurt us because of Bill…'

Dr. Harris remained silent as Clem's voice faded away. Then he said softly, 'But you aren't a child any more. Watch out, young man.' He took Clem's pulse. 'Did you give your name to him?'

Clem shook his head and winced again. 'That soldier was a right little tick.'

Dr. Harris nodded. 'They're the ones to avoid, the puny ones who want to look big.' He checked Clem's nose. 'Boys your age are being sent to prison and some are deported and God only knows what happens to them in France and Germany. The prisons there have a terrible reputation, awful things go on.'

Clem shrugged. '*I'm* not frightened. At least I could escape from prison and make my way overland to join up. No one can escape from *here*. Ruddy sea all round us like prison walls.'

'*This is not a joke.*' Doctor Harris gripped his good arm and looked at him intensely. 'You've lost one brother. Don't break your mother's heart.' He handed Clem the tube of ointment and told him to put it on every evening and morning.

Clem paid him from the medical purse that they kept in the drawer. 'But I want to deck every single soldier I meet.' He raised his voice and said again. 'I flipping *hate* them, even the decent ones.'

Dr. Harris sighed. 'Anyhow, keep those wounds clean and away from muck.'

'Are you calling the soldiers *muck?*' Clem laughed. Then he clutched his sore face. 'Ow, it hurts to laugh.'

Dr. Harris said, 'No school for a couple of weeks. Your face will draw attention.' He put his things away in his bag. 'You're a big lad, Clem. And there's *challenge* in your face. They don't like that.'

Clem managed a lop sided grin, and said, 'good.'

'By the way, that soldier was breaking the rules,' said Dr. Harris. 'You could report him. The Kommandant doesn't like his men behaving like that, beating up locals. It's not allowed.'

Clem thought for a moment. 'It's not worth it. I don't

want to be in the paper.'

When the doctor had gone, Clem went to see Ernest. He leaned over the partition to stroke him, his sore hand on the animal's flanks. The bulk and solidity of the horse seemed to push strength back into him. 'What a sorry state we're all in,' he said. 'What a sorry state.'

Sunday 8th March
9 am

'We'll have to let the vicar know that you can't come to church,' said Mrs. Percheron the next morning. She patted antiseptic on to Clem's nose. 'But I don't know what we can say.'

'I can lie,' said Clem, flinching. 'I'll write a note telling them I had problem with Hotspur.'

Mr. Percheron buttoned up his waistcoat. 'I can lie too, son.' He gave a grim smile. 'And I never thought I'd tell an untruth in church.'

'Plenty of people have upset stomachs,' said Mrs. Percheron. 'Too many turnips and all sorts. I'll tell them that you have that.' She put on her hat. 'I'll send a message next door too, saying to leave you alone in case they catch it.'

Clem tried to smile, but it still hurt. So he picked up his book of birds. 'The swallows will be back soon,' he said. 'That'll make everything seem more normal.'

His mother smiled. 'Everything seems better when they are under our eaves, chattering away.' She picked up her handbag. 'Please stay quietly indoors, son.'

However, as soon as his parents had left the house, Clem nipped outside and whistled loudly and painfully up at Ginger's room next door. The Martins and Braye's did not go to church every Sunday, like the Percherons, so a few minutes later, Ginger came round to see him.

'Crikey. What the heck?' Ginger raised his eyebrows. 'What have you been up to? You haven't been fighting Percy, have you? Like in the good old days?'

Clem shook his head, wincing at the pain. He explained what had happened, then added, 'Rosie saw me bleeding like a pig, so did Billy. Can you tell them I'm quite all right now and it was just a nosebleed, or something? I don't want them blabbing to people.'

'They already have,' said Ginger. 'It's all they talked about when they came back from the orchard, and Rosie was still going on and on when she went to bed.'

Wednesday 11th March
9 am

Clem was up early, feeling more cheerful. He went through his school work, ticking off all he had to do, then joined his parents for breakfast.

'I feel so bad, not helping,' he said. But his father told him he was perfectly capable of running a farm, and that Mr. Braye was enjoying helping him in the fresh air. So he ate his porridge and concentrated on school work all morning.

Ater lunch, he wandered up to the old potato store. Everything ached. His scabs were still oozing blood and pus. He needed to get out of the farmhouse and away from the sympathetic looks from his mother. Auntie Vi had turned up with a small cake. 'Don't ask *me* where I got my sultanas from,' she'd said, slicing it savagely and handing Clem a piece.

Pushing open the door of the potato store he stood for a moment. It felt like being in church. Still and musty and calming. Then he went out and sat on the bench outside. Suddenly, gazing at the yellow flowers and pink blossom below him, he felt such anguish for his beloved island that his heart hurt. He began to cry.

'Stop it, you *idiot*,' he hissed at himself, but he couldn't stop weeping.

The sobs hurt him too much, cramping inside him. As he tried to force them back, he remembered the telegram they'd received two years ago, long before the enemy had arrived. *'Deeply regret to inform you that your son, Able Seaman William John Percheron, is missing, believed drowned, in action at sea.'*

Until now, he'd never let himself believe it.

All at once, he suddenly knew he'd been fooling himself. He'd never, ever see Bill again. And George might die too. He pressed his bandaged hand to his heart, crying so hard that he felt his tears would turn into a river and the river would be a sea and he would drown in grief.

He remembered what Winston Churchill had said, *'I have nothing to offer you but blood, sweat and tears.'* He shut his eyes. 'It's true.'

At that moment, he felt a shadow on him, blocking the spring sunlight. A man's voice said, 'We are all crying, son. We are crying *for* you and *with* you.'

'I'm *sixteen*, too old to cry.' Clem looked up, his heart thudding.

'No one is too old to cry.' A tall man stood before him, his boots tied with string and his clothes ragged. He gave a slight bow and spoke quietly without any accent. 'See? I have some boots now! There is no need to give me your brother's.'

'Oh my word,' said Clem, suddenly smiling. 'It's *you*. I've been wondering where you'd gone.' He looked at the man's feet. 'My brother's boots are much better than those.'

'But too good. They would be noticed.' The man went on. 'You have helped me for weeks. There was one day when I was in despair. Then someone played Russian music on his trumpet and I knew there was hope.'

'I remember,' said Clem. 'And I tried to stop him. He's my friend.'

'Please thank him. Once I slept behind your big pig, the angry one. Other times behind the small ones. I came to say thank you to you, and your mother too. I remember that bowl of food that day, in your kitchen. And the kind doctor.'

'So *were* you one of the prisoners that escaped from that ditch?' Clem said.

'On that misty day.' The man nodded, folding his arms around himself. 'And it was so cold.'

Clem indicated the bench beside him. 'We want to help you all. But it's impossible. We feel so terrible about your suffering in our island.'

'Thank you. But it's dangerous to help. You must think about yourselves, not us.' The man sat down, noticing Clem's arms. 'What has happened to you?'

'This? It's nothing. I'll mend.' Clem touched his bruises. 'But my brother is dead. *That* will never mend.'

'Mine, too,' said the prisoner. They sat in silence, then he added, 'I had a friend. He sheltered with me in the place you made. It gave him rest before he was caught.'

Clem caught his breath. 'How awful. I'm sorry. When did they catch him?'

'Yesterday,' said the prisoner. 'He'll be sent to the castle. The one out at sea. It's very bad there for prisoners.'

'I'm sorry.' Clem pictured Elizabeth Castle, which he'd explored once when he was still at the parish school. It was in the big bay of St. Aubin's and he and Joe had rowed to it in a small dinghy. 'It had such beautiful birds, nesting in the walls. And so many flowers.'

'For now, it is a prison. But one day, its birds will sing again.'

Clem held out a small parcel. 'This is my aunt's cake. Please, take it.' He pushed it at him, but the man refused.

'How can I take food away from a boy?'

'Easily,' said Clem, putting it into his hands.

When he'd eaten it, the man said, 'My name is Sasha.'

'*Sasha*,' said Clem. 'It's a pleasure to meet you properly.

'I took my number off my shirt, 351,' Sasha said, 'and that tore my shirt even more, but it was worth it.' He touched Clem's shoulder lightly. 'Perhaps we will meet again.' Then he climbed on to the narrow wall behind the cottage, before looking earnestly at Clem. 'Please remember. We prisoners can look after ourselves. We have been soldiers. Don't risk danger for us.' Then he did a back flip before running along it with perfect balance.

Clem's mouth dropped open in amazement. At the end of the wall, Sasha jumped off it, picked up a handful of stones. He walked away, juggling them so fast they became a blur.

Later, he told his mother and father. 'He's called Sasha. He speaks good English, much better than we thought when he was in our kitchen. And he's getting stronger because of us. Isn't that great?'

Friday 14th March
5 pm

Clem took the others out into the farmyard, another bruise flowering on his forehead. Joe said, 'What have you done now, Clem? I thought you were mended.' He pointed at the bruise. 'Got into another fight with a soldier?'

'No,' Clem grinned. 'I had a problem with Hotspur last night. I decided to keep him in the yard as our watchman, but I forgot I'd let him out and he had a go at me.' He waved at the new gates he'd put up round the yard. 'No one will dare come anywhere near us if they've got any brains.'

'Good idea,' said Ginger, inspecting the gates. 'No unwanted visitors if Hotspur's on the loose.'

'It's just at night, or life will be a nightmare,' said Clem. 'And I want to show you something else.' He pushed open the barn door, hurried past the Peggy and the piglets' sties and jumped onto a straw bale. 'Follow me,' he said. He scrambled up a huge stack of bales until he was near the rafters, his head brushing the barn roof. He looked down at the others, then groped between two bales to pull aside a board. 'Going through,' he exclaimed, showing them a narrow gap and beckoning. 'Come on, don't just stand there.'

As the others clambered up, Clem squeezed through

the gap until only the soles of his shoes were showing, then he wriggled further and vanished. After a minute, he waggled a hand at them, through the gap. 'I've tied a ladder to the other side, so you can get down all right. So, come on everyone, who's first?'

'I am.' Spinner was already at the top, brushing aside the spider webs. She squeezed through and felt for the top rung with her feet. 'Come on, you two. What are you waiting for?' she called out as she climbed down after Clem. 'There's loads of room this side, a bit of barn we didn't know about.'

Joe and Ginger followed and soon they were all standing in a long, narrow space, lit by small windows in the roof. Clem said, 'Dad and I made an emergency hiding place here last year but we never used it, a sort of false wall. So I disguised it with straw bales.' He led the way to the corner. 'Look.'

Spinner gasped. 'Has someone actually hidden here?' She gazed at the mattress and pillow, a makeshift table with a washing bowl on it and a tin jug of water. 'Like the man Ginger saw?'

'Listen everyone,' said Clem, keeping his voice very quiet. 'I want to tell you about someone I met yesterday. He's called Sasha and he's an escaped prisoner.'

'Blimey.' Joe gave a long low whistle. 'Anyone we know?'

Clem nodded, then he explained everything and said, 'So, we've helped one and now we can help more. Don't talk about it to anyone. Specially in front of that little toe rag, Billy Cliquot.'

'Blimey, Clem. As if we flipping would.' Joe clapped Clem on his shoulder so hard that the older boy flinched. 'Good work, mate.'

Ginger had stayed quiet. 'How do you know you can trust him?'

'For some reason, I just do,' Clem replied. 'There's something about him. He looks you in the eyes.'

'Fair enough,' said Joe. 'My dad never looks me in the yes. Anyhow, do you think we should show him the gold coin? It might come in handy for him.'

'But,' began Spinner. 'Think about it. How can he look after a gold coin when he's on the run?

'I'm always on the run,' said Joe. 'Usually from my dad. I hang on to things all right. Chewing gum, toffees, cigs. You name it.'

'Let's not get carried away,' said Ginger. 'What do you say if we hang on to it until we really trust him.'

The others agreed, then Clem said, 'I've talked about Sasha with Mum and Dad. We've told him that this is a safe house. There's a hatch behind some of these bales, for escaping. It's really strange because there's a sort of tunnel behind it that leads to the back and up the hill. Dad thinks it was from the days when Jersey was hiding the old king. But no one know why it's there.'

'Crikey,' said Ginger. 'I'll go and look that up in the library. An escape tunnel. Fantastic. Though of course, there are those tracks down to the sea for criminals. Safe tracks. They led from the church. Maybe it was part of one of them. The Perquages, they called them. They're still there.'

'Yeah,' said Joe. 'You couldn't be arrested on a Perquage. But times have changed since the Middle Ages, Ginger. You can be arrested anywhere, these days.'

'That's not the point,' said Spinner. 'At least there are tracks and we can tell the prisoner to follow them. Or prisoners.'

Saturday March 22nd
9.30 am

Nothing seemed so bad, now that spring was coming. The hens were laying, the cows were out in the orchard again at night and everything was in blossom. Sasha had vanished again, but all week, Joe had suddenly felt inspired to draw tiny swallows and swifts all over the place, on barn doors, beside the pig sty, over Spinner's woodshed. He explained, 'The swifts have longer tail feathers.'

'They're so beautiful,' said Spinner. 'It's nice that you're drawing again. You're so good at it, you should be an artist one day.'

'Fat chance,' replies Joe. 'Dad'll force me into the fishing trade. Though, come to think of it, I could always chuck him into the sea and nip off with the boat to America.'

Ginger said, 'I'd like to play my trumpet in New York. There's so much jazz going on there. I might come too.' He looked up at the drawings. 'Nice birds, Joe.'

Clem pointed up at the eaves under the barn roof. 'Actually, the real birds are returning already. I hope the guns haven't frightened too many away. I saw a couple last week, nesting outside Bill's old room.'

In the barn, they leaned over the edge of Peggy's sty.

Clem said, 'These last piglets must go as soon as possible. I should have done something weeks ago. They're growing like weeds.'

'Their mother's fed up with them. She's kicking one,' said Ginger.

Clem picked up a piglet with his good hand. Its trotters flailed in the air. 'This one's ideal for Billy's father,' he said. 'He'll sell it for lots of money.' He put the piglet into a crate beside him and the little creature bashed at the wire gamely, as though he had been given a new challenge, squealing loudly. 'Right. One down, four to go.'

Joe said. 'I reckon Auntie Vi will take a couple. She's a practical woman, used to dealing with Dad.' He reached into the sty and took out two hairy piglets. 'Just her type. She'll soon sort them out.'

Spinner said, 'That's cruel. Auntie Vi hates a mess. She won't stand having them in her house. She'll be *furious.*'

Joe smirked. 'I don't think she will, Spinner. She loves animals.'

'There's a couple of chaps at school who want pigs,' Ginger added, 'I'll take one a day on my bike.'

Joe tucked a piglet inside his scruffy coat and held out another to Spinner. 'Want to bring the other one?'

Spinner thought for a moment, then said she would. She took the piglet and they set off towards the lane. It was warm against her chest, grunting gently. They hurried through the fields and were soon at Auntie Vi's bungalow. As they turned into her garden, Beaufort growled and Spinner said, 'I think he can hear a patrol coming.'

Joe hurried towards the back door. Bursting into Auntie Vi's house, he said breathlessly, *'Patrol alert, patrol alert*, Auntie Vi.' Spinner rushed after him, the piglet scrabbling under her jumper.

Auntie Vi was sitting at her table with her friend Auntie Albie, who had a teacup half way to her mouth. She put her hands on her hips. 'And what do you mean, walking into my house without an invitation, pretending to be Germans. Look at your feet, Joe Le Carin. Filthy.' She wrinkled her nose. 'You been in a pigsty or something?'

Auntie Albie smiled at Spinner and sipped her tea. There was a bird on her hat, just like Auntie Vi's, but blue.

'As a matter of fact, that's exactly where I've been.' Joe smiled innocently. 'Because I've bought you some company.' He whipped his piglet out from under his coat and dumped it on the floor. 'Sorry they're so hairy.'

Spinner put hers down too, muttering that she was sorry the piglet's trotters were mucky.

Auntie Vi gasped. 'Get them filthy animals out of my house this minute.' She shoved the dog out of the way and tried to round up the piglets, but then they spotted her shoe laces. One grabbed a lace and pulled it hard, its curly tail sticking up in the air. Auntie Vi yelled, 'Get them out, you horrible boy.'

Beaufort pounced round the kitchen, playing with the other piglet while Spinner tried to grab its tail. Auntie Vi yanked her shoe away, but the piglet stayed attached, whirling about as she tried to shake it off.

Joe said, 'OK, OK, Auntie Vi. I made a mistake. I just thought you might like some nice pork for lunch one day, but I was wrong.'

Suddenly, Auntie Vi froze, the blood draining from her face as there was a rat a tat tat at the front door. 'Bolt the back door. Do something useful for once.'

Spinner looked at Joe. '*The patrol,*' she said. 'They must have seen us.'

Joe bolted the back door as Auntie Vi limped towards the front door with the piglet still attached. Joe wrenched it off and raced back to the kitchen.

'Oh dear,' said Auntie Albie. She took another sip of tea and smiled serenely. Then she pulled a large carpet bag from under the table, which had been hidden by Auntie Vi's best tablecloth. Taking some scones from the plate, she crumbled them and popped them into the bag. Shoving the piglets in, she said, 'In here, dears, quickly.' She buckled it up and pushed it under the table.

Joe and Spinner sat down and shared the last scone. As Auntie Vi brought a soldier into the kitchen, Albie said, in perfect German, 'I must apologise for the horrid smell. I've had the most awful tummy upset. Everyone is having them in the island these days.'

The soldier backed away, quickly inspected the kitchen and hurried out of the room. 'We are looking for escaped prisoners,' he said over his shoulder. 'One has been seen in this parish. Be careful. He is a dangerous Slav and has been on the loose…how you say…for weeks.'

When Auntie Vi had slammed the front door on him, Joe said, 'That one's Big Lips. He couldn't catch a fly. I bet he's scared of the prisoners.'

Auntie Albie opened the carpet bag and made a face. 'Crumbs. These two don't half stink.' She let the piglets out and they roared around the kitchen again as Auntie Vi gave a big sob.

So, Joe said, 'I'm sorry Auntie Vi. I didn't mean to upset you.'

'Oh, I don't care about *them.*' Auntie Vi watched the piglets playing catch. She laughed grimly and said, 'Let them mess up the place.' She showed them a letter. 'Look at this damn thing.'

Joe and Spinner glanced at each other, and Joe said, 'Language, Auntie Vi. There's a young lady here.' He nudged Spinner. 'She's very delicate about swearing.'

Auntie Vi rolled her eyes. 'It's a letter from the authorities and it says,' she scowled, then added furiously, 'I have to have three soldiers living with me and give them breakfast every day.'

'Blimey,' said Joe. 'What a horrible thought.'

Auntie Vi ripped off her bird hat and blew her nose loudly. 'Leave them pigs here and let them do their worst.'

4 pm

That afternoon, Auntie Vi bought her suitcase with her to the Percherons. She plonked it down and announced she'd be staying, talking rapidly about piglets and soldiers and billeting officers and how she wouldn't stay in her house another minute and certainly would never cook for the blooming enemy.

Clem drew up a chair for her. His mother passed Auntie Vi a cup of parsnip coffee and some toasted potato bread. She said, 'Never mind, my love. You can stay here as long as you like.'

Mr. Percheron came into the room. 'You're welcome, Vi. But we'd better let the authorities know today. No-one's allowed to stay with anyone else without permission.'

Auntie Vi crossed her arms and spat out, 'Pah! Who cares? I'll just tell them I've come to look after you.'

But Mr. Percheron insisted. He said, 'I don't need looking after. I'm better now.'

After supper, the others came round and heard about

Auntie Vi. Spinner said, 'We've had a letter too. We've got to have soldiers in the flat. Actually, we thought they'd come ages ago, so we're used to the idea.'

'Blimey, fancy living above Hotspur,' said Joe. 'His war efforts are the deadliest weapons in the island.' Everyone in the room burst out laughing, even Mr. Percheron.

'Flipping heck,' said Joe. 'You say you're used to the idea. But flipping having them so close isn't that good. I hope your dad didn't have a heart attack when he read the letter. Doesn't he do something dangerous up in his study? Forging identity cards or spying, or something?'

'Rubbish,' said Spinner quickly. 'Of course he doesn't.'

Ginger glanced at her. Then he whistled. 'So, the enemy will be right at our door.'

Sunday 22nd March
10 am

Auntie Vi was much more cheerful the next day. She fussed over the children and then announced that it was time for church, but Clem said he had too much to do, even though he had missed the Sunday service for three weeks.

Auntie Vi jabbed her finger at him. 'Shame on you. Who do you think you are? Think about your eternal soul, my boy.'

Clem tried not to laugh, then he said, 'All right, Auntie Vi. I'll come with you.'

When they returned, Auntie Vi was in commanding mode. Clem followed her indoors with a heavy bag.

'I fetched my stores on the way home,' she said. 'Put the bag on the table and fetch the other one, Clem. Hurry up. No spilling, thank you very much.'

Clem went outside and returned with another bag. 'You've been hoarding, Auntie Vi. Very naughty.' He pulled out two small blue bags of sugar, another of dried fruit and one of white flour. Then he found a tin of cherries in syrup and two of sardines. He looked at Auntie Vi with admiration. 'Where the heck did you find this lot?' He kept on unpacking the bag. 'And there's more.' He held up two packets of jelly, custard powder in tins, packets of tea and some Saxa salt.

Auntie Vi tossed her head and clamped her lips tight. She pointed at the other bag. Soon the table was covered in glory. As well as the food, there was a bar of soap, some bandages, a bottle of Dettol and two whole packets of needles and pins. Clem picked up a tin and rattled it.

'Buttons,' said Auntie Vi, smiling triumphantly. She thrust her hand into the bottom of one of the bags and held up a bunch of new bootlaces. 'We can keep respectable on Sundays and wash with proper soap instead of that stuff they give us that does nothing. That'll show the enemy, laughing at us for using string when,' she swallowed and went on, her voice wobbling a little, 'they have *reduced* us to it.'

The Percherons stared at Auntie Vi, not knowing what to say. Clem's father gazed at the full table. He picked up the tin of cherries and gave her an anxious look. 'None of it's black market, is it, my dear?'

'Mr. Cliquot's mixed up in that,' said Clem. 'Did you know?'

'*Pineapples*,' said Mr. Percheron, grimly. 'I told him what to do with them.

Auntie Vi gave Clem a look like a gimlet. 'That devil? Do you think I got these on the black market? I saved them for a rainy day, and I reckon that rainy day's right here.' She folded her arms across her chest and gazed proudly at the table.

'That's very kind of you, Vi,' said Mrs. Percheron, smiling gently. She touched the bag of white flour as if it was gold dust. 'What a treat. Let's tidy it away.'

'We'll hide some of it,' said Auntie Vi. 'You know what the enemy are like when they come searching.' She reached into her handbag. whipped out a packet of dates and held them up high. 'We'll keep these for emergencies.'

Clem looked at the dates longingly.

Auntie Vi bit her lower lip as if to stop herself from boasting. Then she put the dates on the table, a long packet with camels on it and curved ends. She looked round at them as though she had been caught doing something naughty at school. 'We all need a treat now and then. Let's have one now.' As Mr. Percheron coughed again, she added, 'We have to keep up our strength.'

After everything was tucked away, Auntie Vi made tea. While it brewed, she handed round dates and the room was quiet while the Percherons enjoyed their treat, taking their time.

Afterwards, Clem said, 'That was wonderful, Auntie Vi. Thank you.' He stood up and gave her a hug, towering over her. 'It's very kind of you to share with us.'

'Silly boy.' Auntie Vi pushed him away, but everyone could see that she was pleased. 'By heck,' she said, 'those piglets have made a mess of my house and the messier the better as far as I'm concerned. Let those flipping soldiers suffer.' Then she went on. 'It's a pity that Auntie Albie's fetched them. I nearly left them there to go on making more and more and more stink.'

Auntie Vi stamped upstairs to unpack. She set about opening and shutting drawers in Bill's room so loudly that the ceiling shook.

'Crumbs,' said Mr. Percheron, laughing again so loudly that everyone joined in with him.

'As well as all those treats, we've got a proper Sunday lunch,' said Clem, taking out a bowl of potatoes to scrub under the yard pump.

'The Lord be Praised,' said his father. He opened his

bible and began to read as Mrs. Percheron put a very small chicken in the oven to roast.

1 pm
An hour later, Joe turned up with Arthur, Diddie and Beaufort. He was covered in mud and grit. 'Sorry to turn up like this.' He put down a suitcase. 'Our roof's got another hole in it from blinking shrapnel. Water's pouring in. Can we stay a night or two?'

Mrs. Percheron was about to speak, when Auntie Vi came downstairs. She folded Arthur in her bony arms, grabbed Diddie's hand, and said to Joe, 'Follow me.' As Clem laid the table, he heard her saying, 'I'll sort everything out with Mr. and Mrs. Percheron, but not unless you swear to behave every single minute you stay here.'

When they all came down, Mrs. Percheron was taking roast potatoes out of the oven and basting them with the juices from the tiny chicken. 'How lovely that you're all here,' she said in her quiet voice. 'Now we have a houseful.'

It was nice to have so many at the table, thought Clem. When everyone was ready, he carved the chicken into thin slices and shared it out so that all the children had a piece with a pile of boiled cabbage and carrots and a few roast potatoes. The grownups all said they were full and couldn't possibly manage any chicken and that vegetables were all they wanted.

'Yum,' said Joe, rubbing his stomach. 'Best lunch I had in ages.' Auntie Vi glared at him. 'Yours are good too, Auntie Vi. You make lovely conger soup. Mrs. Percheron, please may Beaufort lick the plates? He does all our washing up.'

After lunch, Mr. Percheron asked for a pen and paper. He wrote a note in a shaky hand, using a tray to lean on. Then he gave it to Clem, saying, 'Sorry, son. I thought I was better, but it's a long way to town and I'm not quite up to it. We'd better register our guests, even though it's Sunday. We should have done it yesterday.'

Clem said he didn't mind nipping into town at all, adding, 'At least there won't be any room for soldiers here. We're full to the brim.'

3 pm

Clem set off on his bicycle, rain sloshing down his collar. He pulled his cap low and battled against the wind, singing to make himself feel better.

Nobody was about. Even the soldiers were cowering in shelters, staring dejectedly at the grey sea.

He decided to take the long route over Mount Bingham, so he could look at the harbour, but the view depressed him. The quays were covered in German army trucks.

Something about the sight made his heart ache, the greyness of the lovely harbour and the army trucks. He thought of Bill and how they'd waved him goodbye nearly two years ago.

'*Cheerio,*' he'd said, shouldering his kit bag. '*See you soon.*'

'And we never did and we never will.' Clem murmured. Then he free wheeled down the hill and into town, splashing as many Germans as he could on his way. When he'd posted his father's letter, he pedalled home on the inner road. Half way home, the rain became a downpour. Clem took shelter amongst a clump of trees, wondering when it would ever stop.

Suddenly, someone called out the usual islander exchange in Jersey French. '*Coumme est qu'tu'es?*'

Automatically, Clem answered, '*J'sis mangnifique!*'

Clem looked round and he gasped. 'Sasha.'

The prisoner put out his hand. Clem shook it and said, 'How do you know our language? You didn't try it when you spoke to me not long ago.'

Sasha said, 'I'm learning it, bit by bit.'

Clem looked at him in amazement. 'Where are you living now? We've been wondering.'

Sasha kept silent. Then he said, '*Nyet*. I must not tell you. It is possible that you might be questioned. I hear that soldiers will be staying next door to you soon, so I must…' he searched for the English words.. 'lie low. But I'll be near. And will see you when it is safe.'

'Good.' Clem smiled at him.

'I'll be away for a few weeks,' Sasha went on. 'don't fear for me. All will be well. But,' he looked earnestly at Clem, 'not all prisoners are trustworthy, or kind. Be careful.' Then he was gone.

'*A betot,*' called Clem after him. 'Until we meet again.' He set off again on his rickety bicycle. The sun had come out, and the island blazed with spring. Suddenly, he found himself singing at the top of his voice.

Monday 23rd March
5.30 am

Clem was out of bed before dawn as usual, dragging on his farming clothes, wishing slightly that his father would recover properly so he could sleep a little more at least once a week.

He tiptoed along the landing, noticing the new sounds in his house: Arthur snuffling and Auntie Vi snoring in the spare room and Diddie silent in Bill's room. He could hear Joe scrabbling about in George's room, looking for his clothes and muttering to Beaufort. His father was coughing as usual.

Clem tapped gently at Joe's door, then hurried downstairs in his socks past the grandfather clock and into the kitchen.

The fire was still glowing, so he hung the kettle over it. Then out in the dark farmyard, he pumped icy water into a bucket, took off his shirt and jumper and sloshed it over his top half, gasping at the cold.

When he went back indoors, Joe and Beaufort were in the kitchen. 'Bit flipping early, isn't it?' said Joe, as he let Beau out for his morning run.

'There's so much to do. No Bill, no George and now no Dad for a while,' said Clem, rubbing himself down with a towel. He shivered, yanking his shirt and jumper over his head, then grabbed a coat and put on his boots. 'You coming with me?'

'Yep,' said Joe. Then he frowned. 'Someone's outside. I can hear them...' He shoved past Clem. 'Where's Beau? He should be barking his head off.'

Clem grabbed the heavy torch and they both rushed out. But the yard was empty in the moonlight. Joe yanked Clem's sleeve. 'I can hear something.' Next door there was a soft squeak, then a scuffle of footsteps. Joe whispered, 'Someone's stealing Spinner's rabbits.' They held their breath, trying not to make a sound.

There was a low, menacing growl.

'Beau to the rescue,' whispered Joe. He let go of Clem's sleeve and clicked his fingers, but the dog didn't come to him. Beau growled again a little nearer. '*Beau*,' he whispered. '*Come here, boy.*'

There was another growl, deeper in the dog's throat, and suddenly a dark figure leapt towards them over the garden gate between the houses and raced into the farmyard, then into the orchard. Clem yelled. 'What the heck do you think you're doing?'

Joe yelled, 'Go get 'em, Beau.'

Clem turned on the torch, raking the orchard with the narrow blackout beam, so the buds and the twigs stood out against the dark like skeleton fingers. There was no one to be seen. Beaufort had vanished too, though they could hear the thump of his paws on the ground. Ahead of him, there was the sound of racing boots.

'You go up by the potato shed,' shouted Joe. 'I'll head down to the lane.'

But just as they separated, there was a sudden yelp, then silence. Joe rushed into the dark. 'Beaufort!'

Clem hurried after him with the torch.

As they reached the orchard there was suddenly a voice quite close. 'Stop. There's a dangerous man out there. I have the dog. I will carry him indoors.'

'*Sasha,*' whispered Clem. 'I thought you were staying away.'

The prisoner emerged from the orchard, Beaufort in his arms. 'He has been hit on his head, but he is alive.'

Joe ran up to him. 'Poor Beau.' In the first light of the day, they could see a wound on his head. 'Who did it, Beau? Tell me.'

'Come,' said Sasha. Very gently, he carried the dog to the barn, blood dripping down his clothes and seeping into the ground. He said, 'As I said to you, not all the prisoners are good people. I came back to tell you that again, before I went away. And now this has happened. So you know.'

He put the dog down on straw and added, 'He will heal. It is only a shallow cut.' Then he said goodbye in perfect Jersey French, adding, 'Remember what I said about prisoners. You must be careful.' Then he was gone.

Joe looked at Clem with an open mouth. 'He doesn't look at all like the prisoner we saw in the fog. He's just like a Jerseyman. Amazing what a good haircut can do, isn't it?'

10 pm

Long after everyone had gone to bed, Mr. Braye sat at the kitchen table, drinking a cup of watery cocoa. He was puzzling over a message someone had sent him, written in ugly capital letters. There was no name on it.

'What on earth?' he muttered. Then he read it out softly to Lizzie's cat, who was sitting on his lap. '*We know what you are doing and so do they.*'

After a while, he sighed, tore the note into tiny pieces and threw it on fire. The pieces glowed for a minute, then flamed and spluttered out. 'Horrid people,' he murmured, trying to dismiss the words from his mind.

He went round the house, checking that everything was locked and that the blackouts were shut. It was a school night, so everyone was asleep, even his sister Edie. She was always tired after a long day with Rosie.

Just as he went to lock the back door, he heard the purr of a motor engine in the lane. He thought of the note and his heart sank. *We know what you're doing and so do they.'* Then he straightened his back and went outside, trying to still his racing heart.

A German truck was parking outside the gates, and a minute later, a uniformed officer stepped out and walked towards him. '*Guten Abend,*' said Mr. Braye, keeping to the back door step. 'Good evening.'

The officer saluted him politely, then said, 'I have been sent to ask you to come with me. We must ask you something, but we have respect for you, Mr. Braye. You speak good German.'

For a moment, Mr. Braye relaxed. Then he blinked, remembering the note once more. He reached for his coat and said, 'Thank you. Of course I will come.'

Soon, he was travelling along the dark inner road to town, then up the hill to College House. His heart began to hammer. He had heard about College House and what went on there. None of it was good.

The driver opened the car door, and the officer accompanied him into the building, so he felt reassured as he was taken into an ordinary room with a large desk covered in files. Behind it sat a man he'd never met before. There was no seat, so Mr. Braye stayed standing, holding his hat in front of him with both hands.

The door shut behind him. Suddenly, they were alone together, except for a brute of a guard who was standing against the wall, watching.

The man behind the desk was icy, speaking English fluently. He gazed at Mr. Braye over rimless spectacles. 'I hear you are fluent in our language. Why is that?'

'I'm a music teacher, sir. I have lived in your country. I felt it polite to learn German when I was there. Indeed, it was necessary so that I could teach. I enjoyed my time there.'

'Some people say that you are spying, by pretending to be a helpful Jerseyman, but in fact you are sending information to England.' The interrogator's eyes were pale grey behind his spectacles. He narrowed them. 'By all methods.'

Mr. Braye stayed silent. Then he said, 'There is no way of sending messages to England, except by the Red Cross. And they are censored.'

The other man banged the desk. 'Morse code, radios, sending information with fishermen. You know one of them, Mr. Le Carin?' As he raised his voice, the guard from the back of the room moved close to Mr. Braye, gripping his arms tightly and pulling them behind his back, hard, so that his hat bounced on to the floor and rolled under the desk.

'We all know each other,' replied Mr Braye, keeping his voice calm. 'We grew up together, it is a small community. As for Mr. Le Carin, his boat is as you say, *kaput*. Broken. I do not know morse code and I cannot operate any sort of radio device. As I have said, I am a musician and a teacher, and I translate for the courts. That is all I can say, sir.'

There was a nasty silence, but at a sudden signal, the guard released him and went back to his place. The interrogator glared at him, then said, 'You have been informed upon by someone. Perhaps it is a lie, but if you are mixed up in any spying, you will be shot.'

Mr. Braye found that he was shaking. He said, 'May I ask who told you this?'

'You may not.' The man waved him away and the guard opened the door, propelling him out into the hall.

'My hat,' said Mr. Braye, turning round. Then he tried not to smile as the big brute of the guard went back into the room and picked up his hat from the floor. He returned it to him, staring at him with steely eyes and then gave a slight bow.

An hour after he'd been taken away, he was home, his legs trembling. He put a few more coals on the fire and tried to calm himself. But nothing would take away the terror. Even playing some of his beloved records didn't help. He stayed up late, keeping watch and wondering who on earth had made up such a story about him. Or who, perhaps, had crept into his study and searched.

We know what you are doing. The nasty little words echoed over and over in his head until at last he fell asleep with his head cradled in his arms at the table.

Tuesday 24th March
8 am

'Beaufort's all right now,' said Joe, standing at Spinner's kitchen door. 'Mr. and Mrs. Percheron are looking after him today. But if Sasha hadn't found him, I reckon he'd be dead.' He swallowed. 'I'm going to find the man who hurt him, I'm going to, the flippin' beggar.'

Spinner touched his arm. 'Don't do anything silly. What would happen if you found the man? He sounds violent.'

Mr. Braye was nursing a cup of tea, yawning. He said, 'It's best not to take revenge. Some people are enjoying being horrible at the moment. Just make sure you keep Beau on a lead. And lock the doors.'

Spinner looked puzzled. 'What do you mean by that, Daddy? About people…'

Mr. Braye shrugged. 'Nothing, darling. It's just that a few of them are full of anger for their own reasons. Then war comes along and their anger gets bigger. The main thing is that Beau's going to be fine, isn't it, Joe?'

Joe shrugged. 'Yeah, well, I want to show him.' He bit his lip.

'You'd better clean up. You've still got some blood on you from Beau,' Spinner said, handing him a damp cloth. She took her school hat off its peg and said goodbye to her father.

As they set off to school, Joe told her about the incident. She touched his arm again. 'How horrible. Poor old Beau.'

'I was flipping furious,' said Joe.

'But you haven't told me about Sasha,' said Spinner. 'What does he look like? I'm the only one that hasn't seen him.'

'He's tall,' Joe said. 'Skinny but not starving, and...' He stopped dead as he heard a bike behind them. 'Who's that, speeding like the Olympics?'

'Spinner! Joe!' Ginger screeched to a halt beside them. 'Want a lift to school, girl?' He showed them his sports bag. 'I could do with some help.' As he spoke, the bag moved, wriggling from side to side.

Spinner leapt backwards. 'What's that? Another conger?'

'It's a piggy,' said Joe. 'Remember? Ginger said he'd take one to his friends.'

Ginger pushed his glasses on. 'It's quite difficult to cycle with this jolly old piglet dancing about.' He patted the luggage rack. 'Come on Spinner. Give us a hand.'

'All right.' Spinner looked down at her clean uniform. Then, slinging her satchel on her back, she took the wriggling sports bag and climbed on to the luggage rack. 'I hope it doesn't flipping wee on me.'

'If you smell of pig wee, the soldiers won't inspect you.' Joe held his nose and chuckled.

Spinner blanched. 'Do I *look* suspicious?'

'*Very*,' said Joe. 'But luckily, they're bored with stopping school kids. They prefer to annoy old people at the moment, like Dad.'

Spinner clutched Ginger round the waist, squashing the sports bag between them. The piglet wriggled a bit more, then was still.

'See?' said Ginger. 'I knew you could do it.'

'It's gone very quiet,' Joe said. 'Blimey, Spinner. Best check if it's still breathing.'

'Course it is. I know how to carry animals.' Spinner looked at him scornfully. 'If I can manage a lobster, I can cope with a piglet.'

Joe waved goodbye as the bike wobbled off towards town. 'See you later,' shouted Spinner. Then they were gone. The last thing he heard was a shriek from Spinner. 'He's *done* it. It's a HUGE wee. I told you he would.'

Joe grinned as he watched them out of sight. He was blowed if he'd go to school on a day like this. He perched on a low wall, enjoying a moment of freedom. The daffodils were out in the fields and he thought of his mother, and how she always loved to pick a bunch and arrange it for the kitchen table.

He looked up at the sky. 'We're all right, Mum.' He gulped back a sudden tear. 'But Dad misses you.' Then he jumped down from the wall, ran to the coast road and hitched a lift to town from an army truck, clinging to the back with his feet on the bumper all the way.

A sea breeze was sweeping up the litter on the pavements and piling it away into corners. Everything looked grubby. So many of the shops were boarded up and soldiers had trampled over flower beds, but all the same, Joe felt a sudden lift to his heart, because it was spring. He jumped off the truck then whistled as he made his way to his uncle's yard.

When he arrived, Mr. Cliquot was sitting in the sunshine on a pile of bricks, eating a bun, as if there wasn't a war on. 'Wotcha,' he said, taking a big bite and then another, quickly polishing it off when he saw Joe.

Beyond him, roof tiles were stacked against the wall.

Joe glared at his uncle. 'Those are *ours*. I'd know those seagull footprints anywhere. My Dad will throttle you, Uncle Philo.'

Mr. Cliquot laughed. 'No he won't. I know *far* too much about him and what he's up to these days. And I know about that Mr. Braye, with all his German chat to the soldiers. He brushed crumbs off his moustache and lit a cigarette. 'Look, boy, all I'm doing is making an honest living. I've got a good customer for those tiles and I'll tack some felt on your roof.'

'You blimming thief,' Joe said through gritted teeth.

'Why aren't you at school?' Mr Cliquot stood up. 'You want to watch it young man. Someone will report you to the College House and they'll send you to Germany to work in the factories.'

Joe laughed. 'Oh yes? I wouldn't mind travelling a bit. I could see the world.' He looked longingly at the cigarette. 'I was going to mend the roof. That's why I skipped school. The rain's coming in.'

'There's no need to skip school.' His uncle took another drag on his cigarette. 'I was only kidding. Of course I'll mend the flipping roof. I've got some other tiles coming my way from France. Bit cheaper. Anyhow, I hear you're nice and cosy staying at the Percherons, so what's the flipping hurry?'

'We don't like cadging off other people,' said Joe. 'Not that you'd know about that. I got special permission from school to mend the roof today.' At this lie, he folded his arms and looked away, adding, 'I can't stand being educated no more. They make us learn German.'

Mr Cliquot's eyes narrowed. 'I could give you a lift to the school if you like, and explain why you're late.'

Joe rolled his eyes.

'Or, I've got some other work on today while I'm waiting for your new roof tiles from France. If you come and help me, I'll give you a hamper and we won't say a word to your dad or your Auntie Vi about missing school. Or..' he narrowed his eyes…'the truant officer.'

Joe ignored the last sentence. 'A *hamper*? Pull the other one. How come you can get hold of a *hamper*? When your own kid's stealing jam to fill his stomach?'

'Is he? The little devil.' His uncle laughed and tapped his nose. 'Wouldn't *you* like to know? Come on, jump in.' He opened his truck door and they set off along the coast road. Soon, they were at the beach and Mr. Cliquot chucked Joe a spade. 'Put your back into it, lad.' He lit another cigarette and leaned against the truck.

Joe hurled the spade down. 'If you think I'm going to fill that truck on my own, you've got another think coming. I've got a bad hand.'

'I heard about that from one of my German mates. You've been a naughty boy, going out after curfew then accepting a pile of sandwiches from the enemy. Whatever next?' Mr. Cliquot took a shovel from the truck for himself.

Joe rolled his eyes, but he picked up the spade and dug with his left hand. For half an hour, they chucked sand into the truck. Then Mr. Cliquot paused. 'Oi oi,' he said, pointing up the road. 'There's a blooming patrol coming. Let's scarper.'

'What's the hurry?' asked Joe, when they were accelerating away from the beach.

Mr. Cliquot raised one eyebrow. 'I don't want anyone to know I get my sand from the beach.' He roared with laughter. 'I sell it to the Germans. It ruins their concrete because of all the salt. Your brainy friend Ginger would have something technical to say about it.'

'Yeah,' said Joe, nursing his hand. 'He would. Anyway, where are we going?'

Mr. Cliquot pressed the accelerator. 'First, we're nipping up to Mr. Braye's place to mend a fireplace in the flat and sweep the chimney. The Germans are moving there.'

'I heard that too. I'd make a bad job of it if I were you.'

Mr. Cliquot swung the wheel right and winked. 'I usually find it takes *at least* three visits to mend things for the Germans. They always pay on time, every time. Very efficient, Germans.'

Joe looked sideways at him again, but his uncle was driving along without a care in the world. The truck was hiccoughing as though there was dirt in the fuel. 'Where do you get your petrol from? It must be filthy stuff.'

Mr. Cliquot sailed on. 'This time, I used petrol from my own store. Big mistake.' He tucked his cigarette behind his ear. 'The German petrol's much better than mine.' He grinned at Joe. 'It's best to be a teeny-weeny bit friendly with the Germans, I find. It always pays off. They often fill up my tank for free.'

Thursday 26th March
5 pm

After school, Spinner plonked her satchel down on the floor and hugged her father. 'Nice day at school. We were allowed to do gym, for once.' She hung up her school things, noticing that her father was strangely quiet. So she said, 'When are the soldiers coming to stay, Daddy?'

'Quite soon, I'm afraid. It's such a nuisance.' Then Mr. Braye brightened up. 'The good news is that the chimney in the flat is badly blocked with a crow's nest,' he said. 'So we're spared for a bit longer.' He gave a little smile. 'We *must* be careful when they come, you know. They have a duty to report anything suspicious.'

'We aren't doing anything suspicious, so that's all right.' Spinner threw her arms round him again, then she drew back and said, 'Daddy, you're trembling.'

'I forgot to eat any lunch. That always makes me shaky. I'll soon be better for a nice hot drink. Now, I wonder if we have any bread. Perhaps a little toast would …'

At that moment, they heard shouting outside. Spinner raced out of the house, followed by her father. Mr. Cliquot was carrying a beautiful wicker hamper out of the farmhouse and loading it on to his lorry, followed by Joe. The hamper had the name of a German city painted on it in white: *FRANKFURT. DELIKATESSEN.*

Mr. Percheron was watching from the farmyard, a rug round his shoulders. His voice was raised as he said firmly, 'I'm not having a *black market* hamper in my house. Foreign MUCK. You can take it and put it where the sun doesn't shine.'

'Excuse me, Sid Percheron,' said Mr. Cliquot in an oily way. 'The hamper was not for you, it was for this young man.' He turned to Joe, 'I'm sorry, Joe, if your friends won't let you have what is due to you.'

Mr. Percheron looked puzzled. 'What do you mean by that? *What is due to you?*' He took Joe by the collar. 'I hope you haven't got mixed up in anything you shouldn't have, young man.'

'The hamper was my wages, sir,' said Joe, folding his arms across his chest. 'I worked all day for that.'

'Pah,' exclaimed Mr. Percheron. 'If you were working for your Uncle Philo, I can tell you something. Anything due to you is *the wages of sin.*' He turned and stamped away, coughing while Joe glared at his retreating back.

'Fair do's,' said Mr. Cliquot. 'All the more for me.' He lobbed the hamper into the truck, jumped into the driver's seat and roared off down the lane. Joe followed Mr. Percheron into the farmhouse, his face screwed up in outrage at the loss of the glorious hamper that he had wanted so much.

Mr. Braye said, 'Oh dear.' Suddenly, he found laughter bubbling up inside himself as if it had been squashed ever since his horrible night time visit to College House three days ago, and then again this morning. He caught Spinner's eye, and they rushed indoors, trying to control themselves.

'We mustn't laugh at Mr. Percheron,' he said. 'But it was so funny. *The wages of sin.* Poor old Joe. What a disappointment.'

Later, Spinner decided to catch up with her diary. She sat at the kitchen table while her father read The Evening Post, and wrote:

Spring has come and we are feeling better. At least the prisoners can sleep outside without freezing if they have to. Poor things. The piglets have all gone except one which we are calling Betty. She is also hairy, like her Uncle Hotspur.

The swallows and swifts have come back, and they are burbling away under the eaves. It feels like a wonderful sign that all will be well. There are more than ever, perhaps because Joe has drawn welcoming signs.

She drew Betty under the apple trees, with the first blossoms above her, then added swallows and swifts swooping through the sky. 'I'm trying to be careful,' she said to her father, 'but the war better had be over soon or I'll run out of colour.'

'We can't have that.' Her father glanced at her over his newspaper, admiring the picture. 'I'll have to send for some from Harrods.'

'Very funny, 'said Spinner. 'As if you could.' She looked up and grinned, then she froze. There were large bruises on his arms, where his sleeves were rolled up. 'Daddy, what are *those*? They look very painful.'

Mr. Braye shrugged. 'Oh, *them*? I walked into a lamp post the other night. You know how difficult it is walking into town in the dark.'

'But you've got bruises on both arms,' said Spinner, anxiously.

'They're terribly hard lamp posts,' said her father.

'And it's dark without street lights these days.'

He seemed perfectly cheerful. Then he wound up the gramophone as if the bruises didn't hurt a bit. So she said, 'That Jitterbug's the really fast dance isn't it?'

'I bet Mummy dances to this in England.' Mr. Braye turned the music louder and sang along with the words. But Spinner knew he was sad. His voice sounded wrong, like a violin string wound too tight.

They'd played the record twice when somebody knocked loudly on back door. Mr. Braye said, 'I'll go.'

'Your sleeves. Roll them down,' said Spinner. 'It looks…'

Her father touched her cheek gently. The knocking came again and Spinner felt sick. Clutching the cat, she followed her father to the back door. Two young men stood there in Wehrmacht officer uniform.

Mr. Braye spoke to them in German and one of the officers said, stiffly, 'I am Franz. My friend here is Otto. We are from Hamburg.'

'Indeed,' replied Spinner's father, reverting to English. 'And I am Mr. Braye. This is my daughter, Miss Braye. *We* are from Jersey.'

Spinner gulped. She'd never heard her father so icy. He was usually so polite to the Germans. She looked past him to the two men and gave them a tight smile. They gave her a nod, as if they were pleased to be welcomed by one person at least.

'We are junior,' the other officer said. He indicated the garage. 'The apartment is for us on Monday. It will be good. You will be safe. There are bad people in the island. *Untermensch.*'

'*Monday? So soon?*' Mr. Braye ignored the last few sentences. His voice remained unemotional. 'If you must, then so be it. But you will find that it is a simple flat.'

'It will be in order? Clean?'

'Of course.' Mr. Braye was abrupt. 'And I will give you the name of a man who's been mending the fireplace. He's swept the chimney, but you might want him to sweep it again. We have a problem with crows here.' He scribbled a number on a piece of paper and handed it to them.

'Crows? The big, black birds?'

'Indeed. They nest in the chimneys when they aren't being used,' explained Mr. Braye. 'They've done it for generations.'

'I am from the country too. I know about these birds. Some people say they mean bad luck, but I do not.' Otto smiled, peering at the telephone number Mr. Braye had given him. 'Ach, this man. He is kind to us Germans.' He showed the paper to his companion, whose eyes lit up.

'Mr. Clicko,' he said. 'A good man.'

Mr. Braye changed the subject. 'I am a music teacher. So, you will understand that some nights my pupils play in a very noisy band.'

'We Germans are musical,' beamed Franz. 'We will be very happy together. Do you know of our great composer, Wagner?

'The name is familiar,' said Mr. Braye, raising an eyebrow. Then he said politely, '*Guten Abend.* Good evening.' He didn't offer to shake the soldiers' hands, pulled his daughter gently inside and shut the door in their faces.

'What does *untermesch* mean? I've forgotten,' said Spinner, for no reason in particular.

'It's a horrible word. It means sub human. That's what

Hitler thinks about the Slavs: Russians and Moldovans and the others like them. And jazz musicians. The list goes on.'

'And gypsies, and Lizzie's family...' Spinner blinked. 'I remember now. How horrible.' She leaned forward. 'Hitler even hates circus people. And they're wonderful.' Then she looked at her father. 'Is that why you've changed, suddenly? You don't seem to like the enemy very much, but you used to be so polite to them.'

'I enjoyed living in Germany before the war. But it's a different place now,' said her father.

Friday 27th March
6 pm

The next evening, Mr. Braye decided to walk down to the sea. He turned up his coat collar and pulled on his hat firmly. As he walked down the lane, he hummed, despite everything he had gone through. They had come for him again and once more taken him to College House. But then, like a cat with a mouse, they'd let him go, with another couple of bruises where he had been held tightly once more.

At least, he thought, *Spinner doesn't know about it, even if she's seen the bruises.*

When he was opposite Green Island, he sat down on a bench and took out his pipe. He hardly ever smoked. For a start, there was no tobacco to be had. So he used his supply very rarely. After tamping down the tobacco into the bowl of the pipe, he lit it carefully, so as not to use more than one precious match.

There was no one about. So in between puffs, he talked to his wife in his head.

'They suspect me,' keeping his voice quiet. 'They interrogated me. Today, they took me to College House, and on Monday night too.' He took a deep breath, thinking of the infamous place. 'That's the girl's school. The girls have been moved out. So it makes it all worse that horrible things go on there. Interrogation.'

He pictured his wife. For a moment, it seemed as though she really was beside him, sitting on their favourite bench as they used to only a few years ago.

'It wasn't too bad. A few bruises, a bit of nastiness. More threats.' He swallowed. 'They think I'm spying.' He managed a small laugh, checked around himself and said out loud. 'I am of course.'

Then he sat in silence, listening to the ripple of the tide around the grassy island and the call of seagulls. As the sun set, he stood up, sighed and set off for home.

Sunday 29th March
8 pm

'Dad's a bit glum these days,' said Joe, leaning against the table at Spinner's house. 'I told you ages ago he filled the shed with tins of black market pineapple.' Spinner nodded, so he went on, 'Then somebody pinched it before he could sell it.' He laughed. 'Shame really but at least he won't get caught and end up in prison.'

'I could do with some tropical fruit,' said Ginger. He made a show of licking his lips, then added, 'It's a real shame you couldn't keep the hamper, Joe.'

'It was full to the brim with German goodies. I never thought Mr. Cliquot would actually stick to his promise and bring it. All I did was help him dig some sand from the beach.' Joe clutched his stomach, then moaned. 'And Mr. Percheron made him take it back. All that lovely grub. Tins of ham and...'

'Maybe he'll give it to Billy,' interrupted Spinner. 'He's a hungry lad.'

'Fat chance,' said Joe. 'There were chocs and cake and everything. But Mr. Percheron called the hamper *the wages of sin*. He stuck to me like a limpet until I got Mr. Cliquot to come and fetch it. It's a flipping pain. Beau loves ham.'

'Who wants *enemy* ham and chocs anyhow?' Spinner

frowned. 'And their sausages?'

'*Me*,' said Joe. 'It's gorgeous stuff.' He smirked. 'But I did have a few moments alone with it, so I took a bite off a sausage. Actually, loads of bites. They were different from our sausages, but when you got used to them, blimmin' glorious. And I had a choc or two, shared some with Diddie. Took a spoonful of blueberry jam, yum. Opened the biscuits and we ate the lot.' He fished in his pocket. 'Here, I kept two for you.'

'*Traitor*,' said Ginger, 'eating enemy food.' He held out his hand, brushed fluff off the biscuit and ate it. 'So, you ruined the hamper and Mr. Cliquot won't be able to sell it to anyone.'

Joe gave a biscuit to Spinner. 'I only tasted a little, so it looks like the mice had a go. I left the tins of oysters. We've got plenty of our own.'

'Clever mice, taking off the jam lid,' said Spinner, nibbling the edge of her biscuit. Then she made a face. 'This tastes funny. Have you got anything else in your pocket? Something smelly?'

Joe fished in his pocket and pulled out a crab claw. 'Only some bait.'

'Eeeugh,' shouted Ginger and Spinner together, spitting crumbs.

Joe grabbed the biscuits from them and stuffed them in his mouth. 'You're too choosy.'

'Mr. Cliquot's matey with the enemy.' Ginger spat out the last few crumbs. 'He might tell on you.'

'He won't. I made little mice teeth on all the packets, so there's proof they ate it, not me.' Joe looked at the clock. 'Best go back to Clem's place. I have to entertain the little kids and keep them away from annoying his dad.'

Tuesday 31st March
5 pm

The next afternoon, everyone returned home to find a German motorbike parked by the wall in the Brayes' back yard, with a sidecar. In the flat above the garage, men were speaking loudly in German, against a background of strident music.

'Gosh,' said Ginger. 'They're playing Wagner. Hitler's favourite music.'

They listened for a minute and Spinner said, 'It's very powerful.'

'It's a blimming racket,' said Joe, stuffing his fingers in his ears. 'I'm not listening.' He pushed his bike through the gates to the farm, shouting over the music, 'Best find Clem. I bet he's flipping furious they've moved in.'

'I can hear him, even through this noise.' Ginger hurled his school bag onto the back doorstep and Spinner did the same. Soon they were racing after Joe to the old potato store, with Beaufort catching up, the bandage uncurling from his head like a pennant.

The door was shut. Behind it, there was a thump, thump, thump. Beaufort sat on his haunches and howled. Spinner frowned. 'Shouldn't we leave him alone?'

THUMP, THUMP, THUMP.

'Maybe,' Ginger muttered.

THUMP, THUMP, THUMP.

'He might do something stupid,' said Joe. 'You know what Clem's like when he's really angry. Remember the fight at the school? When he nearly killed Percy?' He tried the door. 'His hands have only just healed. They'll be a right mess now.'

'Perhaps he's kicking it,' said Spinner.

All of a sudden, the thumping stopped and the bolt shot back. Beaufort turned tail and raced down the hill. Spinner gasped Clem wrenched open the door and burst out, his eyes blazing and his face red. His hair was matted with sweat.

'What the *hell* are you doing?' Clem glared at them. 'Leave me alone. Just ruddy go home.' He turned and slammed the door behind him. Then the bolt shot into place. He began to kick the punch bag again, yelling, 'The island's full with wretched prisoners being beaten to death. And now we're giving a roof to a couple of soldiers.' The thumping stopped and he yelled again. 'So we're *all* traitors now, aren't we?'

'We didn't *invite* the Germans to stay,' said Spinner fiercely. 'They just turned up. So we jolly well aren't traitors.' She folded her arms and stomped down the hill.

Ginger said, 'And we aren't *collaborators* either.'

'You don't say,' said Joe. 'Well, *I'm* not going to treat them as if they're my best mates.' He took out his catapult and shot a large pebble at the roof of the flat, then another and another so that the tiles were covered in them. But the new tenants were still listening to their music, turned up too loudly for them to notice.

Spinner said, 'Don't frighten the birds. Poor things.'

6.30 pm

When he'd kicked away his anger, Clem decided to walk the farm boundary. They'd planted wheat instead of tomatoes for the first time ever, on one of the fields by the coast. Everyone needed flour, so they didn't have much choice.

He hid the punchbag as usual, ran his hands through his hair, put on his sweater and left the door unlocked. Then he set off downhill towards the coast. Just as he reached the wheat field, there was a loud shout.

'Wotcha, Clem.' A tall boy was waving at him from the end of the field.

Clem's heart lifted. '*Legs*,' he shouted back, gathering pace. 'What are you doing this side of the island?'

Legs was sitting on a wall with a stone cider flagon. He patted the stone beside him. 'Want a drink?' he said. 'My auntie gave me some of her best. I've just been to see her.'

'*Aunties*,' said Clem, sitting beside him. 'Always up to no good.'

'I should say,' said Legs. He peered into the flagon, shook it and said, 'It's a bit strong.' Then he handed it to Clem, who tipped it back and the cider ran down his throat, icy and sweet.

'You're right. It *is* flipping strong.' Clem wiped his lips. 'Better not have any more. Jobs to do, secrets to keep and all that. Anyhow, Legs, I said what're you doing this side? Apart from seeing Auntie?'

'Hitched a lift, came to see what's happening.' Legs frowned and looked in the direction of the coast. 'Those Germans ain't half messing up the place.' He aimed a pebble at a gatepost and went on. 'It's ruddy annoying me, I can tell you. Soldiers everywhere, beating up those poor fellows.'

Clem said, 'I'm annoyed too.' He waved away the flagon. 'What they do to those Russian prisoners is *disgusting*. They treat them like slaves. Even some of the decent soldiers laugh at them.' He lowered his voice. ' I wish I could escape.' He jabbed his finger in the direction of the French coast.

'How would that help?' Legs stared at him. 'You'd be caught. It's horrible over there. Worse, maybe.'

'Yeah. I know. I'm kidding.' Clem sighed. 'I can't go. Have to pass my exams... except they aren't real exams now we're cut off...and help Father on the farm. He's not been well. Lack of food, really.' He looked out to sea again. 'I feel like a coward, not fighting like my brothers.' He corrected himself. 'Brother, I mean.'

Legs nodded. 'My brother's gone too.' He spoke about his brother Helier and how they'd heard that he'd died, months afterwards. Then he passed Clem the cider again. 'Have a bit more.'

Clem shook his head. 'My head's spinning from one sip. Your auntie must be tough to drink this stuff.'

'She's dynamite,' said Legs. 'You should hear her with the soldiers. Won't have any nonsense.' He chuckled and went on, 'We have to do what we can to fight back. Sabotage for a start. Keep cheerful. Show we don't care.'

Clem agreed. 'And help the prisoners.'

'True,' said Legs. 'But risky. Very risky.' He stood up, wobbling a little. 'If you ever need a hand with anything, let me know. I can run, remember.' He laughed loudly. 'Though not today. Auntie's cider is too strong.'

Clem put a steadying hand on his shoulder. 'Thanks, Legs. I was in a right state this afternoon. Blimming Germans moved in next door and I can't stand them poking their noses in.'

Legs said, 'We've got soldiers too, right in the flipping house. Three of them. Very polite, very clean. Spend their time writing home or watching us.'

'Ruddy hell,' said Clem. 'Can't you poison them?'

Legs laughed, much too loudly. 'I could give them Auntie's cider.' Then he added, 'We're having a party tonight, in her barn. Want to come?'

Clem's eyes lit up, then he shook his head. 'Another time. Too much to do, Dad's still not back to full strength. Thanks, though.'

'Plenty more parties to come,' said Legs. He waved the cider flagon at Clem. 'Plenty of this too.' He put an arm round Clem's shoulders. 'You look like you've got the weight of the world on you, old chap.' Then he wagged his finger. 'Don't forget. Your old pal Legs will help out any time.'

Easter Saturday 5th April
2 pm

In the afternoon, everyone went off to decorate the church as they always did for Easter. Joe decided to stay back at the farmhouse to clean the shoes so no one would feel *reduced*, as Auntie Vi said many times, by looking shabby.

Spring sunshine poured into the open back door. Beaufort lay on the mat on his back, his sore head mended and his tail wagging lazily as he enjoyed the sudden warmth.

Joe started with Arthur's small boots which were old ones of his own. First, he tacked on new soles, then polished the leather until the boots shone. He cut new laces from a ball of brown string, careful not to waste a scrap. But as he threaded them into the lace holes, his dog suddenly sat up and growled, deep in his throat. Then he rushed out, barking wildly.

Joe laughed. 'Silly boy. You'll never catch a seagull.'

He gave the boot a final shine and put it down. Then for some reason he picked up the tack hammer and went out to call back Beaufort. But the dog had stopped his noise. He was crawling along on his belly towards a barefooted stranger who stood in the shade against the milking parlour wall.

Joe clicked his fingers, but Beaufort ignored him.

The man looked up from under a tatty old cap, then sidled along the wall away from the dog, holding out his hand to Joe.

Joe gripped the tack hammer more tightly. He muttered to the dog, 'Come here, boy.' Then, more firmly, '*Come here.*'

The stranger stared at the dog, then back at Joe. After a while, Joe said quietly, 'What do you want?' Then he remembered what Sasha had said, that not all prisoners were good people. So he stepped backwards, urging Beaufort to come with him by clicking his fingers again.

Suddenly, the man said, 'I am friend of Sasha. You help me too.' He waved his hand at the farmhouse and the Bray's house next door. 'All good people are here who help prisoners. And I see bird pictures, like signs to show you are safe houses.'

As he waved, his sleeves fell back and Joe froze. The stranger's wrists and forearms were completely clean. And when he glanced at the man's feet, he noticed that they were unscarred, even though his toes were dirty as though he had walked through the field. *He's only just taken off his boots*, he thought. *And he's not desperate. He's not even trembling.* All at once, he knew that the man was a fake.

'I don't know Sasha. That's not a Jersey name.' He stepped towards the dog and grabbed his collar. 'We aren't allowed to help. I am very sorry.' He pointed at the flat. 'We have German soldiers living here. So we obey the rules.' Before he went inside, he added, 'I like drawing, but haven't any paper. That's why I draw the bird pictures. They're swifts and swallows and we love them in the island.' Then he went inside with Beaufort and locked the kitchen door firmly. He felt shaky.

4 pm

When the others came back, Joe told them about the stranger. Clem and the men searched the outbuildings and the shed, but there was nothing to be seen. Clem said, 'I bet he was a stool pigeon. An informer.'

'If he was, he was useless,' said Joe. He explained what he'd noticed and held up a grubby arm. 'I could do better.'

Ginger said, 'So, someone thinks your bird pictures are a kind of code? Oh dear.' He tapped his head.

'What a bunch of prats. I've drawn birds everywhere. It's the enemy's fault because we haven't any paper to draw on. I told him that.' Joe rolled his eyes, then said he was off to collect Billy because Auntie Vi wanted him to come up to the farm for Easter.

He didn't have to look far. As soon as he reached the beach, he noticed a small, lonely figure on the beach amongst the rocks, poking about with a stick. 'Billy,' he yelled. Billy looked up and his face was unwashed and pale. His hair had been shaved off. 'Nits,' muttered Joe, racing down the wooden steps to the beach. 'Poor kid.'

Billy was shivering in the icy spring wind. Joe ran down to him. 'Here,' he said, ripping off his sweater as Beaufort raced round and round. 'It's not a very good colour, but Auntie Vi made it nice and long.'

Billy shoved Joe away, but Joe gripped him tightly with one arm and yanked the sweater over his head, pulling it down to his knees. Then he dragged Billy along the beach, making him run on his wobbly legs, until he stopped shivering. 'I look like a tube of mustard,' said Billy, looking down at the yellow sweater in disgust.

'Needs must,' said Joe. 'Anyhow, like I said, what are you doing tonight?'

'Mucking about,' said Billy. He showed Joe a small bag of winkles. 'Catching my tea.'

'Blimey.' Joe peered into the bag. 'That's not going to do you much good. Here, come with me. Auntie Vi wants your company.' He grabbed Billy's hand and pulled him up along the beach and up the lane until they were nearly at the Brayes' house. 'You're spending Easter with us.'

Billy's eyes lit up, then he said 'Flipping stop going so fast. I need a break.'

Joe put his finger on his lips. 'Shh. Something's happening in the yard. Stay with Beau.' He tiptoed towards the big gates and put his eye to a crack in the wood.

Rosie was sitting on the back door step in her thick coat, entertaining Franz and Otto. Joe heard her explaining, 'You must be very careful living here. There is a strange man who visits us, but Clem doesn't mind at all. Clem is his best friend.'

Joe saw Franz raise an eyebrow.

Rosie ploughed on. 'So,' she crossed her arms defiantly. 'You must be nice, specially to the man with dirty clothes. He's very hungry.'

Joe beckoned Billy and Beaufort, then he pushed open the gates and dashed in. He forced a smile at the two soldiers. 'We might be doing a band practice tonight.' Suddenly remembering that it was Easter Saturday, he added, 'There'll be a lovely hymn and I know you Germans are church people. Want to come? After supper.' Then he scooped up Rosie, took her indoors and a few minutes later, hurried over to the farmhouse with Billy, left him there and raced back to the Brayes' to ask for a band practice, telling them why.

In no time, Auntie Vi was at the pump, sloshing water over Billy, who had been undressed to his ragged pants. 'This boy's filthy,' she said, turning him round and attacking his back with a sponge. She peered at his shoulders. 'And he's got scabies.'

Joe came out of the Brayes' back door and looked at Billy's skin with an exaggerated gasp. The boy stuck out his tongue, so Joe said, 'They're not as bad as Rosie. She's covered in spots. I've just seen them. Looks like a volcano has erupted over her back, poor little kid.'

'*Spots?*' Auntie Vi rubbed Billy with a rough, grey towel. 'There's measles all over the island thanks to no soap.' She stabbed her finger accusingly at Otto and Franz, who were watching over the wall. Then she dragged back the yellow jumper over Billy. 'Come on, boy. Indoors with you and we'll get out the Home Doctor book.'

Joe followed them into the kitchen. While everyone was busy checking Billy's rash, he took Clem to one side. 'Rosie's just told the Germans that there's a man with dirty clothes who comes here. So I've asked for a band practice to divert their attention and show them how nice we are.'

'Oh, God,' said Clem. 'How on earth has she noticed him? He keeps a very low profile.' He sighed. 'Oh well, we'll just have to tell them that he's a farm worker if they ask. Anyhow, last time I saw Sasha, he'd had a haircut and he's learning Jersey French. He's well-scrubbed too.'

'We're going to play *Ain't Misbehavin*,' Joe smirked. 'But their English isn't good enough to understand.'

6.30 pm

Billy snivelled and looked down at his knees. 'I don't like that blue stuff you've put on me. I look silly.'

'It's called Gentian Blue,' explained Mrs. Percheron, kindly. 'And thank goodness we've still got some in the medicine cupboard. It'll get rid of those sores. You've only got impetigo. It's not as bad as measles.'

Billy stuck out his tongue again, drumming his feet on the floor.

So Clem said quickly, 'Chin up Billy.' He pulled a funny face, waggling his ears. 'You can stay tonight and go home tomorrow. You'll be better in no time.'

'What about my dad? He'll be cross.' Billy pouted, drumming his heels louder.

'We'll let him know,' said Clem. 'But first, we're going to cheer up Rosie. She's really sad because of her measles, so we're going to have a band practice out of doors and she can listen. You can join in.'

Billy scratched a sore, but Auntie Vi yanked his arm away. Billy scowled and said, 'What about the pigs? Do they like music?'

'Sure,' said Clem. 'Those soldiers love a good tune.' He fetched his sousa. 'Come on, Billy. Stop sulking and bring some chairs. We're going to have fun.'

A few minutes later, everyone was outside in the yard, warming up their instruments. Overhead, the swallows soared to and fro, feeding their young under the eaves. From upstairs, Rosie looked out of her bedroom window, her mouth in a furious square and her face dotted with calamine lotion.

Clem opened the top half of the milking parlour door. 'The cows are going to enjoy this. Listen to them mooing.'

Mr. Braye said, 'We're going to play *Ain't Misbehavin'*

and *Your Feet's Too Big*, followed by a nice hymn because it's Easter.

'My fingers still don't work properly,' said Clem. 'But I'll do what I can.' As Clem played, he thought of Legs La Motte and how he laughed at the enemy. *We won't let anyone beat us*, Clem thought. *Ever.* Then he noticed Franz and Otto stealing over to listen. So he turned his back.

'Excellent,' said Mr. Braye, as they finished the first two pieces. 'Billy, you were magnificent on the triangle.'

Suddenly, a shower of potato pellets ricocheted from Rosie's window. She waved the potato gun furiously, then yelled again, 'Bang Bang, soldiers.' Otto and Franz whirled round, staring upwards for a moment, then bursting into laughter.

As everyone gazed at Rosie, Spinner noticed something. Behind the two soldiers, an arc of pebbles whirled through the air in the lane, juggled higher and higher by a tall, skinny man in the lane, neatly dressed like a proud Jerseyman. Then suddenly he was gone.

'And to end with, ' said Mr. Braye solemnly, 'We'll play our favourite island hymn, *For those in Peril on the Sea.*' He glanced at the soldiers. 'In memory of our men, lost at sea in this terrible war.'

The two soldiers bowed their heads.

Easter Sunday 6th April
10.15 am

Everyone had a decorated egg for breakfast, with little hats and faces made by Spinner. There was an extra slice of toast as well. Then it was time for church.

The girls and women put on Sunday hats trimmed with flowers. The men wore buttonholes of violets and primroses, but Mr. Percheron stayed at home to look after Billy and the animals, while Mrs. Martin kept Rosie next door.

The church was bright with daffodils and nearly every seat was full. A tall stranger, neatly dressed, nipped in during the first hymn and sat next to a row of German soldiers. Just before the organist played the last piece of music, he nodded his goodbyes and slipped away again.

After the service, everyone scattered around the churchyard to admire the flowers on the graves and catch up with each other's news, but Mrs. Percheron hurried home. Back at the farmhouse, Mr. Percheron had just come indoors with Billy after visiting his cows. 'A bit of fresh air has done us good, *Ma Chiethe.*' He sat down, trying to catch his breath. 'What a lovely day.'

Billy said, 'It's going to be even more lovely when we have lunch.' He watched hungrily, scratching his spots as Mrs. Percheron checked the roast pork, which she'd put in the old bread oven before they'd gone to church. 'Where did you get *that* from, Mrs. P?' He rubbed his stomach. 'It smells lovely, that pork.'

Mrs. Percheron didn't reply for a moment. She put potatoes round the meat. 'We're lucky to live in the country,' she said after a while. 'Friends help each other out, don't they?'

Billy agreed. 'Like you help me,' he said. He looked anxiously at the meat. 'Is there enough for everyone? It's not very big.'

'Mr. Percheron is very good at carving,' said Mrs. Percheron. 'Now, Billy, why don't you go outside again and fetch your cousin?'

Joe was washing his hands under the pump. 'What's up, mate? You're looking a bit glum. And spotty.'

'I want to stay here forever,' said Billy, turning down the corners of his mouth. 'It's much nicer than where I live. There's cows and pigs and roast pork and everything here and a fire sometimes. And visitors dropping in, like that man who sleeps in the barn. I was watching the swallows early and I seen him. Then I went back to bed.'

Joe tried to look puzzled. He waved at Ginger as he came home, holding Rosie's hand, raising his voice. 'I don't know who you mean by a man sleeping in the barn. I expect he was the ghost.'

'Ghost?' Billy's eyes lit up. 'Is there a real ghost here?'

'So, people say,' said Joe mysteriously. 'He always comes back to help when times are bad, so people say.'

Billy drew in his breath. 'And times are bad now, ain't they? With the enemy here and the war and everything. So the ghost has come back. Blimey...'

'It's marvellous how ghosts understand situations,' said Joe. 'Anyhow, never mind about the ghost. Maybe you could stay on at the farm for a bit longer.'

Billy's eyes welled up. 'Dad won't let me stay here forever. He gets extra food from the Germans because of me. He drags me in front of them and says how hungry I am. They give him stuff, then he sells it.'

'He's a beggar your dad, isn't he?' Joe patted Billy's head. 'I dunno. It takes all sorts, doesn't it?'

Billy began to snivel. 'He's got lots of German friends and all.'

'Has he now?' Joe said.

Billy looked back at the farmhouse. 'Do you think lunch is ready? I heard the others coming back.' Then he spotted the soldiers. Running up to them, he said, 'There's a ghost what lives here. He's come back to help us because of the war and you and everything.'

At that moment, Ginger rushed across the farmyard, covered in a white sheet.

'Booo!' he shouted.

Billy shrieked. 'I told you.'

Easter Monday 6th April
6.30 pm

It was still light when Otto and Franz came back from town after an evening with their mates. First they crashed into the granite gatepost that led to the field beside the Brayes' garage, bellowing with laughter. They pulled the bike away, examined a dent and groaned, but in a mocking way, banging their foreheads in pretend grief.

When they parked it, Otto caught his foot on the pedal and fell head first into the full cattle trough. Franz pulled him out of the water and Otto shook himself like a dog. As water drops flew into the air, he said, '*Lass uns gehen und mit den Grossen schwein reden.*'

Franz found this very funny. He said, '*Mit den Grossen Schwein*' over and over again.

Up on the farmhouse landing, Joe, Clem and Ginger watched them through the open window. Joe nudged Ginger. 'He's drunk as my dad on a Saturday night, and its only Monday. What's he on about?'

Ginger snorted with laughter. 'He said, Let's go and talk to the big pig. The *GROSSEN SCHWEIN*. He thinks those words are hilarious.'

'They are, actually,' said Joe.

'Oh dear,' said Clem. 'What a shame. I left Hotspur outside again, after the stranger came on Saturday.' He pointed, 'Look, Hotspur's lurking behind the sty and they haven't noticed him.'

Suddenly, the soldiers started to march, German style, goose stepping across the yard with their arms at a stiff diagonal. Otto shouted, '*Links, Recht*, left, right.' Franz followed him, his goose steps almost up to his shoulder. '*Halte*,' shouted Otto. Franz bumped into him and they both fell to the ground, cackling with laughter. As they picked themselves up, Otto said, '*Grossen schwein*, where are you? *Heil Hitler*.'

Franz bellowed, '*Grossen Schwein. Heil Hitler.*'

At that moment, Hotspur charged out of hiding, roared into the backs of their knees and knocked them flying. '*Gott in Himmel*,' they shouted in unison, staggering to their feet again and holding each other up.

Hotspur had backed away to the wall again. He was trampling his trotters up and down, ready to charge again. 'PAS AUF,' yelled Franz. 'Watch out.' He leapt on to the wall, followed by Otto. Wobbling dangerously, they clung together, giggling like schoolboys. Hotspur charged again.

Up on the landing, the three boys muffled their laughter. Then Ginger hissed, 'Hotspur's trying to get them.' He craned out of the open window. 'And now Peggy's joining in. You must have left her out too,'

Clem looked smug. 'It's an emergency. I thought we needed double protection since Joe's tricksy visitor turned up.'

Joe chuckled. 'Peggy's showing Hotspur her technique. She's got hold of Otto's trousers and Hotspur's got hold of Franz's.'

'Go Hotspur. Go Peggy,' Clem mouthed.

There was a tremendous ripping sound and some more

German yelling. Otto and Franz raced off, jumped over the gate and hurried into their flat. Peggy and Hotspur stood happily in the moonlight chewing large pieces of cloth.

Joe screamed with laughter. 'I can see the Germans' underpants.'

Wednesday 15th April
7.00 pm

Just over a week later, Ginger nipped over to Clem's place after supper, saying he needed to sort out some chemistry revision. In the farmhouse kitchen, Mr. Percheron was helping Billy with a jigsaw. He looked up briefly.

'I need to ask Clem about a homework problem,' said Ginger. 'Sorry to disturb you, sir.'

'I thought *you* were the clever one, not Clem.' Billy scowled. 'Come on, Mr. P. Please stop talking. I want to find all the edges before my dad makes me go home. I've been here a nice long time now, and I like it.

Mr. Percheron smiled. 'Clem's in his room, Ginger.' He handed Billy a couple of pieces as Ginger thanked him and went upstairs. 'Look, Billy, you won't be going home tonight. But your impetigo's better now.'

Upstairs, Clem was sitting at his desk, a pile of books beside him. 'Hello there,' he said. 'I'm meant to be revising, but...' he lowered his voice. 'Sasha's been back twice, getting people used to seeing him. He helped Dad with some scything.'

Ginger whistled. 'Risky. With the enemy at the door.' He thought for a moment. 'Are you sure you can trust him? What with that stranger, who was obviously an informer, coming on Easter Saturday?'

'Of course we can trust him.' Clem gave Ginger a reproachful look. 'I can't believe you said that.'

'Come on, Clem. I'm not backing off. It's just that he's probably being hunted and they might track him down here, and that'll put everyone in danger. So we've got to think everything through very carefully.'

Clem took a deep breath. 'OK, Ginger. I get your point. But after all this time, no one will bother to hunt for him. They probably think he jumped off a cliff or something. People do.'

'Fingers crossed they think that,' said Ginger. He checked that the door was shut and kept his voice low. 'Actually, I think he was in our house the other night.'

Clem stared at him. 'Sasha? In *your* house? That would be madness.'

'I heard Uncle Hedley and a man talking and I just had this strange feeling that it might be Sasha. No one breaks the curfew and your father goes to bed early.'

'Blimey,' said Clem. 'How does Mr. Braye know about him? Has Spinner told him? Or is her father secretly working with him and thinks *we* don't know him? I'm sure Mum and Dad don't talk about him. They hardly mention him at home,'

'Who knows?' Ginger shook his head. 'She swore she didn't say a thing.' He lowered his voice. 'I think Uncle Hedley's up to something. He might not say anything, but he's got eyes. Maybe he's giving him a false identity. He's clever, Uncle Hedley.'

Clem gave a long, low whistle. 'There'll be all hell if the enemy find *that* out. For all of us. A false identity? That means fake documents and everything. Tricky.'

'And now we've got those two in the flat,' said Ginger.

'So it's even more tricky.' He smiled. 'Except they seem quite decent. They aren't very interested in the war and spend a lot of time drinking beer. I wonder where they get it from?'

''Who knows? The soldiers have their own bars in town.' Clem spread his hands, then went on, 'I don't mind for myself, but I'd hate Mum and Dad to go to prison, or Spinner, if they found out what might be going on in both our houses.' Clem's face fell. 'I feel responsible for them. And Dad's still not well. He pretends he is. But he isn't. He's so out of breath.'

Saturday 17th April
10 am

Legs La Motte turned up when everyone except Clem and Mr. Percheron had gone to town. He climbed the locked gates and wandered past Spinner's house into the farmyard, calling, 'Anyone at home?'

Nobody answered, so he called again. 'Clem?'

He tried all the doors, tapping on them and then knocking a bit louder, trying the handles. The only door that was unlocked was the one to the flat so he wandered up the stairs after admiring the swallow painted over the door.

At the top of the stairs, Legs peered around, then gasped at the sight of German coats hanging on pegs on the landing. 'Ruddy hell. I forgot.' He shot down the stairs and into the farmyard.

Hotspur was in his sty, grunting. So Legs leaned over to tickle his back. 'You're a monster, aren't you?' Hotspur stared at him with his mean little eyes, the ring in his nose glinting in the sunlight. He snapped his teeth and a thick thread of dribble ran out of the corner of his mouth. Legs snatched his hand away. 'I reckon you could be a secret weapon, my boy. You're built like a flipping torpedo.'

After this, he wandered into the Percherons garden, peering into the greenhouse and the sheds. But no one was to be seen. He decided to check the orchard. Clem was always outside somewhere whatever the weather, doing something useful on the farm. He could be anywhere.

'Come on, show yourself, Clem,' muttered Legs.

At last he spotted Clem at the bottom of the orchard, stretching a thick rope between trees. Legs called out, 'Clem! I'm back. How are you doing?'

Clem whirled round, his face anxious. He glanced quickly round the orchard. 'Morning, Legs. Back again so soon?'

'Auntie needs help with the new calves,' said Legs, reaching Clem. 'So I'm over here for the day. Her farm worker's off sick.' He looked at the rope. 'What's with the rope?'

Clem explained. 'I'm making a tightrope for the kids. They're getting into trouble with the soldiers. We're trying to think of things for them to do. Diddie's learning to ride as well. Rosie's turning cartwheels.' He handed Legs the end of the rope. 'If I go up the tree, can you pass this to me?'

Legs nodded and as Clem steadied himself into the branches, he said, 'Keeping them busy, then?'

'We have to,' said Clem briefly. 'Otherwise they're into everything, mucking about with the soldiers and...' he grabbed the end, 'all that stuff.'

'Good idea. Some of the kids are too pally with the enemy,' said Legs. Then he turned suddenly. 'What's that?'

Clem listened. 'What? I can't hear anything?' Then his face dropped. He hurled the rope to the ground and jumped out of the tree. 'It's Dad. He's calling for help.' He raced back through the orchard, brushing petals onto his shoulders as he called out, 'Dad, Dad, I'm coming.'

Legs ran after him.

Mr. Percheron was lying in the farmyard, clutching his heart. Blood was seeping from the back of his head where he'd fallen. As Clem dropped to his knees beside him, his father groaned. 'Get the doctor.'

Legs said, 'I'll ring him,' and dashed indoors. A minute later, he came out. 'He's out with a patient. Not far away. I'll get him.'

'Take my bike,' Clem said, cradling his father's head.

Legs hurled himself on to Clem's bike and raced through the open gates, pounding the pedals down the lane. Clem yanked off his jumper, rolled it up and rested his father's head on it, trying to keep calm. 'It's OK, Dad. You'll be all right.' Mr. Percheron's face was ashen and his shirt was soaking with sweat.

He looked up for a moment and muttered, 'My boy.' Then he closed his eyes and for an awful moment, Clem thought he'd died.

Panic welled up inside him. He forced out his words. 'You're going to be fine, Dad. We need you.' His own heart was thumping as he held back his tears. 'If I have to carry you to hospital, I will.'

At that moment, a familiar voice called out softly, 'Let me help.'

Clem whirled round. '*Sasha*,' he whispered. 'Thank God.'

Sasha's shadow fell on them both. He put his finger to his lips as he knelt on the other side of Mr. Percheron, listened to his chest and looked up at Clem. 'It's steady. Fetch blankets and pillows, quickly.' He gave Clem an encouraging smile. 'I know what to do. And your father is a strong man.'

Clem rushed indoors and back in an instant, his arms full. He and Sasha covered Clem's father with blankets and propped him higher on the pillows. Mr. Percheron opened his eyes and looked at Sasha. 'You are a good Samaritan.' Mr. Percheron closed his eyes again. Then he murmured, 'I can hear soldiers in the lane.'

Clem's heart lurched. He whispered to Sasha, 'It's probably the lodgers. They don't notice anything.'

'Even so,' said Sasha. 'I must leave. Your father will be all right. Keep talking to him.' Then he was gone.

Clem said, 'Maybe Helmut is out there. He's around this part a lot. Joe says he's nice enough, as long as you don't tell him anything.'

Mr. Percheron nodded and said, 'Quite right, son. Never give away any secrets.' As he spoke, there was the screech of bike brakes and Dr Harris appeared from round the corner on Clem's bike. He propped it up against the wall and hurried to Mr. Percheron' side. 'Well, old chap. What have you been up to?' As he took out his stethoscope, he added, 'Too many wild parties, eh?'

Mr. Percheron gave a weak smile as the doctor listened to his chest. A little colour was seeping back into his face as he said to the doctor, 'Haven't felt too good for a long time. Tried to get better. Failed.'

'It's just your ticker being a nuisance.' Dr. Harris put his stethoscope away and said, 'We'll get you to hospital, straight away.'

'How?' asked Clem. 'We can't take him on the tractor, or on Ernest.'

Dr. Harris indicated the lane. 'I had a word with the soldiers out there. They offered their truck.' He lowered his voice. 'I think the pneumonia has damaged your father's heart, so you're both going to have to swallow your pride and accept a lift.' He cupped his hands and called out in German.

Two soldiers arrived. Soon they had made a stretcher with the blankets and Mr. Percheron was lifted gently into the truck. Dr. Harris climbed in beside him. 'There's nothing to worry about. I promise you, he'll be all right. Ring the hospital later.'

'I'm grateful, Dr. Harris.' But Clem couldn't bring himself to thank the Germans, so he said, 'Good luck, Dad.' Then he waved them off.

Just as the truck drove out of sight, Legs arrived. 'How are things?'

'It was a heart attack,' Clem said.

Legs didn't know what to say, except, 'Come and cheer yourself up tonight. There's a party…'

But Clem shook his head. 'I couldn't. What if Dad gets worse?' He kept his true thoughts to himself. Legs seemed safe enough. But he might not be. He thought of his father's words. *'Never give away any secrets.'*

Legs hesitated. 'Can't hang around much longer. Got to help Auntie.' He punched Clem's shoulder in a friendly way. 'Good luck to your Dad.' As he set off, he said, 'I saw a man in the orchard when I was there earlier. Meant to tell you. Completely forgot with all the drama. Tall chap.'

'Oh,' lied Clem. 'I've no idea who that was.'

He went indoors with a heavy heart, sick with fear and worry about his father. And there was another thing. He wanted to escape and fight. But he certainly couldn't now. His father would take months to recover.

Monday 19th April
7.30 pm

'Dad's in the old man's ward.' said Clem. He gave a wintry smile. 'He looks much better than they do.'

Spinner was putting her saxophone together. 'He's only a few years older than mine and Joe's fathers.' She frowned. 'I suppose there's not room at the hospital, with the Germans taking over one whole floor.'

'He's going to recover,' said Ginger. 'That's the main thing, isn't it? Who cares where he is, if he's OK?'

Joe said, 'Pneumonia and a heart attack in a few months. Flipping heck, most people would have popped their clogs for just one of them. Your dad's blinking strong, isn't he, Clem?'

Clem agreed. 'He's tough, is Dad. But he's got to rest for months.'

'That'll bore him,' said Spinner. 'And you'll have to work even more.'

'At least you won't have time to do anything stupid,' said Ginger. 'Anything more, that is, than you do all the time.' He grinned and blew into his trumpet.

'Anyhow,' Clem went on, 'he's sitting up properly. They're all chatting in Jersey French telling each other secrets about how they're foxing the enemy.'

Joe set up his drums. 'Sounds a bit risky.'

Mr. Braye came into the room. 'Right everyone. Let's get going.'

Clem looked through the window at the flat. He could see the Germans sitting at the table, playing cards. One of them yawned, as though he was almost ready for bed, even though it wasn't late. So Clem said, 'Let's play as long and as loud as we can so they can't relax.'

'Nice one,' said Joe, glancing at the soldiers as well. 'How about playing all night?'

Later, Joe said casually, 'I've found a boat. Didn't even need to pay for it. Been looking out for one for ages. Want to come and see it Friday? Just in case we need it? What with all this helping the prisoners stuff and you being in a punch up last month? And all that?'

'Right,' said Clem. 'But I'm not giving up on helping the prisoners. Whatever happens.'

Friday 24th April
5 pm

The four of them hurried after Joe through the fields. Behind them, Lizzie's cat pounced through the grass, searching for nests of field mice. Soon they were creeping along a thick hedge, then over a stile and past the bee hives that Mr. Percheron kept near the sea in the shelter of some lime trees.

'I left Beau at the farm because of them,' said Joe. 'He's scared stiff of bees. So he barks. We don't want that, do we?' He beckoned them through a gap in the hedge. 'Keep your heads down, loads of brambles.' '

A small farm building stood in the corner of a field, hidden behind a curtain of ivy. Joe ducked under a fence, then crawled towards it, keeping low. He hissed. 'Quick, before anyone sees us.'

Ginger dropped to his knees, followed by Spinner and Clem until they were all at the door. Joe said, 'I don't have a key, so we'll get in my way.' He fiddled with a piece of wire in the padlock until it came undone. 'It's easy,' he said. 'I've watched Dad do this plenty of times.'

When they were inside, he bolted the door as they adjusted their eyes to the gloom. Spinner sniffed, and said, 'It smells of the sea. Salty.'

Ginger wiped his glasses. 'Crikey, look at all that lot.'

He waved his hands at the row of hooks on his left with coiled ropes hanging from them. Between them stood every size of prawning net, from tiny to enormous. 'Who owns this place?'

'Friend of Dad's. Knows every rock at low tide. Fisherman.' Joe brushed away a spider web, then pulled aside a dusty tarpaulin that was draped over a mysterious shape. He whipped it off like a conjuror and beamed. 'What do you think?'

A solid little dinghy sat on chocks, her wooden sides curved and perfect. She had two seats, or thwarts, one in the stern, and one in the centre. There was something about her that shouted, 'Tough and Strong,' despite her size. 'She was washed up at La Rocque the other day,' said Joe. 'French. Dad found her.'

Clem whistled, his eyes alight. 'What a great little boat. Even I might risk escaping in that.'

'She's called *Alouette*,' said Spinner, peering at the writing on the bow. 'That means *Skylark*, doesn't it?'

Ginger nodded as Joe said, 'We might make a false wall in here, in case anyone looks through the window.'

'Fat chance of doing that,' said Ginger, drawing a pair of eyes in the thick dust on the window. He jumped back as something moved outside. 'What the heck?' Then he laughed and put his hand on his heart like an actor. 'Crikey. The cat's staring in at me. That gave me a shock.'

Spinner said, 'She's probably staring at a spider's web. No one can see through that glass. It's filthy.' She turned to Joe. 'If you had a false wall, how would you break it down in a hurry?'

'Say, if one of us needed to escape, pronto?' Clem's eyes gleamed. 'Got into trouble or wanted to go and fight?'

Joe looked scornful. 'You can't just escape, *pronto*, in a boat. Everything depends on tide. You have to plan, Clem. It's not like jumping on Ernest and whizzing into the sunset.'

'Fair enough,' said Clem, laughing. 'Anyhow, I'd be the last person to cross the Channel. Can't sail, can't row, never used a compass. Deep water gives me the creeps. Give me a field to plough and I'll be fine. Give me a boat and I'd be rubbish.'

'You came out with me and Daddy once,' said Spinner. 'And you were brilliant, took the helm and everything.'

'I enjoyed it,' said Clem. 'But on my own, I couldn't do it.'

Joe stroked the little boat's bows. 'Dad and I have worked on her already. He comes down here a lot. Stops him from going crazy with all his thoughts about the last war.'

Ginger ran his fingers over the name plate. 'Skylark. I love that name. They're such cheerful birds and they lay golden eggs. You could paint a skylark on her bows.'

'I'm planning it,' said Joe. He held up a pair of oars. 'We're working on these, then we'll make a mast. Except for a couple of skylarks. we aren't going to paint her because we want her to look old and unused in case anyone finds her. We'll varnish her instead to keep her watertight.'

'How about sails?' asked Spinner. 'Daddy's got some. When the enemy took his boat, he kept most of them. We might be able to use one, maybe cut it down.' She sat in the stern. 'It's so exciting. I'd love to take her out.'

Ginger had been quiet, but then he said, 'Perhaps we should collect emergency rations and medicine and store them here.' He looked round at the others. 'Just in case we really *do* need to escape. Or one of us.'

'Impossible,' said Clem. 'It's a long way to England, and think of all the submarines and the like. It would be better to hide if we were in trouble.'

'One man did it,' argued Joe. 'He got all the way to England on his own, right through the shipping lanes in the channel.'

'It was a few months after the Germans landed, wasn't it?' said Ginger. 'In a dinghy called Ragamuffin.'

'If he can do it, we can too,' said Joe. 'You know the stars, don't you, Spin? Being a Girl Guide? You could navigate for us. Easy.'

Spinner rolled her eyes. 'Very drole. Anyhow, we couldn't all fit in Skylark together, maybe with Daddy as well. We're growing too tall.'

'We might have to,' said Ginger. 'If anyone finds out about Sasha. Hiding wouldn't be enough. Someone would tell.' His eyes gleamed behind his glasses. 'Or the cat would give us away by staring at us. She's such a weird cat. Always staring.'

Saturday 25th April
10 am

All the adults went to town as usual, taking the younger children. So Clem said, 'Let's go and talk to Ernest. I brought him in last night to groom him. He'd like the company.'

'Can't do it for long,' said Ginger. 'I've got a pile of homework that big.' He showed them by spreading his hands.

Ernest had his back to the door, his tail swishing from side to side. When Clem and the others walked in, he whinnied, turning his head as if he was searching for something. 'Steady, boy,' said Clem. He stroked Ernest's flank and edged round him. Then he caught his breath and motioned the others to stand back, his face suddenly ashen.

'*Sasha,*' he whispered. 'What have they done to you?'

The prisoner had flattened himself against the wall behind the horse. His hair was caked in blood. One side of his face was bruised and swollen. 'They tried to catch me.' He gave a painful smile, then put his hand to his ribs. 'But they failed. I won't be sent to the castle after all. No nasty fairy story for me.'

'Flipping beggars,' said Joe, looking round the horse. He reached out his hand. 'They don't like you, do they?'

Sasha shook his head. 'I think not.' Very slowly, he started to struggle round Ernest towards them, gasping with pain and clutching his chest.

Spinner couldn't speak. She saw that Ginger's glasses had misted up. Clem's hands, she noticed, were bunched into fists. So she moved back to the door, stammering, 'I'll keep watch.'

Joe held out a hand to Sasha. 'Blimey. You're shaking like a leaf.'

Sasha collapsed on a straw bale. 'I didn't want you to see me. I came to ask Ernest for comfort, and I should not have done that. It isn't safe for you.'

'We don't care about safe,' said Clem. His face was red. 'Who did this? *Tell us what happened.*'

Sasha wiped a trickle of blood out of his eyes, then leaned forward to put his hand on Ernest's comforting flank. He glanced at Beaufort, who had crept in and was licking blood off his boots. 'You remember when your dog was hurt one early morning?'

'Too right I remember,' growled Joe.

Sasha sat down, wincing. 'I was trying to find the man who did it. I knew he was once a prisoner, but then I find he is paid by the enemy. He looks for escaped men like me. I had to fight him.'

Spinner gasped, turning round from her station at the door. 'What a horrible man.'

'A turncoat,' said Ginger. 'War time's full of them.'

'I bet that was the one I met checking out the farmyard.' said Joe. 'On Easter Saturday. I should have set Hotspur on him. Medium size, suspiciously clean. Brown hair. Twentyish.'

Sasha nodded. 'That is the one. He would say he was my friend. He has done that everywhere. He puts out his hand for food. But he is not hungry. He is given rewards by the enemy.'

'I *knew* it,' said Joe. 'What a creep.'

Sasha nodded. 'I want you to remember something. *No one* is worth trusting except your very own...what do you call it?' He searched his mind...'your friends and family. And even then, they might betray you, without meaning to. That little boy...'

'Billy,' said Clem. 'He says whatever comes into his head.'

'The little girl,' said Sasha. 'They could question her.'

'Let them try,' said Ginger, suddenly fierce.

'And *your* friend, Clem. The one with long legs.' Sasha spread his hands. 'He might make conversation with his family, and *Boof!* He gives something away without meaning to. Or your dog, or even the cat, following you.'

'*I told you,*' Ginger mouthed at the others.

After this, they were very quiet. Sasha said, 'I am sorry to say all this. But I must protect you. Please, I beg you, *stop* trying to help us. It is very kind of you. But now it is summer. We can sleep in the fields. There is food to dig up.' Then he put his head in his hands and for a horrible moment they wondered if he was crying.

But then he looked up. 'I am so tired. For your last help, you could watch for me and I will sleep. Then I will leave until this ...this chase...is over.'

Joe fished in his pocket and handed Sasha the gold coin. 'We found this. It's a lucky charm, mate.'

Sasha gasped. He held out his bloodied hand and took it as though it was everything he had loved and lost. 'It is mine, and I lost it. My mother gave it to me when I left home to fight.' Then he crossed himself the Russian way. 'Joe. Keep it. Give it me when the war is over. Come to see me in my motherland. It will bring you luck too. If I keep it, someone might kill me for it.'

'Flipping heck,' said Joe. 'I hope they don't do that to me.' He put the coin into the depths of his pocket with a smile of thanks, then went to keep guard in the lane with Beau. Ginger hurried to the orchard while Spinner stationed herself on the steep path to the potato store. When everyone was sure that the coast was clear, Clem helped Sasha into the barn and waited at the door as he climbed painfully up and over the straw bales.

They took it in turn all day to be sentries until the soldiers arrived home and went into their flat. Then Spinner and Ginger knocked on their door and kept them talking. The yard rang with the music of Wagner as Ginger asked for more and more records to be played so that Sasha could sleep on, safe from German eyes.

Later, as Clem helped his mother to tidy up after supper, he murmured to her in Jersey French. She filled a can with soup like she had done weeks before and gave it to Clem, who tucked it under his jacket. His mother caught his eye, then quickly busied herself looking after Mr. Percheron.

In the barn, Clem called out softly, 'Sasha. I have food for you.'

There was no reply, so he climbed gingerly up the bales and peered over, balancing the bowl in one hand. Sasha was nowhere to be seen. The spare shirt and shoes had disappeared, the mattress had been covered with straw and every scrap of evidence removed.

7.30 pm

When Clem met Ginger for band practice, Rosie was

wandering about in her nightie and Aunt Edie was trying to persuade her into bed. 'Who is Sasha?' Rosie asked.

'Not a person,' Clem said quickly. 'It's something we learn about at school in mathematics. A Sasha equation. It's very difficult. Ginger understands it but I don't.

Rosie looked dubious, then she asked if she could listen to band practice.

Ginger took his little sister's hand. 'You can listen from bed. I'll play you a special tune.'

When she'd left the room, Ginger played the trumpet softly with the lullaby called Golden Slumbers, which Rosie liked very much, and which their father had often sung to her.

Mr. Braye arrived. He leaned against the door and listened. 'That was very lovely,' he said to Ginger. 'It's not easy to play a lullaby on a trumpet.' Joe and Spinner turned up, so Mr. Braye went on, 'Don't forget, we're playing in the park next week. Special appearance by the Hot Trotters.'

'It's the beginning of the summer season,' said Ginger, happily. 'We could play on the beach sometimes, like we did last year.'

'No chance, pea brain,' said Joe. 'They're mined. Even playing the drums might set them off. Think of the lobsters.'

Spinner had been quiet. Then she said, 'How about we do a Battle of Flowers, like we always did before the war? A parade? We could make a float out of flowers, and everyone can dress up and the band can lead and Ernest could wear rosettes and...'

'And afterwards, we'll throw flowers about,' said Clem. 'Like the good old days when everything was fun. A bit tricky, when people are almost eating flowers though. It would be hard work, and who's got time for that?'

Spinner persisted. 'Even a tiny parade would cheer people up. The float could be a swallow or a skylark. We could have a bird theme. And we don't have to have it on the anniversary. We'll do it in August, like we used to, to show them we can.'

Joe had been thinking. 'I could wear my old lobster costume I wore two years ago. Auntie Vi would let it out. We could sing the Lobster Blues. Actually, I might wear it for the concert. It would be a laugh.'

Everyone laughed, and Clem said. 'It'll be tricky to play the drums with lobster claws.'

'We could parade down the lane and along the inner road, then back again. Hotspur at the front, clearing away any random soldiers. Hotspur's dead keen on doing that.' Ginger took off his glasses and wiped them. 'The thought's misting up my specs.'

Joe grinned. 'It'll annoy the heck out of the enemy, seeing us having a good time.' He picked up his drumsticks. 'Brilliant idea, Spin.'

Spinner's father lifted his baton and they raced through their repertoire. When they'd finished, Mr. Braye said, 'Well played everyone. We're ready for the concert.' He moved his music stand to the corner and laid his baton on it. Then he pulled down the blackouts. As they packed away their instruments, he wove his way between them to the door. 'Goodnight all,' he said cheerfully. 'I'm off to listen to The News.'

Clem noticed a piece of card lying on the floor. He called out to Mr. Braye. 'You dropped something.' But Mr. Braye was gone, in his hurry to catch up on the progress of the war. So he picked it up, glanced at it briefly and then gazed at it more carefully, turning it over and examining the photograph. Then he gave a long, low whistle. The others stopped what they were doing and stared at him. Clem put his finger to his lips, after whispering, 'It's an identity card. And it's not one of ours.' He held it up.

Spinner gasped. 'That's a photo of Sasha. With his new short haircut.' She spread out her hands and frowned. 'But prisoners don't have identity cards. They have numbers. So why does he have one of these?'

Clem read out the details. 'It says he's a farm labourer and lives at St. John. Blue eyes, six foot three inches.'

'Blimey,' said Joe. 'That's tall for a Jersey man.'

Ginger had been thinking. 'More importantly,' he murmured. 'Who dropped it in this music room?'

Joe winked at Spinner. 'Your dad's a dark horse. He's up to all sorts of things. Maybe he's forging identity cards.'

Clem and Ginger caught each other's eyes.

Spinner thought of her father's bruises and swallowed. She dropped the card to the floor as though it was burning. 'If we leave it here, he'll think we didn't see it.' Then she said quietly. 'It's best we don't know anything about it.'

Clem agreed. 'What we don't know, we can't tell.' As he put away his sousa, he said, 'Anyhow, Sasha's gone.'

'Gone?' Spinner stared at him. 'For good?'

Clem spread his hands. 'Who knows?' Then he shrugged, but his eyes were sad. 'Perhaps it's for the best. He told us not to help, didn't he?'

Joe rolled his eyes. ' D'you think we're going to take any notice of that?'

Monday 4th May
9 pm

Spinner sat at the kitchen table making a pirate ship for the children out of cardboard. Billy had cut out a set of miniature cutlasses from silver toffee paper, Joe had cobbled together a few pairs of tiny pirate boots and Diddie had knitted pirate coats. As she worked, she wondered where Sasha was, imagining him hiding in a ditch, or up on the north coast in one of the deep caves below the cliffs.

She thought of the little boat, *Alouette*, snug in its shed. One day her mother would be back and they'd sail round the bay once more.

Upstairs, she could hear her father's wireless in his study. *The News*, she thought, glancing at the clock. She cut out a couple of small sails for the pirate boat, concentrating on her work. Sometimes, it was a better not to listen to the wireless too much. There was nothing they could do, stuck on the island and anyhow, it was upsetting. So much of the news was bad. She imagined her mother, coping with bombs, hiding in cellars for shelter, and said a little prayer for her.

At that moment, she heard her father groan loudly, muffling the newsreader's voice. Mr. Braye thundered downstairs to the sitting room, where Aunt Edie was quietly knitting.

Pushing back her chair, Spinner stood up, her heart hammering. *Mummy*, she thought. *Something's happened to mummy and it's on The News.'* The little sails dropped to floor as she crept towards the door. Even though she knew she shouldn't eavesdrop, she strained her ears as her father said, 'Oh, Edie. Such a sad thing has happened. Three boys tried to escape in canoes last night. One's drowned, and two have been captured. I've just heard it on the local news.'

'*My dear,*' said Aunt Edie. 'How dreadful.'

'They'll be interrogated, I tell you. It's going to be very bad for them.'

'*Prison?*' murmured Aunt Edie, her voice anxious.

'Much worse,' replied her father. 'I knew about their plan and I am absolutely certain that they had maps and photographs. They'll be sent to the camps.' Then he groaned again. 'This war is *terrible*, Edie. It's doing such dreadful things to our young people.'

Aunt Edie agreed. 'But people will cover for them, won't they?'

Mr. Braye's voice was anxious. 'It'll make the enemy mad with rage. They'll follow up every lead, checking for cameras and hidden boats.'

'What about *your* camera? Is it well hidden?' Aunt Edie whispered, but Spinner could still hear her, and her heart thumped. They'd been searched the year before and the house had been turned upside down.

Then the door squeaked and she tiptoed back to her chair. When Mr. Braye came in, she was working away on her project as though she hadn't heard a thing. Without even asking her, he made then both a cup of real tea, a sign that something was very wrong.

'Thanks, Daddy,' said Spinner, sipping. 'This is a treat.'

Her father sat opposite her. His face was white and tired. 'My darling, some boys are in trouble. They've been very brave, trying to take information to England, but their plan has gone horribly wrong.' He patted her hand, and went on, 'It's going to be terrible for their parents.'

'What's happened?' Spinner bit her lip.

Mr. Braye told her what he knew and suddenly reached for her hand. 'Being brave is important but remember this. You are so precious to me and to mummy. Now this has happened. Please, don't do anything silly. No escaping plans...'

'We don't have a boat, so we can't,' Spinner lied, keeping her voice light. Then she saw his expression. 'I promise.' Her father's face was so kind, but he was trembling. 'Please, don't do anything silly yourself, Daddy. I know about the...' she was about to mention the identity cards, then she checked herself. *If he was up to no good, he'd want to keep it to himself. Just like she and the others did.*

Saturday 9th May
10 am

Clem and Ginger cleared out the hiding place. 'It's for the best,' Ginger said, heaving straw with a fork. 'We can still help if he needs us. Two of the boys have been sent to prison camps. They're ruddy awful places. I can't do that to Mother and Rosie.'

'I don't care if I end up there,' said Clem. 'I'm not a ruddy turncoat and I don't like to think of him out there.' He waved outside.

'At least it's not winter, like he said.' Ginger stacked up the wooden pegs Clem had used to build the straw wall. 'And there's food growing everywhere. Spinner's radishes for a start.'

Clem glowered. 'I'll still put food in the shed. So I suppose we can still call ourselves a safe house. In a way.' He stopped for a moment. 'I hate all this. Auntie Vi's right. We're being reduced.'

'Perhaps we can go back to trickery and manipulation,' offered Ginger. 'Like we did last year. Anyhow, we'd better focus on our blinking exams. So much revision and so much depending on the results.'

Clem was still angry. 'They can't be marked by the English examiners. So what's the point?'

'*Keeping on* is the point. Not giving up.' Ginger's voice

was suddenly fierce. 'Don't you think?'

Clem was about to reply, when there was a sudden shout from the farmyard. Spinner appeared, waving a Red Cross message. She said, 'Something amazing has happened. Mummy has actually received one of my letters. I now have proof.'

'Let's have it then,' said Clem. 'Loud and clear so the lodgers will hear that we aren't downhearted.'

Spinner beamed and read out, *'ALL WELL HERE. GLAD ABOUT PIGLETS PINEAPPLES LOBSTER CONGER NICE YOU'RE BUSY. HOPE YOU AND JOE KEEP FISHING. LOVE TO YOU AND EVERYONE. MUMMY.*

Ginger scratched his head. 'That's pretty amazing. Imagine it, a bottle finding its way across the Channel without sinking or being blown up in crossfire. The odds are incredible. Mathematically, I'd say, about...'

Spinner interrupted. 'I'm off to tell Joe. He never believed she'd get them, but I *knew* she would. I checked the tide and everything.'

'He's in the orchard with Peggy,' said Clem.

Spinner charged out of the barn. A second later, there was a bump and Spinner shouted again. 'Ow.' This was followed by 'You blinking idiot, standing there where I didn't see you.'

Clem shot after her, but Spinner was rubbing a bruise on her head. She had her back to him and was glaring at Otto. 'What are you *doing*, hovering about listening, so that people bump into you? There's nothing to see in the barn, but if you must, go and look.'

'I am sorry, Miss Braye.' Otto bit his lip as he saw her bruise. 'I didn't mean to hurt you.' He indicated Franz. 'I am waiting for my friend to start our motor bike. It is very smelly when it starts. And I have what you might call a hungover, so I am getting fresh air.'

'Hangover,' said Spinner. 'It's when you drink too much beer and have a headache.'

Franz was astride the bike, revving the engine. Otto squeezed into the side car and shouted over the noise. 'No more beer for us,' he said. 'We should have learned when we had that problem with the pigs. We had a bad time mending our trousers.' Franz revved again.

'I'm sorry about your trousers,' shouted Spinner, grinning.

Otto gave her a thumbs up and they set off, roaring through the gate into the lane. Clouds of smoke poured out of the exhaust. Spinner watched them, giggling. Someone had wedged half a potato into the pipe. She said to herself, 'I bet Joe did that.' Then she raced on to the orchard.

Joe was leaning over Peggy, who was in a pen under the tree. 'Wotcha Spin. What have you done to your head?'

'Never mind about that,' cried Spinner. *'Mummy's getting my letters.'* She took a deep breath and her words tumbled out in a rush. 'Miracles really do happen.' She thrust the Red Cross message at them, smoothing it so that they could read it. 'I *told* you, Joe. I knew they'd get there in the end.'

'Goodness gracious me,' said Joe. 'Good old King Neptune.'

But at that moment, Peggy lunged forward, baring her teeth. Even though the fence was between them, Spinner leapt back, dropping the message. It fluttered through the wire and the pig looked up with her mean little eyes. Then, with one easy gulp, she grabbed the message and gobbled it up.

'OOOOOH, NO.' Spinner put her hands over her face.

'Spit it out mate,' urged Joe, leaping over. He stroked the pig's hairy chin and yanked at her mouth. But the message had gone. Peggy licked her lips, swallowed and licked her lips again.

Spinner welled up. 'That's the first real message from mummy for two years and she wrote it herself in her own handwriting. *I hate* pigs,' she gulped. Then she stomped off home.

As she passed the farmhouse, she heard Auntie Vi shouting. Her voice was like a trumpet. Spinner peered round the kitchen door. Auntie Vi was in the hall on the phone. She always shouted into the receiver.

'*No*,' yelled Auntie Vi. 'You're his father, Philo Cliquot. Look after Billy *properly* or I'll call the police. He's got rid of his impetigo, he's been properly fed and he's cheered up. Don't you *dare* ruin it.'

Someone spoke at the other end of the line. Auntie Vi raised her voice even louder. 'I'll let you keep him if you *promise* me you'll *take* your wife out of that blooming nursing home. I've been to see her and there's nothing wrong with her that a bit of kindness can't cure.'

The other voice answered, then Auntie Vi shouted again. 'You're a disgrace, Philo Cliquot. *Pah.*' The other end rattled on and Auntie Vi gasped. 'WHAT DID YOU SAY?' She glared at the phone and boomed into it, 'So you think we're hiding a *prisoner*? Are you off your head? We aren't that stupid. Who on earth told you such rubbish?'

The phone was slammed into its bracket and Spinner hurried away. Some of her wanted to laugh, and the rest of her felt sad. She remembered Billy at their kitchen table, struggling with his Sunday letter to his mother. He always said, when he finished it, *'She never answers my letters, and she can write much better than me.'*

In their house, her father was putting on records. 'This is about a Spanish man, Don Quixote. He tries to fight evil by being a perfect knight.'

'Like us,' said Spinner. 'Sort of.'

Saturday 16th May
5.30 pm

On the day of the concert in the park, Mr. Jument's truck rattled into the yard on the dot. 'I've scrubbed it,' he announced, smiling broadly. He held out his hand for the instruments, loaded them carefully into the back and covered them with a dust sheet. 'Crumbs,' he said, 'You lot are looking tidy.'

Clem straightened his tie as Mr. Jument said, 'You're a giant, young man.' Then he looked beyond Clem. 'What on earth is that?'

Joe was hopping out of the farmhouse, dressed in a long blue tube. He was carrying a big head dress with long feelers waving about in the air. As he hopped, he flicked a blue cardboard tail from side to side. 'Wotcha, Mr. Jument. Like my lobster costume?' He did a curtsey, then a bow. 'Bit difficult to walk in though.'

Ginger helped Joe into the truck. 'Did Auntie Vi really make that? She's a wizard.'

'She had to let it out, but it's still too tight. I can't really breathe.' Joe spat on his hands, smoothed down his hair and said, 'The lobster head really messes with my good looks. It's blooming hot, too. At least I left the claws behind.' He showed them a bag of sweets. 'Nicked these from Helmut for the kids.'

'Nice one,' said Clem, straightening his tie. Spinner checked her pigtails. Ginger felt in his pocket for a spare pair of glasses, then everyone else crammed into the truck with Mr. Braye and the Percherons squeezed into the front with Mr. Jument.

'We're off,' said Mr. Braye out of the window. The engine spluttered into life. Mr. Jument pressed his foot on the ancient accelerator, and they bounced out of the yard.

Soon they were in town, setting up on the bandstand. Joe hopped about, putting the board out with the band's name, which his father had repainted. *The Hot Trotters*. The crowd was gathering, so he hopped among them with the head dress on, lobster feelers waving. 'Give me a wish and I'll make it come true, and if I can't do it, I'll give a sweetie to you,' he said in a muffled voice.

'A fish?' said Auntie Albie, as she settled into the front row. She turned to her friend. 'I think the sun has gone to the boy's head. He was always a funny one.'

When Joe had finished handing out Helmut's sweets, he struggled back to the bandstand. Mr. Braye picked up his baton. 'Time to start,' he said. 'Let's here it for the blue lobster.' Joe bowed, then took off his head dress, saying it was blooming hot inside a lobster's head. Then Mr. Braye winked at the crowd. 'We'll start with *Ain't Misbehavin.*'

The band struck up and the audience cheered as Spinner sang. At the end, they shouted, '*AGAIN.*' Mr. Braye waved his baton again and the Hot Trotters repeated the song. Everyone roared, '*AIN'T MISBEHAVIN.*'

After this there was Ginger's solo. Mr. Braye introduced it, saying that this was the music for a dance about a Spanish noble. '*DON QUIXOTE*' he announced, telling them that it was about a man who tried to fight evil. 'Something we are all trying to do in this island,' he added, staring at the soldiers.

As Ginger played the short piece, Spinner watched the audience's faces light up. A little boy at the back began to leap about on the grass, and so did Otto and Franz, at the back of the crowd.

At last Ginger put down his trumpet and Joe stood up. 'I am the magical blue lobster, to appear at our very own Battle of Flower parade, date and place to be announced. You will be able to tell me your wish and I will try to make it come true. Plan your wishes, Ladies and Gentlemen. But for now, we'll play our very own new tune, The Lobster Blues.'

Then they were off, giving it all they could as the sun began to set. Afterwards. Mr. Braye said he was sorry they couldn't finish with the national anthem, as of course it was banned. 'Instead, we'll play *Beautiful Jersey*. Please join in.'

As the lovely tune filled the air, Spinner felt tears welling up inside her, and she could see that everyone else felt the same. Even Joe was biting his lip at the island song and Clem was glaring to keep himself under control.

Afterwards, Joe passed round his school cap. 'Our friend Percy Du Brin is running a soup kitchen. I haven't any money, but if you have, please could you give some. Percy's a brilliant cook and so many kids are hungry.'

As he returned to the bandstand, three soldiers drew close. Joe scowled, covering the money, but they walked straight past him to the truck, where Clem was sitting with Spinner and Ginger. There was one with high cheek bones and grey eyes. He pulled Clem's sleeve and said,

'You attacked one of our men. And there are other things that we hear about.'

Clem looked at him scornfully. 'Says who?'

The man sneered at him. 'It'd be a shame if you couldn't play in the band any more. We watch you.'

'Good gracious, are we that important?' Joe gave the heavy cap to Mr. Braye then climbed in next to Clem. He leaned out of the truck and said, 'You lot really know how to spoil a nice evening, don't you?'

Saturday 23rd May
2 pm

Mr. Cliquot turned up with Billy in the afternoon. He was carrying a big basket and Billy had hold of a bag. Spinner was in her garden, weeding round her carrots. Everyone else had gone for a walk with Mr. Percheron, except for Joe, who was helping his father with their fishing boat.

Spinner looked up. Billy was wearing a grubby shirt and his knees were scabby again. 'How are you doing, Billy?'

Billy scowled. 'All right.' He glanced at the farmhouse. 'I liked being there.'

Mr. Cliquot lit a cigarette. Spinner noticed that it was German, as he waved it about. He said, 'I got some nice stuff for you all. Bit of chocolate. Lav paper. Soap. You name it.'

Spinner kept her voice neutral. 'That's very kind of you, Mr. Cliquot. Shall I make you a drink while you wait for the others to come back? Glass of water? Parsnip coffee?'

'Parsnip coffee?' Mr. Cliquot snorted with disgust. 'I got some proper coffee in this basket. Your dad will like that.' He pulled out an oblong packet and sniffed it ostentatiously. 'Mmm, wonderful. All the way from Brazil.'

Billy kicked the gravel beside Spinner's vegetable patch. He muttered, 'Yeah. I know where you found that coffee' His father gave him a swipe and he ducked. His eyes pleaded with Spinner.

She put down her trowel and took hold of Billy's hand. 'Let's go inside and see what we can find.' She smiled politely at Mr. Cliquot. 'It's hot out here. You can cool down in the kitchen.'

When they were indoors, Mr. Cliquot gazed around. 'I hear your dad's busy translating for the Germans. I guess he's friendly with your new lodgers. Has them round in the evening, that sort of thing?'

Spinner froze. She said casually, 'He lived in Germany once and he liked it very much. That's where he met Mummy. But we don't let the *enemy* into our house.'

Mr. Cliquot took a long drag on his cigarette. Billy drank water noisily. 'And your Mummy's in England, isn't she?

'What's it to you?' Spinner stared at him.

Mr. Cliquot smirked. 'I bet your dad's passing information to your mother. She could be doing all sorts with it in England.'

Spinner glared. 'Are you saying my parents are *collaborators?*'

'Only joking,' said Mr. Cliquot. 'I just thought, seeing as how you have visitors to your house a lot, you could have secrets. That tall young man, for instance…'

Spinner's hand shook as she poured tea for Mr. Cliquot. 'So what? Everyone has visitors.'

Mr. Cliquot raised an eyebrow 'I've heard there's a chap that helps on the farm now and then. I need a hand myself.'

'Legs lives miles away,' Spinner said. 'He's a friend of Clem's. He wouldn't help *you*.'

Mr. Cliquot stirred his tea. 'No, not him. I mean the other tall chap. Very good with animals, Billy said.'

Billy looked from one to the other. 'He's probably the ghost, Dad.'

Spinner shrugged. '*I* don't know who helps on the farm. Sometimes we all do. Sometimes other people come in for the day. Mr. Percheron's been *ill*, you know.'

'Keep your hair on, girl,' said Mr. Cliquot. He stubbed out his cigarette on the saucer and picked up the basket. 'I'm getting a lot of work from the Germans and I need a big strong man to help.'

'I'll ask them,' said Spinner, firmly. 'But they won't take stuff from your basket. The Percherons are very religious. They won't take black market food. They didn't touch that hamper, remember?'

Mr. Cliquot looked injured. 'Come on Billy. We know when we aren't wanted.'

As soon as they'd gone, Spinner stormed over to the farmhouse. Mrs. Percheron was in the kitchen, mixing lard into potato flour, adding water to make pastry.

Spinner's voice was furious. 'Mr. Cliquot's implying that we're collaborators.' She took the pastry from Mrs. Percheron and whacked it down on the table. As she shaped she went on. 'He was disgusting.'

Mrs. Percheron said, 'Well, my love, I've known Philo Cliquot all my life and I've never trusted him. He was as bad in the playground, and I've never believed a word from his mouth ever since.'

'He's an instrument of the devil,' muttered Mr. Percheron from behind his copy of the Jersey Evening Post.

'Who is?' Clem came into the room with Ginger. Mr. Percheron muttered and went back to his newspaper, so he asked again.

Spinner told them what had happened. 'Just wait till I tell Daddy,' she said. 'He'll hit the roof.'

'He won't.' Ginger laughed. 'Uncle Hedley's never angry.'

Spinner disagreed. 'If he sees injustice, he *BLAZES*.' She took a bowl of mashed swede and spread it on one side of the pastry. Then she folded the other side over. Dabbing her fingers into a little bowl of milk, she wet the edges and crimped them together. 'Done,' she said, giving it to Clem's mother to put in the oven.

'You boys can take it with you on your bike ride,' said Mrs. Percheron. She looked at the clock. 'It'll take half an hour, then you'd better be off and make the most of the day.'

When they were alone, Clem said to his mother, 'We'll be looking out for Sasha. He's probably up north. You never know.'

Noon

Clem and Ginger reached St. John's church earlier than they planned. Clem said, 'Let's see if the puffins are back. We could visit Legs on the way home.'

Ginger agreed, so they cycled on until they reached the north west, the highest part of the island, its steep cliffs crammed with birds' nests. They turned right along a narrow track. Above them, the sky blazed with blue, and they could see the houses on the French coast.

'We'd better hide the bikes,' Ginger said. 'This'll do.' He jumped off and shoved the bike under a prickly gorse bush covered in yellow flowers. Clem padlocked his bike to Ginger's, then they headed off to find the puffins.

Clem wind-milled his arms to stretch them. 'Isn't it brilliant to have a day off from exams?'

'Only Greek translation to go, 'said Ginger. 'Then we're finished. Let's have our lunch when we get to the best spot. The puffins are usually around here. If we're quiet, they'll get used to us and...' Then he stopped, grabbing Clem's arm. He pointed over the cliff. 'Listen. There's a lot of shouting down there.'

Clem stopped whirling his arms about in the sun and paid attention. 'Maybe someone's fallen over the cliff.' He listened and peered into the sea. 'Can't see anything.' He glanced into the distance, to their right, then frowned. 'Hey, look at all those trucks. Where did *they* come from?'

'They're carrying railway sleepers,' said Ginger, after a while. 'Legs told me that they're laying railways everywhere this side of the island. I reckon that's where the shouting came from. Look at all those workers,' Ginger said, passing Clem his pocket telescope. 'They're shifting concrete, hundreds of workers and guards.'

'Poor men.' Clem watched, biting his lip. 'They're so thin. I wonder how they find the strength.'

Ginger took back the telescope. 'Let's keep away from there. I'd rather watch puffins on our day off.'

Soon they found a sheltered dip among the ferns, with the sun pouring into it. To their left, they could see where the puffins usually nested and settled down to eat their lunch. Clem took out his diary, ready to make notes. But as Ginger unwrapped the pastry, there was another shout, much closer.

Ginger frowned, the pastry halfway to his mouth. 'That sounds pretty angry.' He listened again, then suddenly grabbed Clem's arm and dragged Clem to the ground. He made a shushing wave with his hand and peered through the gorse. Then he gasped. 'Oh, my God in Heaven. *That poor man.*'

He pointed through a gap in the gorse bush, whispering, 'There's a prisoner on the path down there.' He pointed to the bottom of the cliff, far below them. 'He's being chased by a guard and the poor man's tumbling over and trying to escape, and the soldier's laughing at him.' Ginger stopped for breath, then he covered his face. '*He's laughing at a terrified human being.* I can't be seeing this. It isn't true.'

Clem peered round the gorse bush. 'Ruddy hell, Ginger.'

Ginger looked again. 'He's out of sight.'

But suddenly, quite close there was the sound of frantic scrabbling and ragged panting as though the hunted man had been cornered. Ginger said, 'He's got him.'

Clem shot out of their hiding place and yelled, waving his clenched fists. Then he slumped down again, pulling bracken over both their heads.

Ginger stared at him. 'You're flipping crazy. Don't you know *anything?*'

Below them, the soldier had stopped in his tracks. His pale blue eyes raked the gorse bushes. He called up, 'Wherever you are, you will be next if you help these Russians. They are *untermensch*. Understood?'

'Sub-humans,' explained Ginger, gathering up the picnic. 'Let's get out of here.'

'That's outrageous,' Clem began.

'Don't react. It won't help anyone. We know that.' Ginger peered through the gorse bushes again. Then he gasped and put his head in his hands again.

'He's jumped off the cliff.'

2.30 pm

Soon they were far from the scene, pedalling as though their lives depended on it, taking the back routes away from marching soldiers and avoiding Legs's house in case they were being watched. On the way, they tried to keep their heads down, but over and over again they saw terrible things, a prison camp, men behind barbed wire, and something much worse.

'Don't interfere,' said Ginger, as they cycled along a secret lane after seeing yet another miserable group of prisoners. 'It won't help anyone.'

'How can they treat people like that?' Clem pedalled on, his face dark with rage. 'We'll have to tell Uncle Hedley. I bet he doesn't know the half of it.'

Ginger glanced at him. 'You think?' He stopped for a moment to wipe his glasses. When they were on again, he said, 'I think he knows everything and he's finding ways to report it to England. And that's why he keeps warning us. He knows what the enemy is capable of.'

Clem kept quiet, then he said, 'So why don't our boys come to the rescue? Why are they leaving us here to rot? A handful of islands, left alone by their great protectors? So much for the Royal Air Force!'

'Big questions, Clem,' said Ginger. 'But if they tried, the whole island, and all the others...' he waved at the other Channel Islands in the distance...'would be bombed into nothing. Smithereens, as Diddie would say.'

'I suppose so,' said Clem. 'I see your logic.' They turned into St Peter's Valley, dark and mysterious, now that the trees were in full leaf. 'I used to love this valley. It's good grazing, too.' He pointed at the cows in a meadow full of buttercups. 'At least there are a few cows left, but the rest of it's ruined.'

'Keep your head down and don't look,' said Ginger. 'There as many soldiers here as there are buttercups in that field.'

An hour later, they cycled up the lane and into the Brayes' yard, dusty from their long ride. Rosie and Arthur raced up to them, but Diddie hung back as she always did, twiddling her plaits. 'When are you going to let me ride Ernest?' she asked Clem.

'Later,' said Clem.

Ginger did his best to smile. 'We're a bit tired.'

'Boring,' said Rosie. She skipped off to play with Diddie and Arthur.

As they put their bikes away, Ginger said, 'I'll tell Uncle Hedley what we saw.'

'All of it?' Clem padlocked his bike.

'Perhaps.' Ginger took his bag out of the basket. He looked at Clem. 'It was bad, wasn't it?'

Clem nodded. 'I'm not saying a thing to Mum or Dad. They'd be so upset.' Then he added, 'Do you think I made things worse for the prisoner? Was it *my fault* that he jumped off the cliff?'

'Of course not.' Ginger wiped his glasses and put them back on again. 'I bet you he was going to do it anyway. Finish his own life.'

'I couldn't forgive myself if it happened because I was an idiot.' Clem stared at the ground. 'So stupid of me to shout.'

Ginger said, 'The prisoner's last thought would be that someone cared about him. That someone stood up for him and risked his own safety. You.' As Clem looked at him, with the beginning of hope in his eyes, Ginger went on, 'Let's not mention anything to Spinner. She's brave, but she has nightmares. And she's worried stiff about Sasha.'

5 pm

Clem's chest hurt. He felt that he'd been hit, but it was only because he had to keep everything that he and Ginger had seen to himself. Diddie was longing for a ride on Ernest and Clem never broke his promises.

So he led Ernest round and round the farmyard with Diddie standing on his broad back, wobbling now and then, but keeping her balance with her arms outstretched.

Franz and Otto were sitting on their doorstep, smoking and watching. *'Zehr Gut,'* they called out, puffing smoke.

'What's it to you?' Clem muttered under his breath.

'What are they saying?' Diddie asked, trying to stand on one leg then the other.

'They say you're very good,' said Clem, speeding up. He kept his back turned to the soldiers as best he could. Even looking at them reminded him of the incident on the cliff.

Diddie plonked herself down and held on to Ernest's mane. 'I don't think I can stand up if we go faster.'

'I certainly couldn't,' said Clem. 'But you might. You're very good at balancing. Let's get away from this cigarette smoke and try cantering in the field.'

'I'd like to canter,' said Diddie, holding on tightly. As they reached the field, she said, 'I want to ride Ernest at a circus wearing a tutu.'

'A tutu?' Clem laughed. 'Fat chance. Jersey's right out of tutus these days.'

Diddie said, 'What's wrong, Clem? You look as if you want to punch someone. You do that a lot, don't you?'

Sunday 24th May
11 am

The rain dashed against the windows, so Ginger stayed indoors, trying to revise for his Greek translation. Normally, he found it easy. But on this day, he kept thinking about what they'd witnessed. Clem had gone to church as usual to lead the choir, almost an impossible task when his mind was filled with dark pictures.

The more Ginger pictured yesterday's scenes, the less he could concentrate. He gazed at his father's photo in its silver frame and wished he could talk to him.

At last, it was lunchtime. His mother served vegetable pie with a flourish, but Ginger wasn't hungry. 'I caught the sun yesterday,' he explained. 'I feel a bit sick.'

'My chickens are in a bad state too,' said Spinner. 'They were boiling yesterday and today they're dripping about in the rain, pecking each other.'

'The chickens are horrible.' Rosie made a face. 'I saw them fighting over a frog. One had the legs and the other had the front legs and they were pulling and the frog bounced up and down.'

'Stop it,' snapped Ginger. 'Stop talking about such things. Poor frog. I hope you rescued it.'

Everyone was silent. Ginger never talked like that.

Rosie's mouth went square, and she muttered, 'FOX, RABBIT, OX, GOAT

Ginger swallowed and said, 'I'm *really sorry*, Rosie. I didn't mean it. '

Rosie blinked away her tears, then she edged on to his lap until she was a huge, warm weight on his knees. Ginger put his arms round her and she snuggled into him until it was pudding time, the only day they had it, their Sunday treat. 'Jam sponge,' announced Aunt Edie. So, Rosie scrabbled back to her place and held up her plate.

As she ate her second helping, Ginger blinked. *This time yesterday*, he thought.

4 pm

Clem managed to get through the day, helping on the farm as usual and leading the choir, then trying to eat the lunch his mother had put together as she always did on Sundays, trying to make a special day of eating, even though there was so little to share.

In the afternoon, he kept away from the others, spending time with the animals. They were all inside because of the drenching rain, so he cleaned and filled the mangers, talked to Peggy and her growing daughter, Betty, and groomed Ernest. There was a new calf, too, born in the night when no one had expected her so soon.

The swallows swooped in and out of the milking parlour, making their usual burbling sounds. Their chicks peered over the edges of the nests, yellow throats opened wide. Clem sat on a straw bale watching them. 'Joe's swallow pictures worked,' he said. 'You found your way home.'

'Yes. They worked,' said a quiet voice.

Sasha had crept in, neat in Sunday clothes, looking more like a Jersey man than ever. He sat on one of the bales. 'I came to see you. I am sorry for what you saw yesterday. I heard that you were near the cliffs.'

'How did you hear? Clem stared at him. 'Who told you?'

'News travels fast among escaped ones,' Sasha said. 'It's passed from man to man like a bucket of water being sent to put out a fire.'

Clem bit his lip. 'We saw worse, later. I knew everything was bad for you, but not that bad.' He stood up. 'I love this island. It's horrible seeing what's going on. But I'd still find it hard to leave.'

'Why should you leave?' Sasha frowned. 'The war will finish one day.'

'I'd leave if I had to save my family, if I was in trouble with the enemy, and it was me or them. I wouldn't compromise.'

'But you won't be in trouble. You have done nothing.'

'But I might. I won't be able to stop, and I know myself.' Clem punched his fist into the palm of his other hand. 'Yesterday, I learned about what you escaped from. My God, the guards were cruel. I saw them before, but I didn't realize that you lived in those sheds. I thought,' he swallowed, 'that you had escaped hunger and some harshness. Not that brutality.' He blinked. 'I'm so sorry.'

Sasha looked at his hands. 'It is not your fault.'

'All we have to give is crusts,' said Clem. He bit his lip. 'We're so *helpless*, trapped in this island by a thousand rules and a dangerous sea.'

'We must help ourselves and we must keep faith, whatever we believe,' said Sasha. He lowered his voice. 'I hear the rumours. My people are dying in their millions,

~ 208 ~

but still, they keep their faith. If you cannot, then you must pretend for the children. Even in the camps they do that, when hell is all around them. They say to them, 'All will be well. Life is beautiful.'

Clem nodded. 'That's what we are trying to do with the kids here. We're planning a parade to make life fun for them.'

'Keep on with it,' said Sasha. He touched his hair. 'See, I am mended. No blood at all.' His expression was sad, as he added, 'That informer has been taken away to prison camp in Germany. His treachery did him no good at all.'

11 pm

When Ginger was sure that everyone except his uncle was asleep, he tiptoed out of his room and knocked gently at the study door. There was a hasty shuffle of papers, then Mr. Braye let him in and ushered him to a chair. 'What is it? Oh, my dear, I can see you are very unhappy.'

Ginger wrapped his arms round his chest and tried to control himself, but he couldn't. His glasses misted over, and he yanked them off and bawled into his pyjama sleeve, trying to muffle his misery.

Mr. Braye leaned forward. 'Has someone hurt you?'

'Everything hurts.' Ginger wiped his face on his cuff and burst out, 'Suddenly, I can't see the point of music.'

'Why do you say that?'

'I thought I could fight with it,' Ginger went on, 'to keep everyone going. But it's not enough, a few tunes on a trumpet here and there.' He put on his glasses again and sniffed. 'Sorry about blubbing.'

'Did you see something yesterday that made you

think like this?' Mr. Braye's face was anxious. 'Tell me.'

'Everything in my head has changed,' said Ginger. 'I tried to be fair to the enemy. Then, yesterday...' he swallowed. 'The day was meant to be fun, a break after the exams. So, we went to look for puffins, so see if they'd arrived. So it would feel like normal.' He looked at his uncle. 'Clem sang all the way there to the north coast.'

'That must have made everyone happy.'

'The blossom was out and the gorse was so yellow, miles of it, blazing in the sunshine.' Ginger gulped, 'But after that, everything went wrong.' He told his uncle about the prisoner jumping off the cliff, shuddering as he remembered it.

'My dear,' said Mr. Braye. 'How dreadfully upsetting.'

'We came home on the lane above the five-mile beach,' said Ginger.

'Where you used to live before you came over to the flat?'

Ginger nodded. 'There was building going on everywhere and anti-tank devices all over the beach.' He blinked and went on, 'There were some very thin workers,' Ginger said. 'They were in a far worse state than the ones this side of the island. Their eyes were hollow, and their skin was...' he searched for the word... 'like tree bark, if you see what I mean. They had no shoes. Like the prisoner I saw after Christmas, through the window.'

'Poor fellows,' said Mr. Braye. 'Those poor things. I knew a little about this.'

'The worst thing...' Ginger gulped. 'The very worst thing...was that they were building a concrete wall with the guards watching them and shouting at them, and one of them stumbled, so the guard pushed him into wet concrete.'

His uncle gasped.

Ginger went on. 'So, the prisoner tried to get out and the guard shoved him back and it happened over and over again, and we wanted to help, but we couldn't. Clem was bellowing at the guards, and they turned on us. So, I told him we must leave, or it'd be no good for us, or the prisoner.' He put his head in his hands. 'We cycled by on the other side of the road. We gave up on them.'

Mr. Braye's voice was gentle. 'They wouldn't want you to be hurt as well. What would be the point?'

'And then we passed a camp with barbed wire round it and huts, and there were people there in a terrible state and one was tied to a pole.' He wiped tears off his face, and said, 'So we came home. And we did nothing to help except give away Clem's pastry.'

Mr. Braye gave him a clean hanky and rooted in the cupboard under the desk. He brought out a little crystal glass and an ancient bottle of brandy. 'Here,' he said, pouring brandy right up to the brim. 'Take this.'

Ginger sniffed it and took a sip. 'Father has this brandy. I'm not allowed it ever.'

'The thing is,' said his uncle, 'however much you want to help, it's best not to deliberately set out to help unless one of them escapes on his own. Then we can organise a safe house for him, like the Percherons have.'

'You know about that Sasha?'

Mr. Braye nodded and went on, 'People are doing this all over the island, but we don't talk about it. We must *never* speak of it.'

'I understand,' said Ginger. 'The less talk the better. Sasha...'

'I really do know him,' said Mr. Braye, suddenly. He put his finger to his lips, then said, 'It takes lots of people to save a prisoner. If one person can no longer do it, another must take over. Everyone can play a part, but we mustn't speak of it. For instance, I can make these,' He showed Ginger a couple of fake identity cards.

'They look genuine,' said Ginger, pretending he hadn't seen the one on the music room floor. He held them up to the light. 'They really do.'

Mr. Braye spoke so softly Ginger could hardly hear him. 'It's almost impossible to hide the ones who can't speak English, but it's different with Sasha. He speaks English, French, Spanish and Russian, for a start.'

'You know him well.' Ginger stared at his uncle.

Mr. Braye went on, 'and he's learning Jersey French quickly. He could be anyone.' Ginger took another sip of brandy, suddenly noticing what was on his uncle's desk, a large map of Jersey. On it were markings and diagrams mostly dotted along the coast. Mr. Braye said, 'I'm doing some research on where the enemy is building. Just for my own interest of course, though best not mention it to anyone.'

'Ah,' said Ginger. 'Clem and I can add to that. We made a note of them. It was the only thing we could do to help.' The brandy was putting colour back into his cheeks.

Mr. Braye put his hand round Ginger's shoulders as he left the study. 'Even in the prison camps, they sing and play music with whatever they can. It keeps their souls intact. But you know that. Music is your small part in this battle, just as mine is the cards and the maps, and other people's is spying and passing on information. Don't forget that. You are a cog in a large wheel, that is quietly spinning in the background.'

After that, Ginger went to bed and slept until dawn, when his mother shook him awake so that he wouldn't miss his exam.

Saturday 6th June
7 pm

On Saturday evenings, the Percherons and Auntie Vi always sat round the wireless to listen to comedy on the Light Programme. This Saturday was no different.

However, just as they'd got to the funniest part, the phone rang, and everyone groaned. 'Don't answer,' said Auntie Vi. But Mr. Percheron picked up the receiver. Mrs. Percheron turned down the volume as her husband spoke rapidly in Jersey French, then listened. He rattled off more Jersey French and put down the phone.

Auntie Vi said, 'Spit it out, Sid, so we can go on listening. Was it important?'

'Yes. It's a horrible blow.' Mr. Percheron slumped into his chair with a sigh. 'All wirelesses have to be given in next week. If they don't, there'll be punishment.'

'That's ridiculous,' said Clem, his voice furious. 'I bet it's because the war's turning against them and they don't want us to know. If we don't have the wireless, what *do* we have? Just the Jersey Evening Post with a German editor writing a load of rot.' He stamped out of the room, saying over his shoulder, 'I'm blowed if we let them take Bill's wireless. If we do, it's like losing him all over again.'

Monday 8th June
7 am

While he was dressing, Clem listened to his brother's radio for the last time. When Bill was eighteen, he had won a prize for showing his pedigree Jersey calf. The prize was a trip to America with other cattle breeders. Included in his prize was some money to cover food and lodging. Bill had lived on American sandwiches instead of proper meals. When he returned home, he had spread his hands and said, 'They're huge. That big, full of bacon and mayonnaise and all sorts.'

As well as waving on meals, he slept in hostels rather than hotels. That gave him enough money to bring presents back to Jersey. He chose records for the family's exciting new radiogram, and a special portable radio for them all to share. It was called a Sparta Sled valve radio, model 557 and it had to be especially shipped all the way from Michigan.

When it arrived, not long before Bill joined the Royal Navy, everyone gasped at the sight of it. It was the blue of a tropical butterfly's wings, with steel slats for decorations. Clem had said, 'It looks like a sort of toast rack,' and everyone had laughed. That was when life was still a joke.

When Bill had left after his last leave, he said to Clem,

'Look after my radio. And if anything happens to me, give it to my girl.'

'Nothing'll happen to you,' Clem had said. But he was only thirteen then, so he didn't know anything.

Two days after the annoying order about the wirelesses, Clem put Bill's radio back into its wonderful American box and carried it to the barn while he decided where they could hide it. They had a week to give in the radios – or wirelesses, as most people called them – so the enemy wouldn't search for them yet.

He covered the box with clean straw, quite high up in case Diddie or Rosie decided to play there. It was raining, and they like to do that sometimes, keeping Ernest company, now that Peggy and Betty had moved to the outside sty next to Hotspur.

After breakfast, when everything was finished on the farm, he set off on his bike to school with Ginger and Spinner. Halfway down the lane, Mr. Cliquot's truck rumbled towards them. He leaned out of the window with a cigarette wobbling on his lip. 'I've come to collect the wirelesses. Special commission from the Germans.'

'So soon?' Clem sneered and turned to Ginger. 'Some people are such ruddy traitors, aren't they, Ginger?'

'A man's got to earn a living somehow,' said Mr. Cliquot cheerfully. 'Cheer up Clem, it's not the end of the world. You'll get them back after the war.'

'Oh yeah? What do you know?' Clem pedalled on and said as he always did, 'Snivelling creep. I can't believe he's related to Joe.'

'You ought to shut up when you see him,' said Spinner. 'You'll turn him against us.'

Clem shrugged. 'Who ruddy cares? I hate the man.'

Ginger changed the subject. 'Your parents have a

Marconi, haven't they? A radiogram. It's a beauty. Great sound.'

Clem glowered. 'It took them years to save up for that. They've got about ten records that Bill brought back from America. Gospel hymns and big bands. They love playing them.'

'We've labelled Dad's wireless,' said Spinner. 'He's so upset. We love listening to the big bands and the orchestras. He said losing his wireless might be the straw that broke his back. But he didn't mean it.'

Ginger added, 'Uncle Hedley's taken a photo of his and he's going to take one of yours too. He said he wanted a record.' Ginger's face fell. 'I loved listening to jazz on that wireless. And Rosie likes *Listen with Mother* and Diddie comes up to listen to *Children's Hour*. It's a such bore.'

They cycled on, nearly at the edge of town. Then Clem said, 'I hope horrible old Mr. Cliquot didn't see Mr. Braye's camera. That's illegal too.'

Spinner glanced at him. 'Mr. Cliquot's making a ton of money out of the war. He doesn't care about anyone's feelings. Even if he didn't see the camera, he'll say he did.' She shivered. 'He scares me.'

4 pm

Mr. Percheron had spent the day making a false bottom for inside of the piano stool. He sanded it carefully, then varnished it. It was a sunny day, so when he was satisfied with his work, he left it outside to dry, out of sight of Franz and Otto in case they wandered into the farmyard.

A sudden breeze picked up a handful of dust and swirled it in a tiny maelstrom on to the varnished board.

When Mr. Percheron came back to inspect it, the dust had coated it nicely. After another session with the sandpaper, the false bottom looked like an old piece of wood. When he'd fitted it into the piano stool, no one would notice that it hadn't been there forever.

'Crumbs,' said Auntie Vi. 'You're a marvel, Sid Percheron. What a relief you're up and running again.'

'Not exactly running,' said Mr. Percheron, 'But not too bad.'

After school, Clem fetched Bill's radio in its box while Rosie out of the way, having tea. He slotted it into the depths of the old piano stool and put the false bottom over it. 'Ruddy perfect, Dad. Thanks.'

'No need to swear, son,' said Mr. Percheron.

Auntie Vi chose a few ancient pieces of music hall music and laid them on top, complete with a couple of spider webs. 'That'll fox them,' she said. Now we can listen to our favourite programmes when we want.'

'*Sherlock Holmes,*' said Mr. Percheron.

'*Crime Does Not Pay,*' said Clem's mother, coming into the sitting room to admire the handiwork. '*Sunday Half Hour.*'

'*Music while you Work,*' said Auntie Vi, flicking a duster over the piano

'The one I liked best was the BBC recording of the nightingale with the Lancaster Bombers flying above them. Couple of weeks ago,' Clem said. Then he shrugged. 'Let's be realistic, everyone. We can't really listen to all that. Otto and Franz are next door. Secret police are listening under windows. Mr. Cliquot's working for the Germans. It's hopeless.'

Mr. Percheron put his hands together. 'Let's keep the faith. At least we can listen the The News and find out what's going on. And maybe we could have *Sunday Half Hour* when all the soldiers are back at the barracks listening to whatever they like.'

'The main thing is,' offered Mrs. Percheron, 'that we've kept Bill's radio.'

Auntie Vi said, 'The other main thing is that we'll have to find another way of entertaining ourselves. If we can't have fun with the radio without the threat of those bl...' She controlled herself... 'those ruddy Jerries putting us in prison just for listening to a blinking wireless, then we must think of something else.' Suddenly, her eyes gleamed. 'We could have sing songs round the piano and invite those two German boys. We can laugh like drains because they'll never guess we had a wireless right under my bum while I play.'

Clem roared and his mother had tears of laughter in her eyes. 'Vi,' she shrieked, 'you *devil*.'

Saturday 13th June
8 pm

A few days later, the Percherons went over to the Brayes' house in the evening. Otto and Franz were sitting on their back doorstep, smoking in the evening sun. As the family passed by, Otto said, 'You are going to a party?'

'Of course not. It is no time for parties when the whole world is in flames.' Mr. Percheron looked firmly at him over his glasses. 'We are having a prayer meeting.' Then he marched stiffly into the Brayes' kitchen, followed by his wife and Clem. The door was firmly locked after them.

Otto puffed out a cloud of smoke, ran over to the locked door and shouted through the keyhole. 'Have a good time. Say a little prayer for me.' Then he went back to the doorstep and smirked at Franz. 'Prayers, hein?'

Indoors, Mr. Braye led everyone to the sitting room, including Auntie Vi. Joe was examining a tangle of wires on the sofa, while Mr. Braye had a small board, a bulb of sorts and a loud speaker, which he was putting together.

Joe said. 'You wait. He passed an untangled wire to Mr. Braye as everyone huddled round the sofa, jostling each other.

Mr. Braye connected wires to the board, then held up his hand. 'This is the BBC,' said a crackling voice like a goblin. 'The Home Service.'

Everyone gasped. Mr. Braye smiled triumphantly and showed them exactly what to do to make the radio work. 'It's not brilliant, but I'm working on it. I'll keep all the parts separately, in case we're searched. But at least we can be in touch with the outside world, even if we only hear the minimum.'

Clem looked at his parents, bursting to tell them about Bill's American wireless in the piano stool. But they shook their heads. 'Don't tell,' mouthed his mother.

Ginger said, 'That's a crystal radio, isn't it? Very clever. It's amazing what you can do with a few wires. Let's have a go, Uncle Hedley.'

After they'd all tried their hand at fitting everything together, Spinner handed out real tea to celebrate, then they spilled out into the yard to go home. The two soldiers were on the step, drinking beer. 'Good prayer meeting?' asked Otto, his voice slurred.

Auntie Vi clasped her handbag to her chest. 'Indeed, it was young man. You must join us another time. We were learning about The Good Shepherd.' Then she beamed at them, showing all her teeth. 'We are having a sing song on Monday evening and would be delighted if you would join us.'

Tuesday June 16th
8 am

Auntie Vi's singsong had been a great success the night before. She had made a list of World War One songs and played on and on without a break until the two soldiers were white with exhaustion. She said, 'I lost my son in the last War against Germany.' Then she played on, smiling brightly, and sitting firmly on the piano stool.

At the end, the soldiers bowed politely and said that they weren't really allowed to join local people's parties, so they were sorry, they couldn't come and sing again.

Everyone else was exhausted by the evening as well. The potato crop had to be dug. Last thing, Ginger said, 'The Germans are doing a big sweeps of the farms.'

'Big sweeps?' Joe raised an eyebrow. 'What the heck does that mean?'

'Looking for prisoners and wirelesses,' said Ginger. 'Suspicious lot, the enemy.'

Clem nodded. 'At least with Sasha away we've got nothing to hide.' He thought of the radio, then quickly moved on. 'We'll start with the flat field. See you tomorrow. We've plenty of helpers.'

They started work early with the neighbours spread along the field in a long line. 'Who wants to be indoors on a day like this?' Joe dug energetically. 'It's great that boys are allowed off school to do this.'

'Poor Spinner,' said Ginger. 'It must be annoying being a girl sometimes.'

Clem broke in, 'I've got a plan. We're going to use Legs as a decoy. I haven't told him, obviously.'

'A decoy?' Joe scratched his head. 'Why? We aren't doing anything against the law. Just digging up spuds.'

'Legs looks a lot like Sasha,' explained Ginger. 'So that's really useful. He's the same height, dark hair, skinny. The soldiers are buzzing around like bees today.'

'You see,' Clem said, 'if someone like Mr. Cliquot's put two and two together and told them about Sasha, we can explain that he must have got it wrong. It was Legs all along not him.'

'Nice one,' said Joe. 'And here he comes. Legs Eleven, as they say.'

'Wotcha, everyone,' said Legs, loping towards them. He held up a flagon of cider. 'I've got some of Auntie's medicine for later.'

They dug until midday, with the sun warming their backs. When they paused, Legs gave them each a sip of cider and Ginger said, 'Anyone listen to the news yesterday?'

'Shh,' Clem hissed. 'We aren't allowed to listen to the BBC.' He indicated the other workers. Then he stood up, staring. Otto and Franz were crossing the far end of the field with another soldier. Little dust whirls flew under the firm tread of their jackboots. Clem whispered, 'Blast it. They've got that nasty blighter with them. The sergeant that hit me. He's a right tick. Watch out everyone, look busy.' He started to dig again, his back to them.

'Crikey,' Legs whispered. 'He looks like a nasty piece of work.'

'Beau doesn't like him,' said Joe, clicking his fingers for his dog. 'He's making that silent growl he's learned lately.' He held up a handful of potatoes as the soldiers drew near. 'Want some? They're excellent with butter. If you have any butter. We don't of course.'

Franz and Otto smiled and thanked him, but the other one brushed away Joe's offer. He said, 'We are looking for prisoners. We have been told by many sources that you have one that works for you.'

'*Many sources?*' Clem raised an eyebrow. 'Who would that be? And why would we do that?' He waved his hand across the field. 'We're busy and it's against the rules to even say hello to one of those poor blokes.'

The sergeant pointed at Legs. 'Who is this?'

'Legs La Motte,' said Legs, beaming. He held out a muddy hand but the sergeant brushed it away as Legs forged on. 'Pleasure to meet you, sir.'

'Identity Cards, please,' barked the sergeant.

'Righty ho,' said Legs, amiably. He fished in his pockets and dragged out a crumpled card. Then he shook it and exclaimed. 'Oh blimey, it's so muddy. I hope it doesn't make your lovely clean hands dirty.'

The cold-eyed sergeant checked the card then thrust it back. He stared at Legs for a long time, but Legs held his gaze, smiling gently adding that he was delighted to meet such a friendly chap. Behind the sergeant, Otto and Franz smirked. Legs smiled back at them. 'Smashing sergeant you have, boys.'

The others showed their cards, then the sergeant wrote something in his book and turned to leave without a thank you. Franz and Otto looked back apologetically and followed him along the field to check the other workers.

Clem grinned as they all had another refreshing drink of cider. 'My plan worked rather well, don't you think, chaps? They really do think you are...' Then he shut his trap. Legs didn't know about Sasha.

11 pm

Ginger stayed up late, even though they'd worked so hard in the potato fields. He and Mr. Braye had laid the map of Jersey on the floor after carefully drawing the black outs so not a chink of light could get out.

He pointed at a spot on the northwest of the island. 'There was a gun site being built there,' he murmured, keeping his finger on the spot until Mr. Braye had marked it on. 'And there and there.' He showed his uncle eleven places where they had seen buildings, as well as the prison camp. 'What are you going to do with the map, Uncle Hedley?'

'I'm not sure. Get it to England, if only it were possible.' Mr. Braye frowned, turning towards the window. 'What's that outside?' He switched off the light and peered round the side of the blackout.

Ginger froze. 'Jackboots. In the middle of the night. What on earth?'

'Go to bed,' whispered Mr. Braye. 'I'll deal with this.' He groped for the map in the dark and shoved it behind the desk. Then he groped for the light bulb, took it out and hid it behind his books, all in the dark.

Ginger felt his way to his bedroom, put on his pyjamas and jumped into bed. He thought of the sergeant today and his cold eyes and how he had implied that they might be breaking rules.

Then he remembered the guards that he and Clem

had seen on their bike ride. *They've tracked us down*, he thought, his heart pounding. He heard his uncle go into his own bedroom. A few minutes later, he went downstairs. Ginger pictured him in his darned old dressing gown, perhaps without his glasses, his hair rumpled.

Ginger heard Mr. Braye opening the door. There was an exchange of words, polite and German. Suddenly, the stair lights were switched on. Footsteps echoed in the hall and Rosie gave a cry in her sleep.

The rumbling of voices went on. Mr. Braye said, quite clearly, 'Please don't wake the children. The older boy has had exams and he's very tired.'

A voice muttered, '*Sei Ruig, bitte.*' Then Ginger relaxed. That's only *Franz*, he thought. He's telling his uncle to stay calm. His bedroom door opened and he clamped his eyes shut, hardly daring to breathe. *Don't tread on my glasses*, he begged silently.

Someone walked across the room, then out again. The door closed. Nobody said a thing. Ginger sat up, straining his ears. The men walked into the study and almost immediately out of it and downstairs.

The back door shut. Jackboots clattered across the yard and there was silence.

'Good God,' whispered Mr. Braye, tiptoeing into Ginger's room. He chuckled. 'What madness. They were sent to feel the light bulbs.'

'*What?* At this time of night?' Ginger felt for his glasses and checked his luminous clock. 'How strange.'

'Someone told Franz and Otto that we have parties in this house and that we use electricity after switch off time,' said Mr. Braye. He continued, 'Honestly, they *really* were ordered to feel every single light bulb in the house to see if they were warm.' Mr. Braye started laughing.

'Luckily, they accepted that my study light bulb was broken.'

'Crikey. That's so crazy,' said Ginger. 'Do you think they'll check the farm?'

'Not a chance. Clem's still leaving Hotspur out at night.'

Saturday 22nd June
6 am

Spinner wrote her letter early, hoping she could send it on the morning tide. She had picked up a couple of beer bottles that Otto and Franz had left outside the night before and rinsed them over and over again to take out the smell. When they were dry, they'd be perfect to send, nicely disguised in the sea with their dark green glass.

> *Dearest Mummy,*
> *The early potato harvest has been finished in record time. There were so many of us, and now we're going to help on other farms, but Clem is stinking mad because the Germans arrived to collect half almost before they'd dug the last one. He is under the tractor already, at this hour, getting rid of his anger, trying to mend it. But he thinks it will be ready for the wheat harvest.*
>
> *They're having a break from potatoes and cutting the hay by hand today. I might have a go with the scythe (only joking).*
>
> *Every Monday, we're going to have a singsong with Auntie Vi in view of the wirelesses being taken. She's also very keen to help with the parade we are planning soon. She has her sewing machine out and*

has taken out all the curtains from her house. She did it when her German lodgers were out on duty and said, 'Too Bad.' They still have the blackouts, so I expect they will be all right.

It is a real bore having no wireless, but we are all too busy anyhow so never mind.

Load of love, Spinner. Xxxxxxxxxxxxxxxxxxxxxx

As usual, she decorated her letter, but this time she had to draw in pencil. All her crayons were used up. 'Hay stooks don't look the same in black and white,' she said to the cat.

Looking at her clock, she decided to send the letter another day. Anyhow, the beer bottles were still damp inside. So she put on her coolest shirt and her dungarees and hurried downstairs. Everyone else was ready to start the hay field, even Aunt Edie, who was in her special farming breeches. Spinner said, 'You look smashing, Aunt Edie.'

Her aunt smiled, then she rolled up her sleeves ready for work and showed Spinner a telegram. 'I heard from the boss yesterday.'

'Uncle Jack?' Spinner pictured Ginger's father, jolly and clever with dark brown hair.

'He's on leave in Devon,' said Aunt Edie, beaming. She showed Spinner the Red Cross Message. 'That means he's safe.' She picked up Rosie and whirled her round and round, then gave her to Spinner's father. 'Could you look after her this morning? It's my turn to help out of doors.'

Mr. Braye said he'd take Rosie to the beach to look for shells. 'There are still a couple of places we can go to,' he said. 'Enemy free places, that is.'

The news lifted everyone's spirits, so after a piece

of toast, Spinner and her aunt headed out to the field. Already, Clem and his father had started, scything in a wonderful rhythm, with Joe and his father following them. A couple of other helpers worked at the far end of the field. Spinner screwed up her eyes in the early morning sunshine. 'Who are those two?'

Aunt Edie said, 'Probably neighbours. We're all helping each other, aren't we?' She took hold of a rake. 'Come on, Spinner, let's put our backs into it. Mrs. P's made some lovely biscuits for elevenses.

Spinner started to rake the hay into neat piles, the sun on her back. Overhead, skylarks soared and she felt as though she would burst with happiness. For once, there didn't seem to be a single soldier in sight. It felt just like it used to. But suddenly, she heard the pounding of feet. Billy Cliquot shot into sight, his grubby face crumpled with anxiety.

He raced up to her and tugged at her dungarees. 'I heard my dad talking about Bill's wireless to a soldier. And I don't think he was very nice about Clem. And I think everyone should...' But at that point, he gasped. 'I can hear a German truck coming. Listen.'

Spinner gave him a hug. The younger boy smelled of dirt and fear. 'It'll be all right, Billy. Don't you worry. There's nothing to hide.'

Billy stared at her. 'What about the escaped prisoner? The tall man. He's there.' He thrust his hand out towards the scythers. 'Look. And he ain't a ghost, whatever Joe and Ginger say.'

Spinner's heart raced. 'I don't know what you mean, Billy.' Then she gasped. A soldier was emerging from each corner of the field, four of them. She grabbed Billy. 'Run for it, Billy. Go and tell Auntie Vi and Mrs. P. They're cooking biscuits and there'll be one for you if you go like the clappers.'

'I want to watch,' said Billy, then added quickly. 'But I really want a biscuit.'

Spinner glanced at the soldiers. The haymakers scythed on, the long grass falling in pleats along the field. Aunt Edie stopped raking and walked calmly towards the soldiers. In her gentle voice, she said, 'Can I help you?'

The soldiers looked taken aback. One, with tortoiseshell spectacles, took off his cap. He said, politely, 'Have you seen any rough looking men around the buildings? There's a dangerous person around here.'

Aunt Edie stepped away slightly, saying that the sun was in her eyes. As she edged round, the soldiers moved too, facing her. Beyond, the cutters worked on impassively. Aunt Edie kept them talking, pretty in her spotted blouse and breeches, her hair in a green scarf. 'Oh dear. What a horrible nuisance.'

Suddenly Spinner noticed that the two tall men at the far end of the field had vanished, almost into thin air. It was as though they had been ghosts. Joe mouthed, *'Sasha..'*

At that moment, there was a shout from the end of the field. A sergeant stood by the gate, barking orders. The soldiers raced towards him, pistols at the ready. Aunt Edie said calmly, 'I'd better go and check on Mrs. Percheron. She'll be very upset if they go into the house.'

In the field, the haymakers paused. Clem said quietly, 'Legs is wearing the same clothes as Sasha. They'll chase him and they'll never catch him or Sasha.' Then he grinned. 'He has a special hiding place.'

11 am

In the farmhouse kitchen, Mrs. Percheron was taking biscuits out of the oven. She had made them with beetroot syrup for sweetness, some of Auntie Vi's secret stash of raisins, potato flour and a dash of butter. As the sergeant burst into the house, followed by two of the soldiers, she looked up and said, 'Usually, it's the custom to knock before coming into other people's houses.'

The soldiers skidded to a halt. The sergeant spat out his words like bullets. 'There is a dangerous man on the run. We have guards outside.'

'Oh dear,' said Mrs. Percheron. She held out a plate of biscuits. 'We'll let you know if we see him. Would you like one?' From the sitting room there came the tinkling of Auntie Vi at the piano. Mrs. Percheron said, 'My friend Vi loves playing Beethoven, your wonderful German composer.' She pushed the plate nearer to the soldiers as Aunt Edie appeared, smiling and friendly, pushing a curl back from her forehead.

For a moment, the sergeant looked confused. 'You don't understand, Madam. I said we are very looking for a dangerous man.' He turned to Aunt Edie. Please explain, Miss.'

Aunt Edie smiled. 'I am glad you think me so young that you can call me Miss. But I can assure you that this lady is able to understand everything.' She indicated Mrs. Percheron. 'Even though she is a Jersey woman.'

Mrs. Percheron kept her voice calm. 'Please feel free to look inspect our house and farm. We have nothing to hide. We have no knowledge of this dangerous man.'

The sergeant asked his men to put their pistols in their holsters. Then he said, 'Please show me around.' The soldiers gazed longingly at the biscuits, but the sergeant gave them a fierce look, so they followed him meekly into the hall. Auntie Vi played on, giving Beethoven her all as the men tramped after Mrs. Percheron, intruding into every room. Aunt Edie asked Billy to come out from under the table where he'd been hiding.

In the implement shed, Sasha was climbing down the well. Legs covered the hatch carefully with straw and pulled the harrow across it. Then he loped back to the farm into the barn, ready to give chase if he needed to.

In the hayfield, everyone worked on under the hot sun, watched by the soldier in the tortoiseshell glasses, stopping now and then to sharpen their scythes.

When the sergeant returned downstairs, he peered into the sitting room door. Auntie Vi's hands raced up and down the keys. The sergeant said, 'You are doing... how do you say it? Justice...that is the word...to our great composer.'

Auntie Vi flashed him a toothy smile. 'God bless the man. Beethoven brings the world together.' She sat more firmly on the piano stool. 'I also have some lovely German songs, which I will play once more when the war is over.'

The sergeant gave a little bow and went back through to the kitchen. He thanked Mrs. Percheron and ordered his soldiers to follow him. As they left the kitchen, Billy said loudly, 'I told you they didn't have no wirelesses. My dad was lying.'

The men looked at each other, but just as the sergeant was about to question him, Legs bellowed from the barn, shot into the open and raced up the hill, his legs working like pistons. 'Come on, boys,' he yelled. 'Catch!'

The sergeant threw his hands in the air and sprinted into the farmyard, ordering his soldiers to follow. Soon they were racing after Legs up the track that Mr. Percheron called the Perqualage, the route where criminals could find sanctuary in the old days.

Joe watched them from the field. Then he grinned. 'I put a couple of tripwires on the track. Legs knows, but they don't.'

'Enjoy the sight,' said Clem. 'I'll just nip down to the shed and let Sasha out.'

5 pm

Legs turned up later, beaming. 'That foxed them,' he said. 'They had a couple of nasty bruises from the trip wires. Clever move, Joe.' He accepted a biscuit from Mrs. Percheron and said they were the best he'd ever eaten. Then he shouldered his scythe and hurried back to his auntie's farm up the hill. 'Cows to milk, pigs to feed,' he said. 'So much to do, so little time.'

The hay was cut and drying in the field, so Joe said, 'Let's nip down and see how the boat's getting on. Dad's been working on her.'

'He's a busy man, your father,' said Ginger, as they set off. 'He was working on the tractor again last week. He's welded lots of new parts.'

'We'll use it soon,' said Clem. 'Poor old Ernest is too old to work.'

Mr. Le Carin was waiting for them beside the boat. 'I've made the mast,' he said. 'It's easy to put in place.' He turned to Spinner. 'Your father's given me an old sail and I've made two new ones.'

'That's wonderful,' said Spinner, admiringly. 'You're very clever.'

Mr. Le Carin looked away, but Spinner could see that

he was proud as Joe heaved the sails out of a canvas bag. 'This is the mainsail, which'll catch most of the wind.' He showed them the smaller one. 'This is the jib. It holds the boat steady.'

'The jib goes at the front,' said Clem. 'At least I know that. Not that I'll need to use it, I hope.'

'You have to feel confident about a boat,' said Spinner. She stroked the varnished sides. 'I'd be fine in this one.'

'Now, you kids.' Mr. Le Carin put his hands on his hips. 'Don't get carried away. I want to tell you something. This boat is here for *emergencies only*, not silly schemes for escaping to the mainland. Keep your mouths shut about her, kids.'

Clem looked curious. 'Do you think she's big enough to escape in, sir? Cross the Channel, for instance?'

'With the right person at the helm and a fair wind, yes,' said Mr. Le Carin. 'But that's no concern of yours. Right, I'm off. I've got work to do. That ruddy tractor, for a start.'

Joe said, 'Thanks Dad.' He opened the door.

After he'd gone, Clem whistled. 'Your father's changed in the last year.'

'Up to a point,' said Joe. He shrugged and went on, 'But he really knows about boats.' Reaching for another bag, he said, 'I've got charts, a compass, life jacket, sextant. Everything for navigating and some emergency rations, sardines and tins of stuff. There's an Aldis lamp with a full battery, to shine at the sail if you need help.'

'Grim,' said Ginger. 'Imagine being alone in the middle of the English Channel in the dark, with battleships bearing down on you.' He shuddered. 'Or a U boat emerging from the deep like a whale.'

'Flipping exciting, if you ask me,' said Joe. 'There's

some fishing line, a knife, some hooks and a first aid tin.'

Ginger was tapping his foot. 'That's all very nice, but what's the point of all this?'

'Get a grip, Ginger,' said Spinner. 'We might not need to use it. But it's here in case we do. *That's* the point, so we can sleep at night.'

Joe smirked as he said. 'I'd never go. I couldn't possibly leave the island all on its own without me.'

10.30 pm

Before they went to bed, Spinner and her father looked out of the study window. It was warm so they kept the window open. The stars were out and the moon was bright. 'How beautiful,' said Mr. Braye. 'A harvest moon.'

'What a day,' said Spinner. 'Everything seems to have happened.'

Mr. Braye said, 'Shall we listen to some music?' He wound up the gramophone and put on a record. 'It's that piece about the man that fights evil. Don Quixote.'

'I love that music. It's so full of life.' Spinner beamed at her father. Then suddenly, she grabbed his arm. 'There's a man dancing in the garden.'

'Really?' Mr. Braye looked out and gasped. 'Good gracious. I think it's Sasha. Just look at that.'

The prisoner was leaping across the grass in time to the music, his legs and arms stretched wide and his face full of laughter in the moonlight. As the music came to an end, he gave a huge, extravagant bow and was gone.

'Did we really see that?' said Spinner. She rubbed her eyes. 'Did I imagine it?' She turned to her father and added. 'Perhaps that was a thank you present. Or maybe a ghost.'

Monday 13th July
5.30 pm

Every Monday night, Auntie Vi was determined to hold her singsongs. She asked Otto and Franz each time, but they always managed to be busy and went out for the whole evening. Auntie Vi laughed, adding, 'The more I ask them, the less excuse anyone will have for searching for that jolly old thing in the piano stool.'

While most of the family were singing along to the piano, Mr. Percheron made the excuse that his lungs were still not quite right, even though he was completely up to strength again. Instead, he sat in the barn with Sasha, teaching him Jersey French and keeping an eye out for visitors in German uniforms, or the ones that pretended to be prisoners. In return, Sasha worked on the farm, scything the verges and anywhere else where he could escape from quickly.

'It's blimming amazing the way that man vanishes,' said Joe. 'Like a puff of smoke.'

'Of course.' Spinner folded her arms. 'He told Daddy he used to be in a circus. He knows hundreds of tricks.'

There were no more inspections from the enemy, so everyone felt safe, though they kept watch. 'They're bored with us,' said Ginger. 'And Auntie Vi's strategy's working very well.'

As well as playing the piano, Auntie Vi was busy making costumes for the parade. Diddie had a tutu, just as she wanted. As there was a seaside theme, she decided she could be a seagull in her white net skirt. Every costume was hung up on a rail, ready for the parade that Spinner had thought of weeks ago.

Joe repainted his lobster head dress and made some better claws. Whenever he snapped them at Arthur, his little brother roared with laughter and said, 'Chase me, chase me.'

Rosie couldn't decide whether she wanted to be a swallow or a skylark, but Auntie Vi made her a pair of blue trousers so she could turn cartwheels on the parade, so she opted for being a swallow. Spinner helped to make wings, with cloth cut into feather shapes and carefully sewn on to a frame that attached to her white bodice, with the back painted black.

'We could put wings on Hotspur and Peggy as well,' she suggested one evening.

Ginger laughed. 'Pigs might fly. Hilarious.'

They were all sitting in the hayfield after tea. The stooks had been made into a haystack, although some of it had been pitchforked into the hay loft above the cattle stalls, ready for winter.

Joe put a piece of grass between his teeth and made up a tune. 'I'll bring some lobster pots and we can stuff flowers between the holes. We can't use them for anything else, so we might as well.'

'Good idea,' said Spinner. 'We could tie them together to make a gigantic conger eel. We could carry it above our heads, like those Chinese paper dragons.'

'It'll be heavy.' Joe tapped his head. 'Crazy days, Spinner. Turning lobster pots into dragons.'

Clem rolled on to his back and stared at the sky. 'The Spitfire pilots might even see it from up there. They'd know we're all right and take the message home.'

However, before they could really give their time to the parade, the second crop of potatoes must be dug, so for much of July, everyone was busy. The potatoes had to be washed and crushed, pulped and dried to make flour and it had to be done quickly, as all over the island, the potato crop was diseased.

'I've never known anything like it,' said Mr. Percheron, helping Clem to work the potato crusher. 'Disease and Pestilence. It's a sign from God.'

Joe rolled his eyes. 'What's next? A plague of frogs?' He was sitting with Ginger on upturned barrels, cutting out bad bits before the potatoes were crushed. When they were halfway through the pile, Mr. Cliquot turned up, whistling.

'My word, you boys are busy,' he said. He pulled a cigarette stub from behind his ears. 'Want a hand?'

Clem muttered under his breath, something about traitors. He nodded curtly at him and carried on with his work. But Mr. Cliquot didn't seem to hear. He lit up and Joe groaned. 'Give us a puff, Mr. Cliquot.'

'Sorry, son. They're German smokes. You wouldn't want to be caught smelling of them.' Mr. Cliquot gave a curt laugh, gazing around. 'I said, want a hand? You short of help?'

'We're doing very well as we are, thank you,' said Mr. Percheron. He didn't look up, but Clem knew what he was thinking. *Turncoat. Not to be trusted.*

'Legs is coming over,' said Ginger. 'Clem's friend. Honestly, Mr. Cliquot, I think we're plenty of hands for the moment.'

Clem glowered at him and Ginger suppressed a grin. He went back to his potato pile. Mr. Cliquot puffed, then said casually, 'I wouldn't mind a piece of bread if you've got any. We're a bit short in town.'

Mr. Percheron stared at him. 'I heard you had a business going, with the Germans, Philo. You had lots of benefits, so I hear. Why bread? They pay you well.'

'Yeah. Well, no longer.' Mr. Cliquot put out the cigarette and tucked it carefully behind his ear again. 'It's folded.'

Joe whistled. 'Blimey. What are you going to live on? Limpets?'

Clem laughed. 'You could help build the bunkers. But,' he added, glancing at Mr. Cliquot's soft hands, 'You'd best find some gloves on the Black Market.'

Spinner arrived with a basket. 'Lunch, boys. Sandwiches and blackberries.' Then she noticed Mr. Cliquot and asked him where Billy was. But Mr. Cliquot didn't reply. Instead, he wobbled on his feet and held the fence post as though he was going to faint.

'Let's be Christian,' said Mr. Percheron, suddenly concerned. 'Share with us, Philo.' He cut his small sandwich in two handed one half to Mr. Cliquot.

Mr. Cliquot gobbled it down, then wiped his forehead with his handkerchief. 'Thanks, Sid,' he murmured. 'I'll say something for you. You're a difficult old Christian, but you live what you believe.' He took a handful of blackberries from the bowl in the basket and smiled at Spinner.

After he'd gone, Joe said, 'How are the mighty fallen. As they say in the Bible.'

'He's not the mighty type.' Clem rolled his eyes. Then he said, 'But he's still one of us.'

When the crushed potatoes were carried indoors, Auntie Vi groaned. 'To think, before the war we could have proper flour whenever we wanted.'

6.45 pm

The hedges were laden with blackberries, so whenever possible, Spinner, Diddie and the boys took them to anyone in the parish who was too old or ill to pick them for themselves. On this evening, Clem stopped suddenly as they made their way round with their baskets. 'Listen. I think that's Auntie Vi, yelling at someone.'

'And here she is,' said Joe. 'Blimey. Stand back everyone.'

Auntie Vi was steaming towards them, her hat askew. She was bellowing at a soldier. 'If I want to put potatoes under the hedge I ruddy well will. It's a free country.' She glared. 'It used to be.'

The soldier had her by one arm. Auntie Vi shook it away. 'Get off me, you little *Pehon.*' Then she spat full into the man's face and repeated the rude Jersey French word. *'Peasant.'*

'Ruddy hell,' said Clem. 'That's going too far. She'll be for it.' He ran towards Auntie Vi, but the soldier held up his hand.

'Halte.' He shouted. 'This woman must come with me.' He thrust her towards a nearby German truck and slammed the door. As he drove off, Auntie Vi pressed her face against the window. Her lips were clamped tight. Without saying a word, the boys leapt on to their bikes and raced after the truck, all the way and up the hill to College House.

'Jesus,' said Joe. 'They're going to interrogate her.'

'Auntie Vi's *old*,' said Clem, as Auntie Vi climbed out

of the car and adjusted her hat. Then she put her head up and marched ahead of the soldier. He said, 'Just as we get lulled into thinking everything's all right, they show us their true colours again. Bloody hell.'

Ginger said, 'We'd better fetch Uncle Hedley. He'll help her.'

They raced back to the Brayes' house but when they burst in at the door, full of their news they found that Otto was in the kitchen, sobbing as if his heart would break. Mr. Braye ushered them out. 'There's been a big bombing in Germany. Otto's family is missing.'

'So?' Clem turned on his heel and walked away. Then he stopped, sick at himself. He put out his hand for Otto's and apologized, adding, 'I shouldn't have said that.'

Ginger said, 'I'm sorry.' He pushed back his glasses. 'That must be awful.'

Spinner wrapped her arms round herself and said, 'How horrible. I can't imagine it.' Otto put his head in his hands, and Spinner went on, 'I'm so, so sorry to have to change the subject, but we need to tell you something, Daddy.'

'It's pretty harsh,' said Clem. 'Auntie Vi's been taken to College House.'

Mr. Braye gasped. '*What?* They must have made a mistake.'

Otto looked at her through his tears. '*Mein Gott*,' he said. 'So now my country is hurting innocent old women.

9 pm

Auntie Vi sat in the garden nursing a cup of tea. There was a bruise on her hand and she flinched as she said to the Percherons, 'It was worth it. He caught me putting out food for the prisoners. I spat at him full in the face.'

She burst into tears. 'Why *can't* we feed the hungry and the sick? The Germans go to church too. They know that's our *duty*.'

Mrs. Percheron sighed. 'Something has gone wrong with the world. People live in fear.'

Auntie Vi wiped her eyes. '*I'm* not afraid. And I told them so. I said, 'Why have you brought me into this place? I have nothing to hide.'

Mr. Braye leaned forward and touched her gently. 'What did they do?'

'They didn't hurt me. I thought they would but they didn't.' She looked at her hand and said, 'Oh, that?'

Mr. Braye let out a sigh of relief as she went on. 'They put me in a room and left me alone to stew. But I said my prayers.' She tossed her head.

Mr. Percheron said, 'We did too.'

Auntie Vi went on, 'Then three of them came into the room. They looked like rats out of the sewer with their greased down hair and shiny boots. But I said to myself, they're only boys and I sat up straight and kept my hat on.'

'Go on,' said Mr. Braye.

'I wasn't going to let them bully me. So I said nothing and they started muttering in German and staring at me. Then they laughed.' Her voice quivered at this and she took a deep sip of tea. 'They said *Alte Frau*.' She glanced at Mr. Braye. 'What does that mean?'

Mr. Braye looked away, but Auntie Vi asked him again, insisting that he translated. So he mumbled, 'It means old lady. It was very unkind.'

'How rude.' Auntie Vi crossed her arms, then managed a grim smile. 'I expect they were talking about someone else. Old ladies don't spit.'

Wednesday 5th August
8 am

Clem brushed Ernest carefully and gave him extra hay. 'You must be on your worst behaviour, Ernest. Otherwise, the Germans will take you away from me.'

Spinner flung her arms round the old horse's neck. 'Why? He's so old. He's no use to them.'

'They've sent their horses home. Now they want ours. Every horse has to go to the Parish Room.' Clem was curt.

'Shall I come with you?' Spinner stroked Ernest's neck. 'He might feel happier with two friends instead of one.'

'Thanks, Spin.' Clem swallowed. 'I'll be better alone. Just me and Ernest, in case it's our last walk.'

'Of course it won't be,' said Spinner, keeping her voice strong. 'You'll both be back in a tick.'

'I'd rather he was *dead* than in their hands,' Clem went on.

'They like horses though,' said Spinner, as Ernest backed into the yard. 'They would treat him well, I'm sure.'

But Clem couldn't reply. He gave Ernest a wizened apple from last year's harvest. Then he led him down the lane, his shoulder against the horse's. She knew by his back view that he was fighting back tears.

Saturday 22nd August
9 am

At last the day of the big parade had come. Ernest was safe. No one had wanted him and he'd come home with Clem, so everyone was able to enjoy the preparations.

Joe and his father wired twenty lobster pots together and all the children, including Arthur and Rosie, collected hydrangea flowers, the kind always used for the island's usual battle of flowers. They worked late in the big barn the night before, securing them to the lobster pots, and adding giant daisies for the conger eel's eyes and a row of paper triangles as teeth.

Arthur and Rosie screamed when they saw it. Joe said, 'We must have got it right then. It really looks like a conger.'

Ernest was brushed until his coat gleamed. Spinner wove flowers into his plaited mane and brushed his huge fetlocks and tail. Messages were sent round the parish with the time of the parade. Even the soldiers agreed to help. Otto wanted to keep busy. So he and Franz attached wings to Peggy on a harness and eventually to Hotspur, after bribing him with their bread ration.

Ginger polished his trumpet. Auntie Vi helped Aunt Edie to button Rosie into her swallow costume. Arthur looked perfect as a little crab and Joe told him that their mother always called him 'Man P'tit Crabin,' Jersey French for 'My Little Crab.'

'My,' said Mr. Percheron. 'Don't you look spiffing.'

When Otto and Franz were out of the way, Mr. Braye took a photo with his Kodak camera, saying to Rosie, 'It's only a pretend camera.'

At last it was time. Joe's father said, 'Who cares if we can't do this sort of thing without permission? Let's show 'em.' Then he, the other men and Clem and Legs hoisted the flower conger to their shoulders and walked into the lane, with Sasha under the head where he wouldn't be seen.

Ginger led the way, playing The Lobster Blues on his trumpet and Joe danced after him in his blue Lobster outfit, with Beaufort dressed in a collar of shells. Behind him came the conger eel, weaving its way to and fro as they passed their cheering neighbours.

'I've got the blues,' sang Joe, clapping his cardboard claws. 'I really got the blues, man. My life has exploded and the mines are everywhere, I got the blues.' Then he threw stolen German sweets to the children and bellowed, 'I'm Lobster Blue. I want to make some wishes and make them all come true. But I can't, Man, so I got the Blues.'

Next came Diddie. She was standing on Ernest's back. As he walked along, lifting his fetlocks solemnly in time to the music, she twirled on his back on tiptoe. Her tutu was made of net curtains, but as far as Diddie was concerned, it was a genuine ballerina dress. She waved her wand at the crowd, exclaiming grandly, 'Sing for Lobster Blue. May our wishes all come true.'

After this, Hotspur and Peggy pulled Joe's fishing cart. Hotspur was strangely quiet, but Peggy was beside him and he always copied her. Clem had found Bill's old Christmas paint, so the cart was streaked with gold. The pigs' harness were scarlet ribbons from Auntie Vi's mending basket, and Legs La Motte had them under control, walking ahead with some of Mrs. Percheron's best biscuits. Their wings flapped in the breeze, but nothing seemed to worry them.

Arthur waved from the back of the cart in his crab outfit, followed by Rosie turning cartwheels and shouting, 'I'm a skylark.' Aunt Edie marched beside her wearing her best blue dress and hat with cherries on it, together with Auntie Vi and Mrs. Percheron with flowers in their buttonholes. Auntie Vi shouted, 'WE will not be REDUCED,' over and over, and everyone joined in.

Then Billy strode along in a top hat that kept falling over his eyes because it was Mr. Braye's. He bowed to the crowds, beaming with happiness, but suddenly he stopped dead. Then he swept off the top hat, gave the biggest bow of all, ripped the rose out of his buttonhole. He raced towards a pretty woman standing quietly next to his father. '*Mummy*,' he yelled. 'Mum. You've come back.' Then he threw herself into her arms and she burst into tears of happiness.

At the back, Clem led along his beautiful cows, collared with flowers, together with the new calf. As the crowd clapped, one woman said, 'They've even taken away half of our pedigree cows to breed. The Devils.'

Ginger turned left at the bottom of the lane and left again. Soon he was back at the beginning. Clem led the animals into the farmyard, while the lobster pot conger eel sat down. Sasha took off the head and slipped off to look after the animals, and nobody even noticed because they were waiting for the most exciting part of all. Clem returned and Mr. Le Carin shouted, 'Now for the battle.'

'Hooray,' yelled Rosie, Diddie and Arthur.

Mr. Le Carin yanked the first flower out of the conger eel and hurled it at Franz into the crowd. Then another and another, and the crowd hurled them back. Soon, everyone was joining in. The air was clouded with flowers and far too soon, the conger eel was reduced back to a line of lobster pots. All the time, Ginger played his trumpet more and more loudly and everyone was crying with laughter and covered in petals.

'Crumbs,' said Mr. Percheron. 'This is just like the old days.'

But suddenly, Otto rushed into the chaos. He waved his arms frantically, telling them to stop. 'The Kommandant is coming,' he shouted, his eyes wide. 'Go home. Take the flowers. I have had a message.'

In an instant, everyone vanished indoors, their arms full of flower heads. Mr Le Carin piled the lobster pots into his friend's truck and they drove innocently home.

Joe stayed to watch from behind the hedge. Five minutes later, the Kommandant's car moved slowly along the coast road at a regal pace. It stopped just the other side of the hedge and Joe craned his ears. The Kommandant climbed out of the car and looked about him in amazement. 'How strange that there are so many fallen flowers here. A sudden gust of wind, perhaps? *Seltsam*. Peculiar.' Then they moved off and Joe hurtled back to his cottage, roaring with laughter.

Before Rosie went to sleep that evening, she said, 'I'll draw lots of pictures of our parade for Daddy. It'll take me ages.'

When Aunt Edie told her brother, Mr. Braye's face

filled with relief. 'So, she won't have a moment to be a nuisance to the enemy.' Then he held up a packet of crayons. 'I was given these today. Thank goodness. She'll be so happy.'

Saturday 5th September
7 pm

After a long day, Clem filled in his diary:

Wheat cut. Threshing machine should arrive next week. A good harvest, thank goodness. The authorities will keep half for themselves. Milk yield high. He looked up at the eaves from his bedroom and wrote on: *The swallows are ready to leave. Their tune has changed.'*

As he put down his pencil, he noticed Joe and Ginger in the yard, so he went to join them. Joe was holding a tatty old bag. 'I've something to show you. Let's find somewhere quiet.'

When they were settled inside the barn, Joe fished in the bag. 'It's only a tide chart. But I thought I'd show you.' He looked at Clem and Ginger. 'Seeing as we haven't had any trouble for weeks, something's bound to happen and one of us might need to leave. The soldiers are getting restless. Something's in the air.'

'What?' Ginger said. 'I haven't noticed anything.'

Joe unrolled the chart. 'I get about,' he said. 'I hear things.'

Clem sighed. 'I hope they don't mess with the rest of the harvest. There's still so much to do. Anyhow, I'm not crossing the ruddy Channel.'

'Fair enough,' interrupted Joe. 'But we should be

prepared.' He showed them a mass of curved lines and arrows. 'The tide comes racing round here and round there.' He pointed at the southeast of the island. 'It's very strong. If you go with it, you can be carried miles without doing anything except steering, but if you try going against it, you won't move.'

Clem puzzled over the arrows. 'I could never be a sailor. I know the tide changes with the moon, but that's about it.'

Just then, there was a knock at the door and Otto walked straight into the milking parlour When he saw the chart, his face was curious. 'What is this?'

'Best be open,' muttered Ginger. He raised his voice. 'In the evenings, we get bored. So, we're learning about our island.'

Joe tried not to laugh. 'See these lines and arrows?' Otto nodded. Joe went on, 'These are the flight lines of swallows. They'll be leaving soon.' He pointed upwards at the eaves. 'You can probably hear them in your flat, getting ready. It's really so..'. he thought for a minute. *'Fascinating.'*

'Ach zo,' said Otto. He grinned and turned on his heel, adding, 'I'm not stupid.' After he was out of range, they burst out laughing, stuffing their fists in their mouths to muffle the noise.

'Right boys, best get on.' Clem yawned. 'There's so much to do. We've even got to work Sunday. Dad is not pleased.'

On his usual evening round, he gave Ernest plenty of time. The huge horse was lying down in his stable, but his eyes were bright. 'It was hot today for an old boy like you,' said Clem, stroking his head. 'Wasn't it?'

**Sunday 13th September
7 am**

The wheat was in, so it was time to harvest the oats. They rustled in the breeze, golden and ripe. Reaping and binding started early and lasted all day. The tractor was almost ready, but at the last moment, it conked out again. So, Ernest pulled the trailer up and down from the farm. It was heavy, piled with straw stooks. His shoulders strained as he did his duty. Clem urged him on, giving him time to rest and drink. From time to time, Ernest leaned his head against him, gently. Beaufort trudged faithfully up and down behind the old horse, dodging his enormous hooves.

At last the field was cut. 'Thank you everyone. There's supper at our place. Come on, folks.' Clem looked at his watch. 'It'll be ready now.'

Everyone washed under the pump for the Harvest Supper. There would be cold pork, sent from the farm where Clem had taken the piglets months before. Potatoes would be heaped on plates and Spinner had provided salad from her vegetable patch. Legs had brought cider from his Auntie.

Clem said, 'I'll groom Ernest and take him to the orchard to cool down. See you later. Don't wait for me.'

As he and the old horse walked in the barn, Mr. Le

Carin came out, waving a crank handle. His grim face was lit up for once. 'Done it. You can give Ernest a rest.'

Clem beamed. 'That's wonderful news. Thanks so much for all you've done. It's about time Ernest retired.'

As Mr. Le Carin went to join in the harvest supper, Clem led Ernest back to his manger, taking it slowly. 'You were a such good boy today,' he murmured, tickling Ernest behind his ears. 'You've always been a wonder. Now you can rest. If it wasn't for you, I'd be gone, off to the mainland to fight. But it wouldn't bring back Bill, would it?'

Ernest whinnied gently as Clem stroked his velvety nose. When his harness was off, Clem groomed him. He brushed his mane and then his fetlocks as Ernest lifted one huge hoof at a time. Then he polished his hooves and buffed his coat until it shone, with long sweeps of the brush.

'That's better, isn't it?' Clem put his arms round Ernest's neck. 'You look handsome now, boy.'

Inside the farmhouse, the Harvest Supper had begun. Clem could hear them through the open door - Joe cracking jokes and Rosie calling out. Arthur was gurgling with joy as he always did even though he was no longer a baby. He heard Didie say, 'I want to wear it again.'

Then Clem heard his father calling for quiet. 'Let's say Grace.' Up in the barn, Clem bowed his head and so did Ernest.

Mr. Percheron said, 'Thank the Lord for all his gifts. Our harvest, our friends and our beautiful animals. Let us be grateful, not angry. Amen.'

Ernest rubbed his head against Clem once more and followed him to the orchard. He looked up at the ripening apples and whinnied again, as softly as a little gust of air. A swallow swooped over his head. He looked up at it, almost with a kind of longing.

Suddenly his legs buckled beneath him and he fell to the ground.

Clem gasped, 'Oh, Ernest. What is it?' He dropped to his knees beside his faithful friend.

Ernest flicked his beautiful tail once more and looked up at the boy he had known all his life. Then he closed his eyes and Clem knew at once that he was dead. He put his head on the old horse's warm body and wept, tears rolling down his face and soaking into the ground.

A minute late, Joe called from the farmyard. 'Hurry up, Clem. Or there won't be anything left.' He rushed round the corner into the orchard, then skidded to a halt. Then he walked softly forwards and knelt beside Clem. He touched the old horse for the last time. Then he turned to Clem and there was silence between them.

10.30 pm

Clem and his father kept watch over Ernest all night. The old horse was covered with a tarpaulin. Mr. Percheron gently laid the rose on it, as though Ernest could not bear any more weight. Then he said, 'Bless Ernest and take him into your loving hands, Oh Lord.'

They both were quiet until Mr. Percheron murmured, 'When I came back from the trenches, Ernest welcomed me.' He glanced up at the stars. 'I'd seen terrible things. We all did - us three men that so stupidly ran away to fight. Ernest was here for us all.'

Clem put his hand on his father's shoulder. 'I remember the rides we had on him when we were kids, Bill and George and I, trotting round the field. He was so gentle.' He kept back tears.

Mr. Percheron nodded. 'They'll take him away in the morning. But we'll stay here all night, shall we?'

'That's the least we can do,' said Clem.

Then his father said, 'I was almost twice your age when I ran away to war. Grown up, too old to fight really. My father was so upset.' He put his hand on his son's shoulder. 'I understand how angry you are, but I don't want you to face the horror we saw. It's selfish of me. I couldn't bear it, as well as Bill.'

'You were brave,' said Clem. 'But I feel such a coward, staying here.'

Mr. Percheron shook his head. 'You are the bravest of us all and I trust you always to do what is right. That is who you are. My brave, fierce son.'

Tuesday 15th September
4 pm

It was the first day of the autumn term. Ginger and Clem were now in the sixth form, almost grown up and prefects. Clem said, 'I don't care. I'd rather Ernest was alive.' But he was glad of something else to think of.

After the first day back at College, Clem and Ginger cycled home, but immediately they noticed a change in mood on their way through town. 'Something's up,' said Ginger. 'It's so quiet.'

An old man was sitting on a bench beside the road, reading the Evening Post. He was jabbing the newspaper with his finger. Clem went up to him. 'What's up, sir?'

The old man jabbed again at the paper. 'The Jerries are sending people to prison camps. I never thought I'd see *this* sort of thing in my island. Women and children, too.'

Clem said, 'Will it help if I take you home?'

The old man shook his head. 'You're a kind young man. But I will find my own way. Hurry on home and find out the news from your own people.'

Clem wished him good afternoon, then he and Ginger sped back along the coast road. They both rushed into Spinner's house and found Mr. Braye standing up, reading out loud from the Evening Post. He broke off when he saw them and waved the paper. 'Such bad news, I'm afraid.'

'What's happened? We heard something in town.' Clem faltered for a moment. 'There's been enough bad news, hasn't there? Has...' he paused, '...Hitler invaded England?'

Mr. Braye shook his head. 'No, it's nothing on that scale. Just on our own little island, but it's really quite awful.' He began to read. *'By order of higher authorities, the following British Subjects will be evacuated and transferred to Germany.'*

Ginger gasped. 'They can't do that. They *promised*, solemnly, to protect the lives, property and liberty of peaceful inhabitants. I remember those precise words.'

Aunt Edie caught her breath. 'How *dreadful*. Who will they send? Is there a list?'

'Not yet. I suppose they'll tell us soon.' Mr. Braye scanned the paper. 'No, no details.'

'Oh, God.' Aunt Edie put her hand to her heart. 'There are terrible stories about places in Germany.'

Spinner arrived home. As she put her school hat and coat on their hooks, her father told her what was happening. 'This is very bad news, my dears. We must be even more careful. They will deport anyone on a whim.'

Spinner sat down, her eyes wide. He father went on, 'This is all we know. *'Persons who have their permanent residence not on the Channel Islands, for instance, those who have been caught here by the outbreak of war.'*

'We'll be all right then,' Spinner said, 'But still, it's awful. How frightening for the whole island.'

Mr. Braye looked suddenly fierce. 'There's more. *All those men not born on the Channel Islands and 16 to 70 years of age who belong to English people, together with their families.'*

Spinner gasped, 'But Ginger's sixteen. And he was

born in England...and his father is English!'

There was a horrible silence. Rosie was eating a piece of carrot, crunching loudly. She paused for a moment and asked, 'Why is everyone quiet?'

'Sometimes, people are quiet,' said Aunt Edie. She tried to smile at Ginger. 'They won't send *you*? *Surely*? You're just a school boy.'

'Fighting age if you think about it,' said Clem, then wished he hadn't. Aunt Edie looked stricken, her eyes filling with tears. 'Sorry, Aunt Edie. They won't take Ginger. He'd be rubbish at fighting.'

Mr. Braye said firmly, 'Of course they won't. Don't think even think about it. They'd only send boys that age if they've been in trouble with the enemy.'

Spinner felt her stomach lurch. Clem said, 'I'd better go and see how Mum and Dad are taking it.' He glanced at Ginger. 'Chin up, Ginge. They won't want a weedy bloke like you. You'd be a liability.'

Over in the farmhouse, Mr. Percheron was also reading the Evening Post. He looked over his glasses at his wife. 'They're *deporting* people. To *Germany*. I knew they'd do it. But they call it *evacuating*.' Then he added a string of very rude words in Jersey French.

'*Sid*,' said Mrs. Percheron reproachfully.

Mr. Percheron ignored her and added, 'They're going for men between sixteen and seventy, and their families. You bet they'll take anyone who's been in trouble, as well.'

His wife slumped into a chair, her face ashen. 'Clem's always baiting the Germans. They might take him.'

'No chance,' said Clem, walking in. 'I'm an angel.'

The telephone rang. Mr. Percheron answered in Jersey French. 'Yes, I've just read it. Dreadful.' There was another torrent of words, and Mr. Percheron said, still in Jersey French. *'In twenty four hours? How cruel.'*

Suddenly a voice rang out on the line. 'Speak in English, please.'

'You Germans...' Mr. Percheron rolled his eyes. 'Listening in again?' He slammed down the receiver. 'The deportees must be at the harbour in twenty-four hours.'

'Typical,' said Clem. 'They just make everything as vile as possible. What a bunch of ...' Then he stopped himself from swearing and stamped outside to check on his cows, avoiding the spot where Ernest had died.

Sasha was sitting on a low wall. He looked up when he saw Clem. 'I heard about your horse. I am sorry. Now, I hear there is trouble for the islanders.'

Clem nodded. 'Thanks,' he said, unable to say any more. 'We have a tractor. So that's bloody *fine.*' The swearing slipped out by mistake, but Sasha seemed to know it was the best way to stop tears.

'The tractor might break again,' he said, 'You'll need more hands. I will come if you need me.' Sasha smiled gently, then he slipped away, circus style, as he always did, vanishing almost like a magician.

When Clem went back to the Brayes', Rosie was in bed. Everyone else was having supper. Joe and his dog had arrived to talk about the new order.

As Spinner gave Beaufort some crusts, Ginger took off his glasses and wiped them. Very quietly, he said, 'Father's an English Naval Officer, fighting the enemy. Rosie was born in Jersey. But I wasn't. Mother and Father lived in England when they were married, for three years. So, I was born in Devon.'

'Blimey,' said Joe. 'That's a bit worrying.'

Thursday 18th September
5 pm

'You weren't on the list after all,' said Joe, kicking gravel.

'Good thing,' Ginger replied. 'I was going to lend you my bike, now I don't have to.'

Joe whistled. 'Blimey, I'm wishing you'd go, now you said that.' He took a cigarette stub from behind his ear. 'Only kidding. Want a smoke? I pinched this from Billy's dad.'

Ginger shook his head. 'Quite a few boys from our school went on Tuesday.'

'Poor blokes.' Joe looked longingly at his bike. 'I like the drop handle bars.' Then waved goodbye and set off for his cottage, puffing smoke.

When they reached home, Mr. Braye was waiting at the gate. His face was screwed up with anxiety. 'I'm so sorry, Ginger. There's some rather bad news.'

'Father?' Ginger's bike clattered to the ground and Franz rushed forward to pick it up. He looked apologetically at Ginger and wheeled it into the yard for him. Ginger glanced at him unseeingly, then said again, '*Is it about Father?*' Then he followed his uncle indoors, his heart like a lump of lead.

Everyone was in the Brayes' kitchen. Auntie Edie stood up, her face ashen. She rushed forward and grabbed his hands. Nobody spoke. Then she whispered, 'My darling boy. Such dreadful news.'

Ginger tried to put his shoulders back. He stammered, 'We must be very brave. I promise you that I'll look after you and Rosie. It's going to be …' He swallowed and added, 'I bet father died in action, doing his duty.'

Aunt Edie pushed back her hair and looked at him in astonishment. 'No, darling. It's not about Father.' She burst into tears. 'It's about *you*.' Then she threw her arms round him. 'You're on the list.'

'This is the order.' Mr. Braye indicated a note on the table. 'But it's ridiculous to send Ginger. What harm has he done?'

As he slowly understood, Ginger blinked and his glasses misted over. Then he broke free of his mother and stumbled out of the door. Aunt Edie rushed after him, but Clem said, 'I'll go. There'll be a way to stop this, I bet.'

Mr Braye left the room. Soon he was on the telephone, protesting in German and then in English. When he returned a few minutes later, he shook his head. 'I don't think there's anything I can do. The Kommandant has tried to stop the whole awful business, but Hitler is determined. He's in a rage, for some reason.'

Aunt Edie had slumped into a chair with her arms wrapped round herself, as though she was trying to hold herself from falling apart. Her eyes were tightly closed aa she swayed backwards and forwards. 'He's so gentle,' she whispered. 'He won't stand a chance.'

Auntie Vi hadn't spoken at all until she said, 'I'm going to offer to go in his place. I'm an old woman and I've had my life.'

At that, Ginger's mother began to weep silently, so

that Rosie wouldn't hear. She said, 'That's the kindest offer in the world, Vi. But the paper has Ginger's name on it. Frederick John Martin. We can't change it to yours.'

'Ruddy Hitler,' said Auntie Vi.

Aunt Edie swallowed. She took the notice of deportation from Mr. Braye and looked 'Let's get started. He's allowed one suitcase and enough food and drink for two days.'

'And my trumpet,' said Ginger, standing at the door. Clem had his arm through his.

7 pm

All evening, everyone helped to pack. Joe arrived to mend Ginger's boots and shoes, then Clem polished them. Mr. Braye talked to Ginger, showing him the Red Cross rules, as well as finding some sheet music that might cheer everyone in the camp. He gave him new exercise books and envelopes and made sure that his paperwork was in order.

Ginger said very little. He sat with Rosie as she played with her doll Vera, then wandered off round the farm, watching the last few swallows. When he came back, he said, 'I expect the swallows will fly right over us in the boat.'

Mrs Percheron found underwear, shirts and trousers that had belonged to Bill. Auntie Vi and Aunt Edie turned up hems and sewed on missing buttons. 'Thank goodness you came to stay, Vi,' said Mrs. Percheron. 'With your buttons and thread.'

Spinner kept Rosie busy. She told her that Ginger was going on holiday and he'd like some of her pictures. She let her draw and colour until she was yawning.

'That's a lovely picture of the cows,' she said admiringly.

'Pigs,' said Rosie. 'And this is Hotspur.' She pointed at a large black object like a spider. 'And this is us.' There was a row of faces with stick legs and arms and underneath them, kisses.

Spinner felt tears rising again. She told Rosie that Ginger would show the pictures to all his new friends when he was on holiday, then she put her to bed. As Rosie settled down she tried to spell holiday in code. Hedgehog, Oryx, Llama. But then her eyes closed. Spinner stayed with her until she was fast asleep.

When she walked into the kitchen, she saw that nearly everything was done. The suitcase was ready. A bag of food stood on the kitchen table and there were two tin bowls, one for drinking and one for eating. 'We'll put in hard boiled eggs in the morning, fresh as possible,' said Mrs. Percheron. 'And I'll bake a fresh loaf with the best flour we have in the morning, when the electricity's on.'

Spinner tucked the pictures into the suitcase. Somebody checked the clock. 'Curfew time,' said Mr. Percheron. He gave a smile that no one had seen for a long time. 'And we don't care a damn, do we?'

'*Sid*,' exclaimed Mrs. Percheron.

Friday 18th September
7.30 am

In my Girl Guide Promise, I said I would Smile and Sing under All Difficulties. It is almost impossible today.

Spinner gave up writing her diary and went to see her chickens. She chose eight of the best newly laid eggs and took six to Mrs Percheron to hard boil. Then she fried two for Ginger's breakfast with the rest of their butter ration.

'It's almost worth going,' said Ginger, trying to eat. He gave a nervous laugh. 'I feel like a condemned man eating his last meal.'

Clem was hovering about, unwilling to say goodbye. In the end, he just said 'We've *got* to go to school. *Orders.* But we're ruddy well coming to wave you off.' He put his hand on Ginger's shoulder. 'I bet they send you straight back when they see you're no use as a fighting man.'

Ginger gave him a watery smile from behind his glasses. 'Sorry I'll miss the Harvest Festival. Spinner's marrows are always the best.'

Joe turned up to say goodbye. 'Diddie sends you a big kiss.' Then he held out the silver coin that he'd found so long ago in the garage workshop. 'It was lucky for Sasha so I reckon it'll be lucky for you. Bring it home so we can take it to him in Russia after the war. We promised, mate.'

Ginger's glasses misted up again as he tucked it into his inside pocket. 'Thanks, Joe. Look after my bike.'

Mr. and Mrs. Percheron said they'd stay home with Rosie. 'All will be well,' said Mr. Percheron, shaking Ginger's hand. He handed him a slip of paper with a prayer on it. 'Keep it with you.'

Mrs. Percheron kissed him and said, 'Be safe, *man p'tit crabin.*'

Ginger wrapped his arms round his little sister and said, ' Best foot forward. I'll try to send you a postcard.'

1 pm

Ginger's mother put on her best green dress to see off her son, and her hat with cherries on it. She used the last of her lipstick, saying, 'The blighters aren't going to see *me* giving in to misery. Then picked up Ginger's blanket by the leather strap that held it in a neat roll, took a deep breath and said, 'Come on, chaps. Let's show them.'

Ginger pushed his glasses into place and picked up his trumpet. 'Yep. Let's do that. They can just …' he nearly said something rude, then smiled ruefully. 'You know what I mean.'

Mr. Braye took his suitcase in one hand and the food bag in the other. Ginger took a long last round his home, kissed Rosie and told her he'd send her some postcards as soon as he could.

As they walked out of the house, Otto hurried out of the flat. 'Thank you for your music. We are very angry that you are being sent away.' Then he stood at attention and saluted Ginger, and stayed at attention until they were out of sight.

When they reached the edge of town, the streets were

lined with people. As Ginger walked between them, they cheered their encouragement. 'Good luck, dearie,' shouted one woman. Another said, 'Give them hell, boy.'

Soldiers kept guard in front of the crowds and some of them faced away, so they wouldn't have to see the long, harassed procession of deportees filing past.

Aunt Edie gave the crowds a thumbs up, then walked on, her best red shoes like berries against the grey, dirty streets. 'Give them a tune, darling. They're so kind.'

Ginger nodded and lifted up his trumpet. Music poured into the sky and echoed against the dingy walls and shuttered shops. He played the whole of the Hot Trotter repertoire, then went into all the jazz he knew and a heady mixture of songs. The crowd crooned along with him, and Aunt Edie and Mr. Braye marched with him, and they held their heads high.

Suddenly a voice boomed out of the crowd, in between tunes. '*One two three four, who the hell are we for? Red heads, that's what.*'

Ginger's face lit up. 'Legs!'

Clem's friend shoved through the crowd and thrust a bag of toffees into Ginger's free hand. 'I pinched them from a soldier and bunked school to give them to you.' He chanted again, '*ONE TWO THREE FOUR, WHO THE HELL ARE WE FOR? G.I.N.G.E.R.*' Then he ran alongside Ginger, dodging round the soldiers.

When they reached the Weigh Bridge Garage on the harbour, Mr. Braye gazed at the long queue ahead of them. 'I think you have to wait here for a medical.'

'*A medical?*' Ginger flinched. 'That's a bit undignified. What do they think we might have? Scabies?'

'They won't send anyone who isn't well,' Aunt Edie said. 'Could you sham it?' She looked hopeful for a moment, then shook her head ruefully. 'I think they'll keep you. You're too blooming healthy.'

Ginger looked ahead. 'There are plenty of kids I know in the queue. If they can do it, I can.' He shook his uncle's hand and kissed his mother. 'I reckon I'm on my way now.' He bit his lip. 'I'll be perfectly all right, Mother. You mustn't worry one bit and I'll be back in trice.'

The cherries on his mother's hat shook for a moment. Then Aunt Edie noticed that a soldier was watching her with cold eyes. She took a huge breath, and said, 'See you soon, my darling. You will do us proud.' Tears welled up, but she shook them off and held him so tightly he could hardly breathe.

Mr. Braye said, 'The Red Cross is *duty bound* to look after you. And we'll write as soon as we have an address. Rosie will send so many pictures you won't know what to do.' He shook hands, then hugged him. 'Goodbye, dearest chap.'

Ginger gazed at them both as though he was etching their faces into his memory for ever. Then he said, 'Cheerio, folks,' in exactly the same way the Clem's brother Bill did two years ago when he set out to fight. He gave his mother a last hug. As they left, he called out, 'They're giving us bread and jam.' He pointed at a table ahead, piled with food. 'Don't tell Joe, or he'll want to come too.'

4 pm

Clem and Spinner cycled to Joe's cottage straight after school. They put their bikes and school uniforms into the coal shed. Joe locked it, then they hurtled along the road until a passing farmer gave them a lift on the back of his tractor. He took them nearly as far as town, then dropped them off. 'Give the Germans hell, kids.' Then he threw back his head and roared with laughter. 'They deserve it, sending people off like that. *The DEVILS.*'

Clem gave him a thumbs up and they set off up the hill that overlooked the harbour, Mount Bingham, where the old fort had stood for years guarding the island. As they hurried up the road, Clem said, 'Ruddy hell, listen to that shouting. There must be hundreds up there.'

'ONE TWO THREE FOUR,' boomed the crowd ahead. 'WHO THE HELL ARE WE FOR?'

An answer came back, fainter. 'J.E.R.S.E.Y.'

'Thousands, I guess,' said Joe, his eyes gleaming. 'Should be fun.' As they reached a large shrub, added, 'Hang on a mo.' He dived into the shrub and there was a great deal of rustling. 'I'm just changing.

Spinner and Clem caught each other's eye. 'You're not going to a party,' said Spinner. 'What the heck are you doing in there?'

There was more rustling, then Joe emerged from the shrub and posed with his hands on his hips. 'What do you think?' He'd squeezed into his Lobster outfit and was carrying the two enormous claws under one arm and the lobster head under the other. 'I want Ginger to have a laugh. Zip me up, someone?'

Spinner giggled and yanked up the zip. 'It's jolly tight. I bet it rips.'

Clem tapped his head. 'You idiot. The soldiers might just notice you too.'

'Who cares? It'll be hilarious. Ginger's favourite word.' Joe pushed the head dress at Clem, saying, 'Help me out, mate.' Then he hopped up the hill with them, saying, 'Let's crack it, chaps.' But just as they reached the top, there was a ripping sound. Joe groaned. 'Oh drat. My costume's torn.' He twisted round and looked behind himself. 'Still, at least I can run now. Good job I'm wearing pants.'

Spinner tried not to look. 'They're quite nice ones.'

'Sunday jobs,' said Joe. 'Just for Ginger. Come on, folks. Let's go.'

The top of the hill was packed with protestors bellowing God Save the King. Clem jammed the lobster head on to Joe and joined in, his deep voice booming across the harbour below them.

Joe staggered about, trying to find the eye holes and singing too, his voice muffled by the head dress. After barging into a couple of nice old ladies, and apologising, he clipped on the lobster claws and leapt on to a high wall, waving them at the boat.

Spinner shouted 'I can *see* Ginger. He's on the boat already, playing his trumpet.'

Everyone roared their approval and started warbling along with Ginger's tune, *Roll out the Barrel*. Down on Pier Road below them, more joined in. Joe conducted, the lobster feelers waggling about and the big claws clapping out the beat.

Clem shouted, 'Give us *Land of Hope and Glory*.'

Soon, the crowds were competing, seeing who could sing the loudest and watching the boats as they were loaded with deportees. Joe clapped his claws on until a woman suddenly pointed at a group of soldiers taking the deportees to the boat. 'Those men have got bayonets. What a bunch of ...'

Her voice was drowned as people began to jeer, surging forward and yelling as another unit of soldiers headed up the hill towards them, dividing the crowd with their rifle butts. A woman screamed as a fight broke out on Pier Road.

Clem eyes were glinting in a way that Joe and Spinner knew well. 'I'm ruddy well going to get stuck in.'

Spinner grabbed him. She yelled at Clem, *'Don't. They've got bayonets.'*

Clem shook her off. Then he hurled himself at the soldiers, his huge fists flailing. He yelled back at them. 'Get off my island, you brutes.'

A soldier shouted a command. Suddenly Clem was surrounded and every soldier wore a tin helmet and carried a rifle with a bayonet. He sneered 'Five against one? Cowards.'

But as he spoke, a sudden shot rang out.

The soldiers froze, staring frantically into the crowd. Clem whirled round inside the ring of men, his face contorted with rage.

Joe was still on the wall. He'd chucked away the claws and was removing the lobster head. 'That wasn't very nice,' he said, as though he was talking about someone making a nasty smell. He dropped the lobster head and pointed at a trickle of blood on his front. 'Flipping heck. That's my costume ruined. Auntie Vi will kill me.'

'Joe,' Spinner whimpered. 'What have they done?'

Joe gave a demented chuckle. He ripped off the costume and added, 'Nothing at all, Spinner. An idiot fired into the air to frighten us. And he got me. Silly mistake.' As he dropped the costume, he said, 'Don't run away, Mr. Lobster. I'll be back for you later.' He glanced at the upturned faces all round him, blood trickling down his arm. 'No need to worry, ladies and gentlemen. It was only a little graze.'

Then he leapt to the ground and charged in his

underpants towards the soldiers circling Clem, dodging in and out like a gnat and pounding the soldiers' backs with his tough, fisherman's fist. As he punched, he panted, 'Needs must, as Auntie would say.'

The soldiers stared at him in disbelief. Then the jeering started again and as Clem struggled to get away, one of them lifted his rifle butt high in the air and brought it down with a thud on his head. Clem fell like a sack of potatoes to the ground, groaning.

Then he staggered back on to his feet, punched the soldier full in the face and ducked out of the circle, racing into the crowd which parted then closed after him.

Joe thrust his lobster costume at Spinner. 'I'm going after Clem. Stay here for Ginger. You can tell him you watched him all the way to France.'

As he disappeared through the crowds, someone yelled, 'They're off.'

Someone started to sing another patriotic song, so Spinner waved the lobster claws so that Ginger could see. 'Poor Ginger,' she muttered, 'Poor Clem.' Tears ran down her face and she began to sob. But suddenly, she felt a comforting arm round her shoulder. Her father and Aunt Edie had pushed through the crowd and were at her side, together with Auntie Vi and her friend Aunt Albie. 'Daddy,' she sobbed. 'It's all so horrible.'

'Those damn cabbage heads,' Albie said. 'The Bosch.' Then she shut her eyes. 'May God forgive me and them and everyone for what's happening.

The boats steamed out of the harbour. All round her, the crowd cheered them as Ginger stood in the bows, playing his trumpet like an angel on a Christmas card.

8 pm

Clem hurtled down Mount Bingham, his boots thundering on the pavement. He jumped on to the back of a German truck, crouching out of sight on the bumper and clinging on like grim death.

Soon the truck was level with the lane from his house. He jumped off and pressed himself into a dark corner, waited until the coast was clear, then charged up the lane towards his home. But halfway there, he stopped dead, his heart racing.

In a flash, he understood what he had done.

'Oh God,' he muttered. 'If I go home, they'll follow me. Then I'll do something worse.' He pictured his parents trying to defend him against the very worst of the soldiers. He imagined them being bundled into a truck and taken away - his brave little mother and his father, who had grown so old in the last year. Then he thought of his father's words as they sat beside Ernest in the night. *'My brave, fierce son.'*

At that, his heart felt that it would break, because he knew all at once what he had to do. There was so very little time. He took a last look at the farmhouse, then turned and ran east, thudding along footpaths and the old tracks when he could, his breath rasping. But for once, there were no patrols. The enemy was busy in town, coping with the angry crowds.

At last, he was tearing across the flat fields towards the old building where Mr. Le Carin had worked so hard on the little French boat that he had found on the shore.

Alouette was out of the shed. It was almost as if she was waiting for him, sitting on a trailer and covered with a tarpaulin, her mast set and the boom ready for the sails. Mr. Le Carin had done the little boat proud.

Clem knew that Mr. Braye had hidden maps in the boat not long after he and Ginger had made their awful cycle ride north. At last his heart stopped racing, and he stood still, listening for soldiers. He thought of George, fighting somewhere, and of Bill, drowned, and he thought, *If I make it to England, I'll have been useful. Then I can fight.'*

The sail bag was in place, together with the emergency food and Joe's tide table. Clem lifted tins of fuel into the boat and attached the outboard motor. Then, with all his strength, he heaved the boat to the roadside, blessing Mr. Le Carin for finding wheels from somewhere, wheels that moved silently and efficiently.

Checking that the coast was clear, he crossed the road to the slipway, leaning back to take the weight as it rolled down the slope towards the sea. When *Alouette* was afloat, he pulled the trailer from under her and made the little boat fast.

Then he staggered up the slipway with the trailer and shoved it into the nearest field, before scraping up a handful of Jersey ground and wrapping it carefully in his handkerchief. He thought, *now I'll have a piece of home with me wherever I go.*

When he was sure it was safe, he shot down to the boat and climbed on board. Listening for the last time to sounds of his island, he sat on the thwart as the boat rocked gently from side to side like a cradle. Then he pushed off.

Alouette glided gently away from the slipway.

Dusk was falling as the tide caught her and pulled her gently away from land. To the east, the moon was bright. For a moment, Clem closed his eyes. He whispered, 'God in Heaven, help me.' Then he took hold of the oars, his heart thundering at the thought of the journey ahead.

Then, just as he dipped the blades into the water, he caught his breath.

A lone figure stood on the edge of the water in College uniform. There was a white bandage on his hand and a dog was pressed close to his leg.

Clem gasped. 'What in God's name are *you* doing there?'

'You flipping *idiot*, Clem Percheron. I had to borrow your bike and your clothes and I look like a twit in them. You eat too much, they're too big. And I cycled so fast it nearly blimmin' killed me. I *knew* what you'd do.'

'So?' Clem growled, 'I don't need you.'

'Oh yeah? Right.' Joe laughed wildly, then flung himself into the water, fully dressed. As Clem gazed at him in amazement, he swam like a demon towards the boat, with Beaufort frantically paddling behind him, spluttering, 'You'll drown without me, Clem Percheron. Farmer boy.'

Clem yelled, 'Who cares?'

'Shut up,' Joe hissed, closing in on the boat. 'Don't be so ruddy noisy.'

Clem wound a thin rope on the outboard motor to start it. 'I'm off,' he muttered, then raised his voice again, 'Look after my cows, Joe.'

'Idiot,' Joe hissed again, popping up beside the boat. He heaved Beaufort out of the water into the boat, followed him and grabbed the motor rope. 'Engines make a noise for miles on the water. You aren't thinking properly.'

Clem glared at him. 'What the *heck* do you think you're doing?'

'We'll have to come with you. You don't know the first

thing about the sea.' Joe grabbed the tiller and pushed his dog safely under his knees. 'You can't even put up a sail.' He pointed at the oars. 'And we've got to row until we're out of sight. It's not dark enough yet and the patrols will be back from town any minute.'

'But what about Diddie and Arthur? You can't leave them,' said Clem.

'Auntie Vi will look after them and Dad's much better these days,' Joe said. 'Then he laughed, 'and I can always make my way back.'

Clem sighed and said, 'All right, Captain.' He took hold of the oars and gazed back at his beloved island. The sky was turning from deep blue to black and a single, late swallow flew over *Alouette*, like a last farewell.

'I'm not running away Joe. I *have* to leave.'

Joe pulled off his wet clothes and pulled a bag out from the locker under the bows. 'See? Dry clothes. You didn't even know that, so how could you sail a boat?' He took out a thick, fisherman's sweater and gave Clem another. 'Be prepared, sailor's motto.'

Clem smiled in spite of himself. 'If I stay, I'll do something much worse than punch a soldier. Then Mum and Dad will be taken away. You know that don't you?'

'Sure I do. That's why I followed you,' Joe said. 'Sasha came with me. He's taking the bike to your home right now and he's going to help on the farm. He gave me this.' He held up the gold Russian coin and it glittered. 'It brought him luck, so it'll do it for us. No problem.'

'*Sasha?* He feels safe enough to do that?' Clem caught his breath. 'That's wonderful.'

Joe shrugged. 'He's not that safe, but he's an acrobat. He'll never get caught, and anyhow, he speaks Jersey French like a farmer these days.'

Clem nodded, then he looked up at the stars. 'Anyhow, your mum's up there, and Bill. They'll look after us.'

'And we've got Beau to keep us warm,' said Joe, patting his dog.

'And Mr. Braye's maps to deliver. We'd better get on with it before they send out a search party.' Clem began to pull on the oars with all his strength and Joe took hold of the helm.

As the oars slipped in and out of the water, Clem began to sing, quietly, until they were far enough for him to sing out loud. Joe joined in as they headed east. Soon, the island was just a long, black shape against the starry sky.

Afterword

Jersey was a happy place before World War Two. Tourists flocked there from Britain and nearby France for the wonderful beaches and pretty countryside full of Jersey cows and flowers. However, in July, 1940, all the Channel Islands were invaded by Hitler's forces and the ultimate British tourist destination was cut off for five years.

By 1942, the reality of occupation was biting. The sea seemed like prison walls, because the outside world was gradually cut off. The local paper was edited by the enemy, listening to the radio was banned, there was no post, telephone calls were monitored and everyone was hungry, particularly those people who lived in the town, St Helier. It was difficult to fish, because the beaches were mined or barricaded with barbed wire. Some people sold what they could for inflated prices. These goods were called The Black Market.

Foreign workers arrived to build bunkers and railways for the German forces. They were given very little money and food for their work, so they roamed the island at night stealing rabbits and cats to eat. For the first time in history, islanders locked their doors.

Later, islanders were upset to see some slave labourers being treated very cruelly. These people, mainly men, were prisoners who had been sent from the Eastern Front of the war and were usually Russians or Slavic people. They worked in awful conditions on the island, with barely any food, shoes or clothes.

There are some paving stones in St Helier, Jersey, which are engraved with quotations from some of those prisoners. One reads: 'No one ever used my name. I was called Number 146. Alexei Konnikov. Slave worker.' It is this stone that inspired me to write about 'Sasha,' the prisoner who features in this book. All the stones send a powerful message: people step on them as they hurry by.

It was strictly against the rules to help the Russian slave workers, but many islanders did what they could to relieve their suffering, giving them what food they could and hiding them in their own houses. This was exceedingly dangerous. Louisa Gould hid one such man for years, but someone informed on her. She died in Ravensbrück concentration camp in Germany. Bob Le Sueur found safe houses for escaped slave workers. He was later given a medal by Russia for his efforts.

Writing about such times is never easy, but I hope that in *Lobster Blues* I have drawn attention to such people as Louisa and Bob, and the other islanders who took such huge risks for the sake of the slave workers. I hope too that by splashing a liberal dose of poetic licence over the hard facts of that time, I have shown the character of Channel Islanders. They are resourceful and witty people – or as one German Kommandant described them, 'wily'.

Acknowledgements

The facts about the German Occupation are very well documented, both in books and archives. Frank Keiller's 'A Prison without Walls,' our cousin Nan Le Ruez's *Farming Diary* and Leslie Sinel's *Occupation Diary* were all of particular importance to me while researching for *Lobster Blues*.

It's always a delight to hear a story of someone's grandfather or grandmother during that time, just as we heard stories from our own family and they really do inform my book. I am so grateful for these stories.

For instance, I know that our great aunt Jane put potatoes under the hedges for hungry prisoners like Auntie Vi does in *Lobster Blues*. Our grandparents witnessed the savage beating of a slave worker by a guard, just as Joe and Clem do in the book.

Thomas Kerr, of Haute Vallee school, told me that his grandfather escaped trouble when he was caught out after curfew by stabbing himself on his hand with his penknife – just at Joe does.

Another man told me that he and his friend got permission to go fishing. They gave their tiny sandwich to a desperate slave worker, only to see him beaten almost to death in front of them, and then to be threatened as well. Clem and Ginger go through the same traumatic experience.

Other stories include the one told me by two ladies I met on a bus, whose father hid a wireless (radio) in an empty cider barrel. Their farm was being searched, and one of the soldiers leaned against the barrel whilst watching the search. Another person who told me of a hidden wireless in the organ seat in a chapel, where a soldier like to practice his playing. There are many stories about pigs and the distribution of piglets.

I am so grateful for all these stories, and for so much help and encouragement from others, such as James Wooldridge, the archivist and librarian at Victoria College, and from Anna Capstick for her family recollections of the occupation.

There have been small but important pieces of information from friends and relations about tractors, tides, wirelesses and army tactics in search operations. Friends have checked that, despite poetic licence, the writing is historically authentic. Thank you to Nick Bailhache, John Crill, Alan Collins. Jo Le Marquand and others for these important details.

Thank you to Sara Skillen for encouraging me to keep going. Thank you to Isla Bousfield-Donohoe for her cover design and illustration skills. Most of all, thank you to Elaine Bousfield of Zuntold, for her editorial input and her faith in me and for publishing this book. I hope you enjoy it and admire the courage of the Channel Islanders and in particular, the people of Jersey.

For more insightful books you'll love,

head to

zuntold.com